Berkley Sensation books by Erin McCarthy

A DATE WITH THE OTHER SIDE
HEIRESS FOR HIRE

A Date with the Other Side

Erin McCarthy

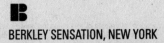

BERKLEY SENSATION, NEW YORK

THE BERKLEY PUBLISHING GROUP
Published by the Penguin Group
Penguin Group (USA) Inc.
375 Hudson Street, New York, New York 10014, USA

Penguin Group (Canada), 90 Eglinton Avenue East, Suite 700, Toronto, Ontario M4P 2Y3, Canada
(a division of Pearson Penguin Canada Inc.)
Penguin Books Ltd., 80 Strand, London WC2R 0RL, England
Penguin Group Ireland, 25 St. Stephen's Green, Dublin 2, Ireland (a division of Penguin Books Ltd.)
Penguin Group (Australia), 250 Camberwell Road, Camberwell, Victoria 3124, Australia
(a division of Pearson Australia Group Pty. Ltd.)
Penguin Books India Pvt. Ltd., 11 Community Centre, Panchsheel Park, New Delhi—110 017, India
Penguin Group (NZ), Cnr. Airborne and Rosedale Roads, Albany, Auckland 1310, New Zealand
(a division of Pearson New Zealand Ltd.)
Penguin Books (South Africa) (Pty.) Ltd., 24 Sturdee Avenue, Rosebank, Johannesburg 2196, South Africa

Penguin Books Ltd., Registered Offices: 80 Strand, London WC2R 0RL, England

This is a work of fiction. Names, characters, places, and incidents either are the product of the author's imagination or are used fictitiously, and any resemblance to actual persons, living or dead, business establishments, events, or locales is entirely coincidental. The publisher does not have any control over and does not assume any responsibility for author or third-party websites or their content.

A DATE WITH THE OTHER SIDE

A Berkley Sensation Book / published by arrangement with the author

PRINTING HISTORY
Berkley Sensation trade edition / May 2005
Berkley Sensation mass-market edition / January 2007

Copyright © 2005 by Erin McCarthy.
Excerpt from *My Immortal* copyright © 2007 by Erin McCarthy.
Cover illustration and design by Rita Frangie.
Interior text design by Kristin del Rosario.

ISBN: 978-0-425-21398-8

BERKLEY SENSATION®
Berkley Sensation Books are published by The Berkley Publishing Group,
a division of Penguin Group (USA) Inc.,
375 Hudson Street, New York, New York 10014.
BERKLEY SENSATION is a registered trademark of Penguin Group (USA) Inc.
The "B" design is a trademark belonging to Penguin Group (USA) Inc.

PRINTED IN THE UNITED STATES OF AMERICA

10 9 8 7 6 5 4 3 2 1

A Date with the Other Side

Chapter One

The man gave a whole new meaning to the words *rise and shine*.

Shelby stood with her hand still on the doorknob to the blue bedroom, the one where the ghost of Nanny Baskins resided, and took a long lingering look at the sleeping male form on top of the white eyelet spread.

The naked man, mouth dropped open on a soft snore, his black hair sticking up, had one hand on his bare broad chest. The other was slung carelessly on the pillow. He didn't look familiar, not a single bare inch of him.

Gran had forgotten to tell her that she'd let the room again.

Yet Shelby couldn't help being a tiny bit intrigued by this tenant. It wasn't quite 9 A.M. yet, and he may have been sleeping, but his thingamabob was ready to start the day with a bang.

"Hey, Shel, you gonna let me in or not?" came Brady's undulating teenage voice. "Bad enough you made us do this at the crack of dawn, but now you won't let us in?"

Shelby started to back up, bumping Brady and his girl-friend Joelle as she retreated, still keeping one eye on that bed. Or an eye on what was on that bed, anyway.

It had been so long since she'd seen a man naked, she'd almost forgotten what they looked like. Besides, her ex-husband had never looked like *that* sleeping. She might not have left him if he had.

"Sorry, Brady, we'll have to move on to the next stop on the tour." She tried to keep her voice down so she wouldn't disturb Naked Wonder.

Brady didn't take the hint. Tossing back his blue hair, he rolled his tongue stud around. "Huh?"

Shelby wondered if kids were still dyeing their hair Easter egg colors or if Brady was sadly dated. Fashion came late to Cuttersville, Ohio. Sort of like getting a flyer in the mail after the sale is over. Cuttersville was always late for the sale.

So even if Brady was way out of style elsewhere, in this town he was a rebel. He was also her cousin, which was why she was letting him take the Haunted Cuttersville Tour at nine in the morning free of charge.

"Shh," she ordered, flapping her arms in her white tank top, giving herself a whiff of her deodorant. "I'll explain in a minute, back up."

With a little luck, she could get the door closed before . . .

"Who the hell are you?"

Too late.

Shelby shot Brady and Joelle, who were straining to see

around her, warning looks. Then she closed the door in their faces, leaving herself alone in the room. With him.

Turning around, she said with a smile, "I'm Shelby Tucker. It's nice to meet you."

The man was sitting up, and he'd pulled the eyelet spread over his lap, but he hadn't taken into account that eyelet spreads by nature are full of many holes. Small and large, affording her interesting glimpses of golden skin and dark hair. Not the comforter of choice for preserving modesty.

Once she forced herself to look up into the dark eyes of Gran's new tenant, she decided modesty didn't suit him. There was something authoritative in his inquiring stare, a brisk calculating gaze that swept over her without moving.

"Well, Shelby Tucker, is there a reason you're in my room or do I have to guess?"

He'd shaken the sleep off pretty quick. He'd caught her name on the first try.

"You can guess if you really want to. But I doubt you'll guess right."

If she had expected him to smile, he disappointed her. An eyebrow rose. "This isn't going to require me to call the police, is it?"

Shelby nearly snickered. Men in Cuttersville just didn't talk like that, and it amused her that he sounded so patronizing, his accent so flat and city-like, when he was bucknaked wearing nothing but her gran's coverlet.

"Why would we be *required* to call the police? Gran just forgot to tell me you were here, that's all." The doorknob rattled with vigor behind her. Shelby slapped the palm of her hand on the door. "Knock it off, Brady!"

Naked Man leaned back on his hands, stretching his

arms out and giving her a great view of his broad, muscular chest, without a single hair growing on it. Geez, did he wax that thing? Men with black hair tended to be hairy, in her experience, which, granted, was limited to glimpses of whoever was swimming in the lake, not from any personal knowledge. Yet this man was satin smooth.

The new position forced the eyelet spread up in the air below his waist. Shelby fought a hard-earned battle not to look. She lost. It just wasn't every day a naked man with a hard-on was presented to her, and she might never get another peep. Of this man, anyway. Surely she was going to see another erection sometime in her lifetime. She was only twenty-six, and what did it matter that her divorce had gone through nearly three years ago now and in all that time the closest she'd come to sex was watching the horses mate?

He was still hard. As a rock. That was the only reason for the spread to be sticking up like that, unless it was his knee she was looking at. The spread hooked him through one of the large holes when he shifted. Nope, that was no kneecap, no siree.

"So, since you insist on being obscure, is your gran my landlady, Mrs. Stritmeyer?"

"That's right."

"What does that have to do with you standing in my bedroom while a teenager with blue hair pounds on my door?"

He really was sharp. He'd had only a twenty-second glance at Brady, while half asleep on top of it all.

"I'm giving my cousin Brady the Haunted Cuttersville Tour. I think he's trying to scare Joelle so he can take her off behind the barn and comfort her."

Shelby heard an outraged female gasp from behind the door. Oops. That might put a dent in Brady's plans.

The naked guy's head fell into his hands and he rubbed. "I don't even want to know who the hell Joelle is."

While he woke up alert, in all areas, he sure didn't have the best of manners.

He fixed her with a frown. "And if this explanation is going to take any longer, can you tell me where I can get my hands on some coffee?"

"The explanation is over. I told you—I'm giving the Haunted Cuttersville Tour." Shelby tucked some hairs that had fallen out of her loose ponytail and wondered if she should warn him that he was about to cut off circulation to a vital area, with the way he was now completely poking through the eyelet hole.

He made a sound of disgust.

She decided to let him figure out his predicament on his own. "And you can get coffee at the diner, but you'll have to get dressed for that."

Boston Macnamara squinted at the woman in front of him. He felt like he'd fallen into a damn rabbit hole. Somebody back in Chicago needed to die for this.

One day. He'd been in this podunk town for all of twenty-four hours and he hated it. Every dusty, tired, tobacco-spitting inch of it.

And the bitch about it was he didn't even know what he had done to Brett, his boss, to be inflicted with the painful punishment of inspecting the plant here in Cuttersville, home of nothing. If he didn't know what he had done, he couldn't fix it. If he couldn't fix it, he couldn't get the hell out of here, and he was going to be forced to deal with country enigmas like Shelby Tucker on a daily basis.

Intolerable.

Having forgotten that he was naked, too busy trying to translate her vague remarks, he glanced down at himself when she made a reference to needing to get dressed. And choked. Holy shit, his dick was caught like a bird neck in a plastic bottle ring. He was surrounded by white lace, the material stretched taut, his skin an alarming shade of tomato red. It didn't hurt, but it looked dangerous.

Swallowing hard, he tried not to panic. He needed this part of him healthy, for more than one reason. He looked up to see Shelby Tucker struggling not to grin, her arms crossed over her white tank top.

"Need some help?" she had the nerve to ask.

"No." He tugged a little at the bedspread, hoping it would pop loose without further interference.

It didn't. Damn. Hoping Shelby wasn't looking, knowing she was, he stuck his leg up trying to block her view while he used his finger to get between him and the fabric and wiggle it a little.

"Don't pull so hard, you'll rip it," she said. "It's nineteenth-century lace from Belgium. My great-great-grandmother brought it over as part of her trousseau when she married Otto Stritmeyer. Gran will kill you if you rip it."

Boston, who had been on the verge of doing just that to free himself, let go and glared at her. Did she expect him to just keep it there indefinitely? Walk around trailing a bedspread between his legs?

"While your family history is fascinating, I'm sure, I don't know how you expect me to get it off unless I pull it."

Shelby rocked back on her feet, sticking her hands in the pockets of her denim shorts. They weren't that short, but he had a nice view of firm, tanned thighs. Overall, her appearance was what he would politely term *earthy*. No makeup, just smooth golden skin everywhere, a narrow waist, and healthy breasts, which were clearly visible in her white tank top.

Her hair looked like a pile of brown fur on the top of her head, sun-kissed wisps escaping the inadequate rubber band and tumbling around her cheeks. Big brown puppy-dog eyes were set above sharp cheekbones and pale shiny lips.

Not his type of woman at all.

That was confirmed when she spoke again. "Well, if you just give it a minute to shrink down, you should be able to get it off no problem."

There wasn't a single woman of his acquaintance who would have just tossed that remark off to a total stranger. He didn't like it. Especially not since, by all accounts, his morning erection should have passed by now. He strongly suspected the reason it hadn't was her.

Apparently women in Cuttersville didn't find it necessary to wear a bra. It must interfere with tossing hay or participating in watermelon seed–spitting contests. Whatever the reason, she was responsible for his boner hanging on way longer than necessary, and decreasing his chances of ever producing children with each passing second.

"I can't just order it to sit and lie down like a dog," he said testily.

She eyeballed him, as if she didn't quite believe him. Her eyes dropped down to the tented spread. "Were you having a good dream? Geez Louise."

He supposed that was flattery. "You know, maybe if you weren't staring at me, we could move things along."

Reaching behind him, trying not to rock anything and cause further damage, he grabbed his pillow and flopped it down on his uncooperative appendage.

"Oh, sorry," she said in a tone that clearly indicated she wasn't. An unholy grin was creeping across her face.

The doorknob rattled again.

Shelby whirled. "Stop rattling that damn knob, Brady, or I'll rip your tongue ring out."

Boston heard a disgruntled voice from the other side of the door. "Shit, Shelby, I didn't touch the doorknob."

Shelby narrowed her eyes. "Maybe Nanny Baskins wants in."

Christ, he needed a freaking interpreter between her country accent and her weird and vague announcements. He was starting to think he shouldn't have rented this house, since the family lunatic seemed to have the run of it.

Shelby added, "Go on home, Brady! Tour's canceled."

Right. The tour. She had babbled something about a haunted house tour. "Can you explain this tour to me again? I can't seem to figure it out." Since she hadn't bothered to explain it.

Shelby shrugged. "Cuttersville's the most haunted town in Ohio. Ghosts all over the place. I run a tour of the most active sites. This house is on the tour."

Maybe they could go back to when he hadn't known anything and then his blood pressure wouldn't be shooting through the haunted house roof. "That's ridiculous. I rented this house and no one said a word to me about any tour. You'll have to remove this stop on the tour."

Her mouth dropped. "You rented the whole house?"

"Yes."

"Why? Are you married or something?"

Boston wondered if he would ever be not confused again. "No. So? I wanted privacy."

She snorted. "You won't get any here. This place is crawling with spooks." She glanced around nervously. "No offense meant, folks."

Happily, the insanity of this conversation had caused total deflation. Boston reached under the pillow and worked the bedspread free. He let out a sigh of relief.

"Everything okay under there, Mr. . . ."

He supposed she could know his name since she'd seen him naked. "Macnamara. Boston Macnamara."

Now it was her turn to look confused. "Which one's your first name and which one's your last name?"

Boston flipped his hair out of his eyes. "My first name is Boston."

"Oh." Her lips pressed together, like she was holding back. Then she put her hands on her hips. "How'd you get saddled with a name like that?"

So much for her holding back.

He was offended. He happened to like his name. It was different and suited him. "Not that it's any of your business, but my parents eloped in Boston."

Understanding dawned. She nodded. "Oh, I get it. Your mom got pregnant there, didn't she?"

Boston didn't know that for a fact, since he had never once felt the urge to get confirmation from his mother about it, but he did know he was born nine months after their wedding. But the way Shelby said it made it seem . . . vulgar.

"I have no idea," he said flatly, feeling that she had distinctly worn out her welcome in his bedroom.

"Because you know that's how Chevy Danforth got his name and Harley Johnson got his."

Now there was a visual he didn't need.

"Oh, and Abigail Murphy."

Boston pondered that one for a second, but couldn't draw any conclusions from it. He shouldn't ask. "How is that?"

"Because that was the name on the headstone of the grave she was conceived on."

He'd had to ask.

Turning, pillow still protecting him, he dropped his feet to the floor. "Well, as charming as this conversation is, I'd appreciate some privacy now, Shelby."

"Sure." She nodded and backed up toward the door. "I'll see you at eleven, then."

He froze on the bed. "Why? What's at eleven?" He had every intention of staying far away from Shelby Tucker, her perky breasts, and her slightly scary speech patterns.

"That's when the first tour runs. Then at five, I have a seniors' group from Warren coming."

Boston was starting to get the feeling that maybe Shelby was being paid money to annoy him. She was just too good at it.

"I told you quite specifically that you'll have to take this house off the tour. I rented it for three months and no one is setting foot in here but me."

Shelby didn't look impressed. "I'll be here at eleven."

"I'm going to call Mrs. Stritmeyer. This is ludicrous!"

Shelby turned the brass doorknob. "You can call Gran, but I happen to know for a fact that she writes it into every lease that you grant permission to allow this room to be viewed on the tour."

Boston's mouth fell clear down to his chest. "That's impossible. I read the lease."

Shelby gave him a grin and a wave. "There's always the fine print, Mr. Boston. Bye, now."

The second the door closed, Boston dove for his discarded clothes, afraid she'd come back and he'd have one foot in and one foot out, further humiliating himself. Underwear secure, he paced back and forth in front of the four-poster bed in his black boxers.

There were only two possible explanations for what had just happened.

He was either the victim of an elaborate reality show joke, or his life was about to take a serious downhill Shelby Tucker–filled slide.

Chapter Two

"Gran, is there something you forgot to mention to me?" Shelby fixed her grandmother with a stern look after kissing her on the cheek.

Gran was having breakfast on her wide front porch, digging around her plate with a fork and an expression of disdain. "This fruit salad is old. That deli at the grocery is going to hear from me. That's what happens when these big stores take over and you lose the personal touch."

Shelby agreed, and normally didn't mind her grandmother saying her piece. But today Shelby wanted to hear about Boston Macnamara in the blue bedroom.

"Forget the fruit salad, Gran, there was a naked man in the White House." Shelby sat down in the wicker chair opposite Gran and kicked off her sandals.

Her grandmother owned half a dozen properties around Cuttersville, each at least fifty years old, all haunted, or so people said. Gran referred to each house by the color of their exterior paint. The one Boston Macnamara was staying in was a white Victorian with black shutters, and was known to everyone in town as Mrs. Stritmeyer's White House.

Putting her fork down, Gran gave her an amused look. At seventy, Gran was slowing down a bit, but she still managed her properties herself and was sharp as a tack. She was wearing capri pants and a coral sleeveless top, which Shelby realized made her own grandmother actually appear more stylish than she did. She had a bad habit of just pulling on whatever was clean and sitting on the top in her drawer.

"Shelby, I thought you said you never see ghosts."

"I don't." That was probably the only reason she could do the job she did every day, guiding tours through Cuttersville's myriad haunted houses. In three years, she'd never once seen a single ghost, heard a single sound that wasn't explainable, or felt a cold spell. Lights never flickered and vapor never flowed past her.

Shelby was solidly in the real world and couldn't count the number of times others had claimed to be experiencing a supernatural phenomenon standing right next to her while she saw diddly-squat. Sometimes she thought it was all a lot of bunk, and other times she was damn jealous. What was the matter with her that no ghost wanted to show her a spectral face and plead for justice?

Except for an hour ago. She'd heard that doorknob jiggle. Of course, that had to have been Brady, acting like an ass, as he was known to do.

Gran speared a melon. "Then how did you see the Old Colonel if you don't see ghosts?"

"I don't know who the Old Colonel is, but the guy I saw was not old, most certainly not dead, and he was sleeping in the blue bedroom."

Naked.

Gran looked surprised. "You mean I never told you about the Old Colonel? He sunbathes in the nude. You'll have to add that to the tour, it's so eccentric. And folks just love eccentric."

Shelby didn't give a rat's hooey about the Old Colonel, though she hoped if a ghost did ever decide to show himself to her, it wouldn't be to flash her.

"I'm talking about Boston Macnamara. You know, you might have told me you let the house before I walked in on the man stark naked." Not that she regretted it, but Gran didn't need to know that.

Gran crossed her little white sneakers at the ankle. "Lucky you."

Shelby laughed. "Don't let Mom hear you say stuff like that, she'll flip out."

Gran snorted. "Your mother's had about twelve boyfriends since your father left. She has no business going prude on me. And I really do think you're a lucky thing to have seen that man without any clothes on."

"Gran!" Shelby laughed. "Behave."

Gran just smiled, her hand coming up to pat her straw-colored hair, trimmed short and framing her face in a cute modern cut. Shelby thought about her own hair, all eight hundred pounds of it, parked on top of her head like a brown octopus. Maybe she ought to think about getting a trim, if her own gran looked better than she did.

"What? I saw the man, and he's quite a hottie. I'm so old,

I've earned the right to say whatever I'm thinking." Then Gran turned sly. "What did you think of him, Shelby?"

That he was a prime hunk of man and that she'd wished she'd been wrapped around him instead of that bedspread. Shelby crossed her legs. Lord, celibacy was catching up with her. "I didn't think anything except that he was naked and in your house."

"He's single, you know." Gran dipped her fork back into the inadequate fruit salad and stabbed a grape. "Works for Samson, of course. Probably rich too. Drives a fancy car and didn't blink when I told him rent was fifteen hundred dollars a month."

Shelby stopped inspecting the dry scaly patch on her left knee and looked at her grandmother in amazement. "You charged him fifteen hundred dollars? That's almost double what he should be paying. You normally only charge two hundred per bedroom."

"And there's five bedrooms," Gran said like that explained everything.

"So that's only a thousand. Where does the other five hundred come in?"

"He's paying extra for privacy. He's got the whole house to himself." Gran waved her hand in the air and didn't look the least bit ashamed of fleecing a city boy. "He gave me three months' rent up front."

Shelby tried to imagine possessing forty-five hundred dollars all at one time and gave it up. "Dang. So what does he do at Samson? Is he here for good?"

Samson Plastics had been in Cuttersville for nearly ten years, and had saved the town from extinction. About half of Cuttersville's fifteen hundred adults worked in the plant, which manufactured two-liter bottles and other plastic items. While it had brought employment, it had also brought outsiders, who didn't always respect that Cuttersville had its own way of doing things.

Boston Macnamara was an outsider if ever she saw one. You only had to listen to him talk for five seconds to figure that out.

Gran shrugged. "I don't know what he does, I just know he must be important. His cell phone was ringing left and right and the whole town's buzzing with his arrival. Seems like nobody knew he was coming, now here he is, and nobody knows how long he's staying. Folks are afraid he's here to inspect the plant, maybe shut it down."

"He can't do that!" Whatever Shelby felt about the changes Samson Plastics had wrought on Cuttersville, she knew it would be a disaster if the plant closed. Half the town would starve.

Sweating in the June sun, even with the porch roof blocking the direct rays, Shelby picked at her tank top and inspected Gran's petunias. White and purple, just like she had every year. There were classic and feminine, like Gran, and suited this tiny Victorian house with excessive gingerbread detailing. Gran had moved into the house in 'fifty-six after her husband, Shelby's grandfather, had gotten too friendly with a bottle of gin one night and his pickup truck had kissed a fence post.

Gran had moved out of the bigger White House, bought the Yellow House, and gotten business savvy enough to spend the next few years snapping up properties nobody wanted and restoring them. Shelby trusted her grandmother's instincts and intelligence more than any other person she knew.

So when Gran said, "If he's here to close the plant, no-body can stop him," Shelby figured she had the right of it.

It was the next thing out of Gran's coral lipstick–rimmed mouth that had her questioning the woman's sanity.

"But who cares about that. He's cute, he's rich, and you've seen him naked. Let me hear your strategy for hooking him."

Boston stepped into the Busy Bee Diner, a copy of his lease under one arm to read over coffee, along with the *Cincinnati Enquirer* newspaper. The first was to prove that he hadn't been stupid enough to sign anything that al-lowed ghost tours through his rental house, the other to prove that the world as he knew it still existed outside of Cuttersville.

Every eye in the place turned toward him as he stood by the front cash register waiting to be seated. Mouths chewed, eyebrows rose, and no one said a word. Boston coolly met each and every gaze that dared to lock with his, and one by one they glanced away. All he needed was a six-shooter and he'd feel like an outlaw walking into a saloon.

A plump pink hand landed on his arm and he looked over at a round, smiling woman with gray hair.

"You need a table, sweetie? Just go on and grab one, we ain't formal here."

"Thank you," Boston said, and picked an empty table against the big picture window overlooking the street. The view was quaint at best. Old cars and pickup trucks lined the curb, and there were a few denim-wearing adults strolling along. The occasional towheaded kid zipped by on a bike, but for the most part Cuttersville was quiet, lazily baking in the summer heat.

The waitress had followed him. "You must be Jessie Stritmeyer's new renter." She held a coffeepot aloft over the mug on the table. "Coffee?"

"Yes to both." He settled in the pleather seat and set his papers down and sighed. He wanted to go back to bed. In Chicago. Where the only women to barge into his bedroom were invited there by him.

"Well, welcome to Cuttersville. I'm Madge."

Of course she was. Every good waitress in Podunk should be named Madge. Boston gave a genuine smile. "Thank you, Madge. I'm Boston Macnamara."

Madge finished tipping coffee into his mug and looked at him in amazement. "That your real name?"

What the hell was so odd about his name? "Yes."

"Some folks like to be unique, I guess." Madge leaned over him, smothering him with her ample breasts, plucked a menu from the plastic holder, and slapped it down in front of him.

"Try the Special, it's the best we've got. And don't worry none about these folks staring at you. They just don't like you because you're corporate."

Though Madge probably meant to make him feel better, it only restored his earlier surliness. He didn't want to be in Cuttersville. He was forced there on a hazy, indefinite assignment that felt suspiciously like a demotion.

He was probably allergic to hay, he wasn't overly fond of grease, and his idea of a good time did not involve haunted houses or cow tipping. Yet here he was, trying to make the best of it, and *they* weren't going to like *him*?

He'd see about that.

With a charming smile over his coffee cup, Boston told Madge, "I'm hurt to hear that, Madge. I'm not a corporate shark, I'm just a poor workingman like anybody else, working too many hours and paying too much in taxes."

Madge chuckled. "That's another reason they ain't going to like you. The girls in this town will be buzzing around you like mosquitoes, with that smile and those city clothes. You look like you stepped right off the TV."

The only local girl he'd met so far had been Shelby Tucker, and she hadn't seemed all that impressed. Amused maybe, but not impressed. But then who wouldn't be amused when confronted with the sight of a man trapped inside a doily bedspread hole?

"Madge, you jawing that young man to death?"

His landlady scooted around Madge and took the seat opposite him. "Get him one of those Specials and leave us to talk."

Boston narrowed his eyes and decided to forgo pleasantries. "Should we talk about your granddaughter waltzing into my bedroom at the crack of dawn this morning?"

The smile Jessie Stritmeyer gave him was smug. "Well, since you brought it up. What did you think of Shelby? Sweet girl, isn't she?"

He was thinking more along the lines of insane, but maybe that's what *sweet* meant in the country. "She seems to think she can bring a tour through the house anytime she feels like it. That wasn't in the lease, Mrs. Stritmeyer."

"Well, actually, it is. It says on the second page that should the landlady find it necessary to enter the house, she is authorized to do so."

*   *   *

Jessie watched various emotions play over Boston Macnamara's face. Incredulous was warring with furious.

"That refers to *emergencies*, like pipes leaking while I'm at work or a fire breaking out."

"It doesn't say emergencies, does it? It says if the land-lady finds it necessary. Well, I find it necessary to help my granddaughter put food on her table." Besides, her houses were the best on the tour, if she did say so herself.

Jessie called to Madge to bring her some herbal tea. She couldn't handle the caffeine in coffee anymore—it kept her up at night and messed with her bladder, and Lord knew she had enough problems with that leaky sieve as it was.

Boston was turning a strange purple, damn near like her petunias. For a second, she rethought her plan, since he seemed a little more uptight than she'd remembered from their initial meetings over renting the house. Then she decided that she had been right. Shelby needed a man with a sense of direction in his life, since she seemed content to float adrift on her own indefinitely.

The girl didn't even think anything of living in her grandmother's house, which was just downright sad for a woman in her prime.

Then this here attitude right now was confirmation that Boston Macnamara needed a woman who was easygoing. Someone to help him slow down, relax, and enjoy life instead of racing to get through it.

"Listen, young man, you're getting all worked up for nothing. The tour only runs twice a day, five days a week, and half the time you'll be at work anyway. When you are around, the tour is only in the house less than ten minutes."

Jessie smiled at him and patted his white knuckles gently. She did not want him to move out.

"You'll never find another decent place to stay on such short notice. There aren't any motels in Cuttersville, unless you want the one out on the old highway that's full up with prostitutes and that bunch of folks who chant at night and proclaim they're aliens." She took in his black shirt and tan pants, expensive watch and salon-styled hair. "You don't look like the chanting type."

He snorted. "Hardly."

"The rent is a steal, you know that. You could never rent a whole house in Chicago for only fifteen hundred dollars. And you have a housekeeper."

She didn't feel a bit of guilt that she was technically overcharging him. It was a steal for him, and a windfall for her. She'd lived too damn long to spend time feeling sorry for folks with money.

Eyeing her over his coffee mug, he asked, "House-keeper? You never mentioned a housekeeper before."

"I didn't?" Jessie feigned surprise. "Well, of course you have one. Mary's absolutely miraculous." She didn't mention just how miraculous. "She pops in two or three times a week and will do whatever needs doing, including your laundry. She'll even cook for you if you'd like."

She sensed she was reeling him in. He didn't say anything, just sat there looking sullen, like Shelby had as a child when she'd gotten in trouble for dirtying her church clothes. Shelby had very little regard for her appearance to this day. Jessie pictured those dusty shorts she had been wearing that morning and shuddered.

Now she wasn't any fashion plate herself—she was too

old and lived in too small of a town to ever be in style—but Lord, Shelby ran around looking like she'd collided with a wheelbarrow full of dirt. It was going to take some coaxing to bring her around to thinking she should set her sights on the immaculate Boston Macnamara.

The little ingrate had actually cussed when Jessie had suggested it over breakfast.

"Mrs. Stritmeyer," Boston said slowly.

She smiled. "Call me Jessie, honey."

He set his mug back down hard. "You know, I don't like the way you've manipulated me. But since I'm only here temporarily, I guess I don't have a choice."

Jessie knew there wasn't anyplace else in town he could stay that wasn't a dump or didn't require a year-long lease. "Oh, you won't be sorry. Trust me." Not when at the end of the day he had her granddaughter keeping him company at night.

"There is one thing, though."

His cell phone rang and he reached for it reflexively before stopping himself.

Feeling magnanimous, Jessie nodded. "You can answer it. Go on, I don't mind."

Hitting the button and holding the tiny phone to his ear, he said, "Samson Plastics. This is Boston Macnamara."

It was enough to make even an old lady shiver. He was sexier than sin, in her opinion, and she knew Shelby wasn't immune to that fact, no matter how many four-letter words she tossed off.

Boston spoke for another minute, giving perfunctory commands, then he hung up the phone. He met her curious gaze and said, as if they hadn't been interrupted, "Shelby needs to knock first. Not on the door to my bedroom, but on the front door, before she and her rubbernecking tourists can come into the house."

Jessie allowed herself a satisfied smile. "I'm sure that won't be a problem."

If she had anything to do with it, Shelby wouldn't need to catch the man sleeping in order to see him naked.

Shelby was on her way to the Busy Bee for a late lunch, annoyed to find she was disappointed that she hadn't run into Boston Macnamara on her eleven o'clock tour. The house had been silent except for the shuffling of her guests, murmurs that they swore the upstairs hall was cold, and the low hum of a fan Boston had left running in his bedroom.

"Hey, Shelby, honey, darlin', sugar, what are you up to?"

Big arms wrapped around her from behind and Shelby was swallowed in a convulsive bear hug from her ex-husband, Danny Tucker. She loved Danny, she really did. All two hundred brawny pounds of him.

He had caught up with her outside the hardware store, next to the diner, and she nearly dropped the keys in her hand from the impact of his embrace. "Hey, Danny. I'm grabbing some lunch. You want to join me?" At least if she had Danny to distract her, she wouldn't be tempted to call up mental images of Boston and the eyelet spread for cheap thrills over her ham and cheese.

"Sure, I'm in town all day. You buying?" Danny pulled off his baseball hat and grinned, his cheeks sunburned from another day out in the fields.

She snorted. "You wish. Dutch, buddy. I don't recall agreeing to any alimony that says I have to buy you lunch."

He laughed, that carefree sound that endeared everyone to him. "Damn, I should have had the lawyer write that in. That's a good one."

Danny was good looking, an all-American boy. Healthy, hardy, blond. A ripped-T-shirt-wearing farmer, and doggone nice to boot. Lack of love or lack of friendship had not been a problem in their marriage. It had been lack of passion.

Shelby felt a pang of something that was either loneliness, regret, or heartburn from going too long since breakfast. Her fingers drifted up to Danny's cheek. "You fool, you got sunburned again. How many times do I have to tell you to wear sunscreen? You watch, when you're fifty years old they'll be hacking half your face away because of skin cancer."

Danny covered her fingers with his, large calloused fingers that always had dirt under the nails. Workingman's hands, unlike that city boy who probably stopped into a salon called Rupert's or something once a week for a sissy manicure.

"That's because I don't have you taking care of me anymore." He took her hand to his mouth and kissed each of her fingertips, his brown eyes teasing.

For the ten-thousandth time Shelby wondered why life couldn't be simple. In a perfect world, she would be weak-kneed with wet panties right now, urging Danny to whisk her off to the back of his truck for a nooner. In her less-than-perfect Cuttersville reality, Danny's kisses were just warm and wet, like a friendly dog.

Yet Boston Macnamara set her thighs burning.

She decided she was a contrary soul.

*   *   *

Boston tried to concentrate on Bob and Phil, the plant managers for the Cuttersville division of Samson Plastics, but all he could do was stare out the window at Shelby Tucker getting mauled by some big brute of a guy wearing a sweat-stained gray T-shirt with the sleeves torn off.

He forced himself to look down at his turkey sandwich, which was loaded with bacon and had a glop of mashed potatoes lying on the plate next to it. Picking the bacon off, he wondered exactly why Bob and Phil were treating him like he was the second coming of Christ.

They were gushing. Hearty. Jovial. Nervous, and sweating like two overfed pigs in golf shirts.

"So exactly how long are you going to be here?" Bob asked for the fourth time in the three hours since Boston had met him. "Mr. Delmar didn't say."

Since Boston had no idea and wasn't about to admit that Brett Delmar had left him dangling on this one, he shrugged. "As long as we feel it's necessary."

For what, he hadn't a damn clue, since he had no idea what exactly he was supposed to be doing in Cuttersville. At his tour through the plant that morning, he had decided to treat it as an inspection, since his duties had not been defined to him by Brett. He would see if the plant was running efficiently, then report back to his boss.

Then beg to get the hell out of here.

Before he dropped dead of a heart attack from excessive fat and grease at the Busy Bee Diner.

He wiped his bacon-compromised fingers on a paper napkin and looked out the window again. Shelby was still wrapped up in the sweaty embrace of Farmer Ted out there. "Who's that guy with Shelby Tucker?" he heard himself say before he could debate the wisdom of it.

Why he cared, he couldn't imagine. If Shelby had a nice local boy to squeeze her day and night, it wasn't his concern.

Except her grandmother had hinted that Shelby was available.

Which still had nothing to do with him, since he wasn't interested in entangling himself with the local tour guide, no matter how firm her thighs were.

Phil set down his barbecued sparerib sandwich and narrowed his eyes to look out the window. "Oh, that's Danny Tucker. Her ex-husband."

A piece of turkey fell from Boston's open mouth to his plate.

Well, well. Another good reason he shouldn't entangle himself with her. An ex-husband who looked to still be very friendly with her. Good thing he wasn't seriously considering doing *anything* with or about her. He was far too rational for that.

The ex-husband appeared to be sucking on her fingers now. Boston tried not to imagine doing the same. "It must have been an amiable divorce."

Phil had gone back to his sandwich, but Bob smoothed back his receding hair and nodded. "Yep. No one was really quite sure why they got divorced. But maybe it was because they got married just about right out of high school. Five years later people change, I guess."

Five years? She had been married for five years? She looked younger than him, and yet she had been married for quite a while and divorced already. Boston hadn't dated any woman longer than a year, and he was leery of even getting a dog. Committing to anything other than his job for an extended period of time, with no closing date, scared the proverbial shit out of him.

Bob said, "You know, our numbers at the plant are really good. We've met production for the last eight quarters and our overhead is low."

Boston forced his mind off Shelby and to the man sitting across from him. Bob was staring at him intently, and Phil had shifted on the cracked vinyl booth. Boston noticed for the first time that the diner was once again hushed, like it had been that morning. While he'd been staring at Shelby out the window, every man, woman, and child inside had been staring at him.

Bob and Phil, between effusive compliments, kept emphasizing their productivity, and Boston finally caught the hidden meaning. Would have caught it earlier if he hadn't been distracted since the minute he'd woken up and found Shelby gaping at his tortured penis.

They thought he was here to check up on the plant and, maybe specifically, to check up on them.

The polite thing to do would be to tell them the truth, that he was apparently on the outs with his boss for some unknown atrocity, and that he had no clue why he'd been banished to Cuttersville.

But his pride wouldn't allow that.

The pride was what had gotten him through childhood, through the heartache and embarrassment when his father had skipped town with a wad of embezzled cash and Boston's eighteen-year-old babysitter. Pride had earned him a spot at the University of Chicago, and then a job at Samson Plastics.

It had served him well, and all the Shelby Tuckers in Cuttersville couldn't force him to part with it.

"Well, after lunch, we'll head back on over and you can show me these fabulous numbers you keep bragging about."

After all, he did have to do something here, and every one of Samson's holdings did need to be watchdogged from time to time. He would just self-appoint himself to the task.

Maybe Podunk wasn't going to be so heinous after all. He had just landed himself a three-month vacation from real work.

Chapter Three

The seniors were getting restless. Shelby recognized the signs. Shuffling of walkers and canes. Griping at their spouses. Fiddling with the false teeth.

She rang the doorbell of the White House again. Gran had told her about the agreement with Boston and she was willing to abide by his rules. But he wasn't answering the door and she had a whole porch full of people with prosthetic parts. They couldn't stand around for very long without locking up.

Knocking with enough force to wake the dead, or at least to rouse Boston, since the dead were already awake, she turned to her audience.

"This Victorian home built in 1886 is home to at least seven spirits. From the nanny who continues to watch over every generation of children in the house and the kindly housekeeper who keeps serving meals, to the forlorn and malicious man who lurks in the basement, there is never an empty room in the house. The current resident is only temporary, while the spirits reside for eternity."

The current resident wasn't answering his damn door, and she figured she'd fulfilled her end of the bargain. Gran had only said she had to knock. Nobody said anything about waiting for Boston to actually let her in.

Oops. Her key fell in the lock and turned.

Since Boston clearly wasn't home, she wasn't going to worry about it. Workaholic like that, he probably would sleep on a couch in his office. Rumpled in his fancy dress clothes, mouth slightly open, arm up, and a sexy little rise and fall of his chest . . .

Hell, what was the matter with her? Fine time for her passionate side to pop up out of nowhere. Hadn't that been the problem with her and Danny? Her nonexistent passion? She had always gone through the motions, knowing damn well she wasn't exactly blowing his mind with her slightly elevated breathing and halfhearted hip thrusts. Since her divorce, no man had really caught her sexual eye, and she had concluded she just wasn't a passionate person.

Until now. Until Boston. She'd felt more urgings today than she had in the past three years, and the man hadn't even laid a soft, city finger on her. Maybe the conclusion she could draw was that celibacy was an unnatural state, and that even mediocre sex with Danny had been better than no sex, because no sex had made her lose her mind and lust after a pretty boy.

"Come on in, folks, and listen carefully for the mysterious sounds of the dead." Shelby entered the narrow entry hall and stepped into the parlor on the left to allow room for her six guests.

"What the hell are you doing?"

Shelby jumped at the sound of Boston's voice coming from behind her. Feeling a guilty blush steal over her cheeks, she turned. "Well, hi there, Boston. How are you?"

He was lying on the couch, damn him, just like her fantasy, only in her dreams he wasn't scrunched on a Victorian chintz sofa too short for him, wearing a tight T-shirt and a scowl. The little wires dangling from his ears indicated why he hadn't heard her knock, and he shifted the MP3 player off his lap, along with a laptop computer, as he sat up.

"Shelby, I asked one simple thing of your grandmother. That you not enter the house without my consent, and here I find you standing in my living room."

The priggish tone set her back up. "That wasn't the agreement! Gran said I couldn't come in without knocking first. I knocked, you didn't answer, then I came in."

Let him dispute that.

His eyes narrowed.

Shelby became aware that the seniors had gone silent in the entryway, hanging on every embarrassing word. She was about to suggest they head on up the stairs, she'd be along in a minute after her argument with sexy city boy ended, when the pocket door to the parlor started sliding shut.

The seniors must be giving her privacy. As thoughtful as that was, she wasn't having any of it.

"That's alright folks, I'm coming on out." Boston could wait. She couldn't really abandon her tour-goers; she needed the money too much to risk alienation. Besides, she didn't want to be closed into a room alone with Boston, even for a minute in broad daylight.

"The door's closing by itself!" one of the seniors called out. She thought it was Ernie, given the gravelly bellow.

There were various startled gasps from others, and something resembling a scream from one woman.

"What?" She strode forward, reaching out to grab the door. It stopped sliding. She stuck her head out a ways, and saw that indeed, all six adults were standing in the hall, none in touching distance of the door.

They gaped at her. "Must have been the wind," she said, trying to push the door back open.

It pushed back.

Shelby pushed harder.

The door gave a hefty shove, sending her sailing back into the parlor, fearing for her head getting caught in the door. It slammed into the wall and she heard the click as the pocket door's little click latch was turned.

"What the hell?" Shelby grabbed the door, rattled it, tried to turn the lock back. Nothing budged.

Boston nudged her, startling her into a yelp. Jesus, she hadn't even seen him come up behind her, she was that freaked out.

"I'll get it."

His ample muscles rippled as he gripped the door and tried to move it. Shelby hadn't noticed all that bulging when she'd seen him that morning. Of course, her eyes had been glued to another bulge. Now with that faded navy T-shirt straining, she had a great shot of biceps.

Scooting back so she wouldn't impede his pushing, she observed that he was wearing jeans. Not butt-huggers, but just enough room there to provide fuel for her imagination without giving it all away. He had an expensive black leather belt, and still wore his pricey watch, but he was barefoot. Even so, he looked out of place in Cuttersville, in the White House's nineteenth-century parlor with fussy lace curtains.

"Whoever locked this door, I suggest you open it immediately. I'm not amused," he called through the door as he struggled with it.

Shelby thought he sounded a hell of a lot like her third grade teacher, Mrs. Gunther. Except Mrs. Gunther had more whiskers.

There was silence for a moment, then came a woman's voice, hushed with awe. "None of us have touched that door. But we all saw it shut on its own."

"Bullshit," Boston said, bending over to run his finger along the door frame and shaking the door violently.

Like that was going to do anything. Shelby called out, "Hey, Ernie, try the door from your side."

The click lock turned back, unlocking the door. Or so Shelby thought.

When Boston pounced on the door and shoved, it still didn't move. "What the . . . ?" He locked and unlocked the latch again and nothing moved. "It's stuck or something."

Wary gaze floating around the room, Shelby ignored the renewed swearing of Boston and the lock rattling of Ernie and waited for a ghost to vaporize before her eyes. She wanted out. Oh, Lord, she was scared all of a sudden. And cold. Maybe the ghost was projecting that on to her. Maybe the ghost was *in* her.

Shelby screamed and launched herself at Boston's back. When she crashed into him and his nose crunched against the pocket door, he said, "Ow, dammit! Get off of me."

There was something every woman dreams a man will say to her.

Her irrational fear disappeared as quickly as it had risen. Replaced by embarrassment that she'd pressed her breasts against his hard back like a bimbo coed in *Scary Movie*.

"Sorry. Something walked on my grave there." She rubbed the goose bumps on her arms.

Ernie called out, "Door won't budge from this side."

Boston rubbed his nose. Shelby rolled her eyes. Like it hurt *that* much. She'd been skipping the Krispy Kremes lately, so he could stop acting like a truck had plowed into him.

"Does your grandmother have a key to this door?"

"I don't know. I never knew it locked before. I could call her and see. Or we could just toss you out the window into the petunias."

His eyes lit up. "The windows. Good point, Shelby. We can climb out the window."

He shoved aside lace, unlocked the flimsy brass locks that had been tacked on the frame of the old window next to the sofa, and grimaced. Boston wiped his hand on his jeans, and Shelby wanted to laugh. Mr. Clean didn't like a little dust and lead-paint chips on his hands.

Then he shoved, giving her a mighty nice view of his back and shoulders straining. The window didn't open. Boston shoved again. And again. Until Shelby was bored with watching him, even that little jerk his cute backside gave each time.

She listened to him swear and move on to another window.

"There's nothing wrong with this window, I don't know why it's not opening. It doesn't look painted shut."

"It's not. There's no air-conditioning in this house and every single window opens."

"Then why the hell won't they open?" He pushed so hard his foot slipped on the hardwood floor.

She sank to the floor and crossed her legs. "Don't you think we should call Gran?"

"Just let me try the rest of these."

Sure, let him get all sweaty. She leaned against the wall and called out to her seniors' group. "Folks, it looks like I'm stuck. I'm afraid we'll have to cancel the tour and I'll refund your money."

There was some grumbling and concerns for her safety for about thirty seconds, then they abandoned her, their footsteps echoing in the front hall, the door slamming shut behind them. With them went her grocery money for the month.

Shelby allowed herself a sigh. Sometimes a girl couldn't catch a break, and if she were a believin' sort, she'd think the spirits were trying to tell her something. Not that she did believe. But if she did, she wished they'd make their desires more obvious.

Because right now they either wanted her to starve to death or be driven to insanity by the stubborn, fastidious, control-freak Boston Macnamara. Neither of which she could claim to be her immediate goals in life.

"Got a phone?" she asked him, sure his cell phone was close to his body in a place of deference. Like next to his heart or in a pocket alongside his third leg.

Boston stopped pushing the last window and turned around, breathing a little harder than normal. She hoped he wasn't going to go postal on her, and throw a lamp through the window. But he just relaxed his shoulders and dug deep in his pocket, confirming its importance in his life to her. He flipped it two feet to her.

"This is unreal," he said.

"So is this phone." Shelby caught it and studied the cracker-size cell phone. She shook it. Tossed it from hand to hand. "Is this thing real? It looks like a kid's toy." And it was metallic blue, showing a whimsical side to Boston she never would have guessed.

"Yes, it's real. Don't you have cell phones in Cuttersville?" He turned and tried the window again.

"There's not much business here that's pressing enough to require instant communication. And if I broke down in Gran's old clunker, it would only take two minutes before someone I know would stop and help me." Shelby pressed random buttons trying to find something resembling *on*. "And it's rude of you to keep implying that we're hicks. Don't they teach manners in the big city?"

Boston watched Shelby double-fist his phone, eyes narrowed, lip bit in concentration, and he felt annoyance all over again. "*I* don't have manners? Who walked into my house without an invitation?"

"That's different," she said without looking up. "I came for the tour."

Then her eyes lit up as she figured out how to turn his phone on, and started dialing, making a face as she left a message on her grandmother's voice mail. He bet her grandma had a cell phone.

Boston wiped his hands on his jeans and tried to ignore the fact that Shelby's knees were slowly falling apart, and that her denim shorts were pulled taut right between her thighs, hugging her body. He also didn't want to notice that the shorts had wide leg holes, and he could see right up them, past lots of golden skin to a flash of red panty. Hot red. Candy apple red. Cherry red.

Clearly the lack of air circulation in the enclosed room, and the irritation of being stuck in a room for no logical reason, had him irrational. Reduced to basic human instincts. Air. Water. Sex. Lots of sex. With Shelby Tucker.

"Mom, I can't get ahold of Gran. I'm stuck in the parlor of the White House and I need you to go get Gran's key." Shelby rolled her eyes as she listened for a second. "It is not my fault. I didn't do anything! And I'm sorry that you have chicken on the grill, but I'm your only daughter and I'm going to die of suffocation, starve, or burst my bladder if you don't get here."

There was a pause and Boston didn't harbor much hope for rescue coming in the form of Shelby's mother.

"And maybe you can ask Dave to bring his ladder or something, and he can try and open the windows from the outside if you can't get the door open."

Another pause. "I know! Geez."

Then Shelby moved the phone away from her ear and glared at it. "How do you turn this thing off?"

Boston stepped over to her and held his hand out. She was kind of cute when she was annoyed, but she also looked like, if given provocation, she could ram his phone up his nose. "Do you really have to go to the bathroom?"

She nodded, placing the phone in his hand with warm fingers. "I think it's just psychological, though."

But her knees squeezed back together tightly.

And he felt the incredibly ridiculous, male urge to comfort her, reassure her that he would get her out of there, beating the door down with his bare hands if he had to. He had never dated women who needed or wanted protection. He dated women who did Pilates and earned six figures without breaking a nail or a sweat.

Shelby didn't look like she needed protection either. But he felt the urge nonetheless and it disturbed the hell out of him. He was in Cuttersville solely for the purpose of getting back out, and it was not supposed to affect him. He liked the way he was, no change needed in his life.

Still, after rattling the door lock without luck for the eleventh time, he paced in front of Shelby. "I know what you mean. I've been sitting in here for an hour working, totally comfortable, and now that I know I can't open the windows, I feel like it's ten degrees hotter." He picked at his T-shirt just thinking about it. It was at least eighty in the parlor.

"You can take your shirt off if you want. I don't mind," Shelby said.

Boston stopped pacing. That sounded . . . suggestive. Or wishful thinking on his part. He glanced at Shelby. A faint pink was creeping up her neck. Definitely suggestive.

"Sorry, that didn't sound right."

"I know you didn't mean anything by it," he lied. If there was one thing he was good at, it was lying to soothe other people. Half his job consisted of soothing clients. Only none of them were cute in denim shorts, and soothing had never sounded so appealing.

Damn, he needed to get the hell away from her. "Is someone coming to try the windows? Can't we just call the fire department or something?"

Shelby looked broadsided by his idea. "I never thought of that. It's not an emergency or anything, but they sent guys out to help Dody Farnsworth unlock her car when she left the keys in the ignition and shut the door. I'll call them and they should be able to get us out one way or another."

Then she grinned at him. "I guess that's why you get paid the big bucks, huh?"

He laughed. "Not big enough yet, but I'm working on it."

Shelby snorted. "Bigger than me."

"The Haunted Cuttersville Tour doesn't have you living in the lap of luxury?"

"No, just in Gran's Yellow House and that's charity because we're related."

"Then why do you do the tour?" He didn't think it sounded like a whole lot of fun, tromping gawking tourists through houses day after day.

"Because it pays better than anything else I'm qualified to do, which is nothing. Cuttersville High trained me to do exactly what I did, become a farmer's wife. Only I didn't stay a farmer's wife, and I'm not book smart, so I won't go to college and torture myself." She shrugged. "I could get a job at the factory, I guess, but I'm not ready for that. Too . . . restrictive."

Boston had heard of people like Shelby. Had even met one or two. He just couldn't fathom how their brains functioned so differently from his. His entire life was consumed by his career and its success. If he stopped moving, stopped pushing and shoving and striving, he wasn't sure what in the hell would happen. He thought it was possible he would melt.

"So why don't you move to Cincinnati or Columbus and get a better-paying job?"

That earned two eyebrows shooting up under her wispy brown bangs. "Because my family is here. I belong here. I'll never leave."

That said, she picked up his phone again and dialed.

*   *   *

"Jessie, we can't do that." Carl Hagan gave her a stern look and crossed his arms. "I'm sending John and Howie out to the house."

"And after all I've done for you, not even a simple request is being respected." Jessie crossed her arms right back. When she had gotten a frantic call from Susan, Shelby's mother, moaning about Shelby in trouble again and burned chicken, Jessie had called her own voice mail and heard the message from Shelby. Shelby was trapped with the hunk—rich hunk—Boston Macnamara. Gee, what a shame.

Sounded like the ghosts were on her side in this matchmaking business, because she knew for a fact that the door to the parlor didn't lock, hadn't in thirty years, and that every one of those windows should open.

Four or five hours trapped alone together could only be a good thing for Shelby and Boston. But Carl was acting like he was going to race the whole fire department out there and bust things up before it even got interesting.

Carl was only ten years her junior, and twice her width, but she had babysat his shiny backside once upon a time while Hitler was racing around Europe, and she'd be damned if he was going to pull professional rank over her.

"Shelby called and said she's trapped, Jessie. We can't ignore her!"

"She's in the parlor, not a cave, for crying out loud. Just for a little while, that's all I'm asking for."

Jessie pulled out a couple of twenties and waved them in John and Howie's direction as they walked past to their nonemergency truck. Both men stopped and looked at her in interest. "Just take a little detour on the way, boys, a little stop over at the Burger King, and get yourselves some dinner. An hour, tops, then you can go rescue Shelby. But if you break one of my windows, you're replacing it, Carl."

"It don't work that way, Jessie. The fire department doesn't pay for the damages made while rescuing people."

"Well, why not? What are my taxes going for?" Took near half her damn income every year, at least the government could replace a broken window.

Lord, it was a good thing she was watching out for herself and Shelby, because no one else was.

Shelby was getting desperate. It had been half an hour since she'd called the fire department, and nothing. She and Boston were still trapped, and as the sun drifted westward, the lace on the windows was no protection from the pounding sunshine, forcing the temperature of the room higher, one hot degree at a time.

Or maybe it was her desire that had the room warm enough to cook a whole platter of ribs in five minutes. Boston had taken his shirt off.

She'd seen that chest before, just that morning in his bedroom. It had affected her then. Now it had her clasping her thighs together and praying she wouldn't whimper.

Even the increasing needs of her bladder were nothing compared to the realization that it had been *three years* since she'd had sex. Three years that had flown by while she'd been living them, and now seemed like an abnormal, painfully large amount of time since her body was quivering and steaming and hissing, like the overheated engine of a Chevy.

Boston, who probably had sex scheduled in on the calendar of his fancy-shmancy computer every week with some suit-wearing, manicure-getting, leggy blonde, looked oblivious to her problem. After a few minutes of polite conversation, he had checked the voice mail on his cell phone, then had moved to foraging through his e-mails on his laptop.

Ignoring her, that's what he was doing. No, that wasn't true. He wasn't ignoring her; he was just carrying on without her. Unimportant, that's what she was. Irrelevant.

Every physical need her body required—thirst, hunger, sex—were all rearing up and begging for attention simultaneously, making her so uncomfortable she wanted to roll around on the floor and groan. Except that would make her bladder pressure worse. Yet Boston just sat with his legs apart, computer in his lap, eyes scanning, clicking and working and looking fit as a flipping fiddle.

He had no right to turn her on doing nothing.

Jerk.

Then he dug into the pocket of his jeans, lifting his hips up a little, a mock thrust, denim pulling, straining . . . and popped a Life Saver in his mouth.

Her stomach cried foul. "You'd better have another one of those."

"Huh?" He glanced over at her.

"That piece of candy. Give me one too. I'm starving." She thought about adding a *please,* then thought better of it. This whole thing was his fault anyway, for being such a dingleberry about letting her in the house. If he'd just been reasonable from the get-go, she wouldn't have walked into the parlor, and they wouldn't be stuck here together.

He'd be stuck alone.

Poor baby.

Boston tucked the candy into his cheek. "I'm sorry. It's the last one."

He looked genuine enough to believe him, but Shelby had male cousins. They'd tell her they were handing her a piece of candy, and wipe a booger into her hand instead. She knew not to trust a man until you'd gotten his measure. She didn't know Boston that well yet.

"Where's the empty wrapper?"

Boston tried to process Shelby's words. Her thoughts moved in directions he didn't understand, and sometimes it took him a minute to follow through to the conclusion. Then he fought a smile. She thought he was keeping a secret stash of Life Savers from her.

Like he needed to hoard hard candy for survival. Despite the slow appearance of the Cuttersville Fire Department, he was convinced it was only a matter of another hour or so before someone managed to spring them from the parlor. But Shelby looked suspicious, and hot, and impatient.

Her forehead was shiny, damp curls sticking to her temples, ponytail drooping, and that white T-shirt was clinging to her breasts. She'd tucked the bottom of the shirt up through the neck hole, tugging it down to create a knot, exposing her stomach. The country version of air-conditioning. She looked like Daisy Duke, feisty and independent and sexy in a really strange, dusty, natural sort of way. If she put on heels with those denim shorts, he was going to be in trouble.

Except that Shelby would probably fall over if she put on heels, and he wasn't supposed to be shopping the local merchandise anyway.

"The wrapper's in my pocket. Would you like to inspect it?" Boston patted his pocket, sucking the cherry flavoring of the candy over his tongue, feeling rude for eating in front of her. He wasn't used to thinking about other people's feelings. He lived alone and he worked hard to get ahead, and while he could schmooze with the best of them, genuine courtesy wasn't really a major part of his life any longer. Maybe it never had been. His parents hadn't exactly been founts of thoughtfulness.

"Toss it this way." She held out her hand.

Boston balled up the empty wrapper and threw it toward her.

Catching it, Shelby gave a heartfelt sigh. "It really was the last one, wasn't it?"

He set his laptop down, not able to concentrate anyway, and dropped onto the hardwood floor next to her. Shelby gave him a disgruntled look and held his empty wrapper back out for him.

Stuffing it back in his pocket, he pushed the candy forward and caught it between his teeth, flashing her a glimpse. She glared at him and lust rose in his gut—plain, vicious, ball-gripping lust—which made him toss her a smile.

"Shelby, I'll share it with you."

Rich brown eyes widened. "Whatta ya mean?"

What did he mean? He wasn't exactly sure, just that he didn't like to see her so uncomfortable, and he was curious if she felt even a pang of attraction for him too.

Retrieving the sticky, slippery candy from his mouth with his fingers, he tapped it against her bottom lip with a light teasing motion. "You can have the rest."

Her tongue slipped out and licked the sugary red droplet the candy had left on her plump lip. "Mmm, that's good," she said, eyes fluttering closed for a brief moment, sending Boston into a frenzy of sexual awareness. "I'm so hungry."

That would be what she'd look like coming apart under him. Hot and damp and dewy-eyed, flustered and sensual, slow movements and sliding tongue. Rolling eyes and murmured approval.

Clearly not dating since Sheila had petulantly declared him a workaholic and walked out six months ago had been a mistake. He was as horny as a fourteen-year-old with a Pamela Anderson download.

But nonetheless, he took the candy and pressed it against her closed lips, forcing her to open for him. Both the candy and his finger slipped inside her hot moist mouth, and when the tip of her tongue traced his skin, he felt a raw groan rush up from somewhere deep in his gut. He managed to stifle it in time to prevent long-term humiliation.

Then she sucked.

He jerked his finger back faster than a stock market crash.

Swallowing and tucking the candy into her cheek, Shelby spoke in a low, breathy voice. "Thanks, I appreciate it, Boston."

"Anytime."

Anytime she wanted to torture him, he was right here, stuck in Cuttersville, with nothing to do but contemplate the many ways he could pleasure Shelby Tucker.

Her eyes widened. "Look out!"

Chapter Four

Sluggish from the sugar rush and the surge of hormones coursing through her body at the feel of Boston's finger in her mouth, it took Shelby a second to realize a lamp was winging across the room right at Boston's head.

She yelled, he turned to look behind him, and Gran's faux Tiffany lamp, with the pink glass tulips on the panes, clipped Boston on the shoulder.

"What the hell?" He jumped to his feet, rubbing his arm and working his shoulder around.

Shelby gaped at the lamp, now resting right side up on the floor, cord trailing behind it, still plugged in to the wall socket. She judged the distance from point of origin to Boston's shoulder to be four feet or more, which was so doggone weird a scream rose in her throat.

Not wanting to look like a wuss, she clamped down on

it, and glanced around the room for any other mobile inanimate objects. "Are you okay?"

"Yeah, it's just my shoulder and it didn't hit with all that much force." He looked a little wild-eyed, left hand still resting on the sleeve of the opposite arm. "But how the hell did that lamp move?"

"I don't know." But she had an idea, one that was more than a little unnerving. One that had goose bumps rising on her skin despite the heat, and she crunched the remains of the candy in her mouth hard, with excess nervous energy.

"Boston, do you believe in ghosts? You know, spirits of dead people hanging on?" First-class skeptic, she'd always been, though now and again she'd wondered if there wasn't some truth to it. But in all her tours, she'd never encountered anything that wasn't explainable.

An acrobatic lamp was unexplainable.

Boston's eyebrows rose. "I know what ghosts are. I just find myself hard-pressed to believe in them. Most sightings occur in the presence of people who want to see a ghost for whatever reason. I don't think that's a coincidence."

"I've never been one to think much of it either, despite my job. I mean, I've lived here my whole life, in Ohio's most haunted town, and never saw a single otherworldly occurrence." She shivered and stood up. "But that was nuts. That lamp just rose off the table and came right at you, like it was aiming for you."

"So you're saying I've offended a possessed lamp?"

Shelby could see the temptation to wing something at him. He was so condescending sometimes, though she wondered if he knew he was or if it was just a by-product of being successful.

"No, you must have offended one of the two ghosts who are known to be in this room from time to time. Red-Eyed Rachel or the Blond Man." Shelby sincerely hoped it was the Blond Man sharing space with them, but she had the sneaking suspicion it was Rachel instead, which made her want to karate-chop her way around the room, clearing the air.

And where the hell was the fire department anyway? She was locked in a room with a sexy Samson VP and a looby ghost. It wasn't helping her overextended bladder in the least.

Boston picked up the lamp, turned it over, inspected the cord, set it down again. He walked the distance between the table and the lamp, then back again, obviously searching for a logical explanation.

"I think it's Rachel. She lived in this house, you know, back in 1887 with her folks."

Boston put the lamp back on the table and sighed. "Oh, God, you're going to tell me a ghost story, aren't you?"

The last thing in the world he felt like listening to was an overexaggerated local legend about some poor biddy who froze to death in the Great Winter. He was starting to feel claustrophobic and was considering calling the fire department again, or just taking the ugly pink lamp and throwing it through the nearest window to escape.

He had no idea how a heavy lamp could have flung off a thigh-high table and nailed him on the shoulder. But it had, and he should be grateful. Another second and he might have actually kissed Shelby Tucker, which was baffling at best, disastrous at worst.

"Of course I'm going to tell you. You'll need to know if you're going to live here and she doesn't like you."

Boston glanced at Shelby, who was pushing her hair

back off her face. She had a lot of hair, the kind that would tease across her nipples when it was let loose. Her shirt rode up and up, the knot still holding, the shirt bunching under each breast and emphasizing its round fullness.

The lamp he was still resting his hand on started to shake, the base clanking on the wood table. He ripped his hand back and stared at it. "Christ, it moved again!"

"Rachel," Shelby said, her head nodding up and down. "She doesn't like men, they say."

"Was she a lesbian?" he asked, picturing that going over big in 1887 Cuttersville.

But Shelby rolled her eyes. "No! She was a regular kind of girl, though a little forceful, everyone says. Christy Levenworth is her descendant through Rachel's mother's sister, and *forceful* would describe Christy too. She flattened me in the Easter egg hunt of nineteen-eighty-four trying to get that purple speckled one."

The really incredible thing was that he knew Shelby wasn't making this stuff up. "So, okay, Rachel, regular girl . . . and then what? She died, I take it."

"Eventually, but first she caught her fiancé diddling with the girl-of-all-work her family had, right here in this very room. Seems the rat was picking her up for an afternoon carriage ride about town, and Rachel had just gone upstairs to fetch her bonnet, and tore her dress trim on the way up the steps. Mending it took her a few minutes, and when she came down, he had the girl in a lip-lock with his fingers in an inappropriate place."

Boston wanted to laugh at Shelby's modest phrasing. Inappropriate was something he could certainly imagine. "So she banished him from the house in tears and wasted away from a broken heart?"

Shelby shook her head. "No. She picked up a candle-stick and bludgeoned him to death right on the spot while the maid stood there and just screamed like a ninny."

Despite his best efforts to remain cynical, a shiver raced up his spine. If he believed in ghosts, which he didn't, he might be a little alarmed to share space with Rachel, the candlestick-crazed ghost. "Holy shit. Don't mess with Rachel, huh?"

He preferred the image of a young woman reclining on a couch, sniffling into her handkerchief and sinking into spin-sterhood, over the idea of some poor guy getting whacked in the parlor. The parlor he was currently trapped in.

"They locked her up, of course, and her parents sold the house and moved to Marietta to escape the scandal. But Rachel overdosed on opium in the nuthouse and since then has been seen from time to time moving back and forth in this room and waiting at the window, searching for her long-lost lover."

Shelby was good at telling the tale. Her eyes had grown wide, her head moved up and down in reassurance from time to time, and she paused for effect at just the right spots. It was obviously a speech from her tour. Which made it dismissible.

Except that a lamp had levitated and tried to take a piece out of his head. "So, you think it's Rachel getting riled up? Has she thrown things before?"

It took a lot of effort not to turn and make sure the lamp wasn't leaping at him again.

Shelby rubbed her arms, goose bumps racing across her golden skin. "Only once that I know of. But she walks back and forth, loud footsteps and cold air, when men are in the room. Men she doesn't like."

His ego was taking quite a beating today. Not a single soul in Cuttersville, living or dead, seemed to like him. "Why doesn't she like me? Do I look like the cheating fiancé?"

With a shrug, Shelby stepped forward, glancing around the room as if Rachel might be watching. She whispered, "Maybe she didn't like what you were doing. How close you were sitting to me. Maybe when you gave me the candy, she thought it was—"

"Inappropriate?" he provided, logic overcoming fear. There was no way a ghost could throw a lamp at him. No way. It must have been a draft or an electrical surge or something.

"Uh-huh."

She nodded, looking warm and soft and very, very close, her shiny moist mouth parted just a little, her breasts dangerously close to his chest. A little shift, a little turn, and they could share a cherry Life Saver again.

"Did you think it was inappropriate?"

"No." Her expressive brown eyes had flecks of gold in them, and as she spoke, they dropped level with his own mouth. "It was probably the best way to do it. If you had taken the candy out and tried to hand it to me, we might have dropped it. You were being cautious, right?"

Caution. Yeah, that's what was driving him.

"Right." Boston touched a wisp of hair that was falling across her cheek and wrapped it around his finger. "And I also wanted to see if maybe, just maybe, you were even the slightest bit attracted to me like I am to you."

She licked her lips. "I do feel a small attraction to you."

They were touching now, and Boston wasn't sure who had leaned in first. He just knew that her breasts were resting up along his chest and her mouth was close enough to his that he felt her breath caress his lip. Her hair tickled his cheek, and he could smell the cherry, musky, floral scent of her.

"How small?"

"Smaller than an ant's butt."

"That's small," he said, even as he tilted, heading toward her lips.

"Very small," she agreed, eyes drifting closed.

Pounding on the window scared the crap out of him and sent Shelby leaping three feet back. Half of his brain panicked as he turned, expecting to see a ghost with a candlestick bearing down on him; the other half moaned at the injustice of the timing.

That half actually groaned out loud when Boston saw a man in a CFD baseball cap peering in the window curiously.

"They take an hour, then show up now?" he asked wryly as Shelby ran toward the window, all thoughts of attraction apparently abandoned.

Shelby yelled, "The door won't open and the windows are all stuck, Howie. Try and open it."

Howie, who didn't look like a deep thinker on his sharpest day, lifted his hat and scratched his prematurely balding head. "Shelby, I'm trying and it won't budge." He tugged again while balancing on a ladder. "And your gran says I can't use a crowbar, it might break the window."

"I'll pay for the window," Boston said, thinking it wasn't really his responsibility but he needed to leave this parlor sooner or later. Not that anyone was listening to him. Howie probably couldn't hear him and Shelby ignored him, giving a sound of disgust.

Heads popped up in two other windows. One was a thin

guy wearing a blue Cuttersville Fire Department T-shirt, and the third was Farmer Ted, Shelby's ex-husband. Which seriously annoyed him. Especially when Shelby raced past the second window and Boston like he and cherry Life Savers had never existed, and gripped the frame, hugging her body against the pane of glass and, in effect, her ex-husband.

"Oh, Danny, thank God. Get me the hell out of here."

Boston found himself rolling his eyes. She didn't have to act like she was being tortured. Nor did he think it was anything less than disgusting when Danny Tucker touched the glass with a finger, mocking a caress. Didn't the guy have a field to plow or something?

"Shh. I'm here, darlin'. Are you okay?"

Shelby nodded. "I'm fine."

"Alright, back up then. Keep going," he urged when Shelby took only a step or two.

Still balancing on the ladder, the guy peeled off his T-shirt, revealing a chest twice as wide as Boston's and sporting a full six-pack. Boston tried to gauge Shelby's reaction to Stud Boy over there, but she looked nothing more than faintly worried, her arms crossed.

"What are you going to do?"

Danny wrapped his shirt around his hand and rammed it through the window. When the sound of shattering glass abated, he winked at her. "Break the window."

Boston fumed, irrational fury and jealousy rising in his gut. Damn it, but that made him look stupid. Like he wasn't man enough to just break the window and get Shelby out. He had been *polite*. Waiting for the fire department, following the proper channels. And instead of looking considerate and professional, he looked like a pansy.

"Oh, God, are you okay?" Shelby rushed toward Danny, her sandals crunching on broken glass. "Let me see your hand."

"It's fine." Danny was knocking the few remaining shards out, but he paused to give Shelby a loud smacking kiss on her cheek. "You look hot."

Which was a damn tacky thing to say, in Boston's opinion.

Shelby didn't seem to mind. She shrugged. "It's stuffy in here."

Like the guy had been referring to temperature.

Boston started forward, intent on repairing the damage to his image. He gently tugged on Shelby's arm to pull her back. "You're standing in the glass. Be careful."

But before Shelby could answer, Danny snorted. "Shelby's not delicate. Come on, babe." He gripped her waist and forcibly hauled her through the window and into his arms.

Boston absolutely hated men who went around showing off their strength. He could bench-press as much as Danny Tucker, worked out in the company gym five days a week, but you didn't see him dragging women through windows like a caveman. Or a farmer.

After Danny had carried Shelby down on the ground and enveloped her in another one of those smothering hugs that made him wonder why the hell they had bothered to divorce if they couldn't keep their hands off each other, Boston climbed out the window himself. And met the steely gaze of Mrs. Stritmeyer. She shook her head, clearly disappointed.

"What?"

"I just thought a slick businessman like you, a city boy,

you might work faster than the cowpokes around here. Guess I was wrong."

And with that charming insult, she turned and yelled at the fireman. "John! Get that ladder off my house, you're chipping the paint."

Boston descended the four rungs of the ladder, not the least placated that the fire department had three men and three ladders scattered window to window yet it had taken Danny Tucker to spring them from the parlor. No, it didn't make him feel better at all.

Shelby had left Danny's arms, but he still shadowed her as she went and helped John pull the ladder off the house. "John, you smell like a burger and fries. Is that what took you so long to get here?"

The guilty flush on John's extremely youthful face gave truth to what Boston suspected had been a joke on Shelby's part.

Danny laughed. "That's where I hooked up with them. I was having a cheeseburger, and they sat down with me and told me what was going on."

Shelby smacked John on the arm. "How could you do that? Run off and eat a big old cheeseburger when I was stuck?"

Boston had to agree. If they had gotten there sooner, he wouldn't have been cuffed with a demonic lamp or come close to kissing Shelby, who was a flake and a distraction and not why he was in Cuttersville.

Except he didn't believe that Shelby was a flake, and he didn't want to be saved from himself anymore. He still wanted to kiss her. Especially when her shirt rode even higher as she reached for the second ladder. The underside of her breast flashed him and he gave himself up for lost.

Danny reached out and stuck his fingers between Shelby's breasts and undid the knot so her shirt fell back into place. "You were showing us your hooters, hon."

Shelby grabbed at her shirt, tugging it down farther. "Oh! Sorry."

"I've seen them before, I'm happy to say, but the other guys might mind," Danny said with a grin.

Boston knew right then and there what Danny Tucker was up to. He was making it clear that he had been married to Shelby, knew her and her body, and that he still had a claim on her.

It should be a reminder that he, Boston Macnamara, Samson executive, had no business messing around with Shelby Tucker, haunted house tour guide. That she belonged to Danny Tucker or another man just like him. A local.

But it didn't. It only sent his blood pounding and his lust soaring, and he wanted. With the intensity he had wanted that scholarship to U of C. That first job. That VP spot at the age of twenty-eight. This he couldn't have.

Only his body didn't like that answer.

Howie stuck his head out of the broken window, standing in the parlor. "Hey, I'm confused. If you all were stuck, why did the parlor door just open for me when I pulled on it?"

Shelby looked at him and shivered.

Jesus. Now he actually found himself believing in a ghost named Red-Eyed Rachel.

Chapter Five

      "Right about here, hovering between the graves of an old Episcopal minister and his wife, is where some folks swear two pale white hands can be seen intertwined on dark nights as the happy couple rests in the hereafter together." Shelby gave a dramatic flourish with her arm to the grassy knoll in the Cuttersville Memorial Cemetery and enjoyed the appreciative murmurs of her latest tour.

It was bunk. It was theatrics. It was the power of suggestion and she knew that. There had to be a scientific explanation for why she and Boston had been locked in Gran's parlor together. One that didn't have to do with disembodied beings with a hatred of testosterone.

A kid tugged on her shorts. Shelby looked down into his round moon pie face, a little sticky around the edges, an empty popcorn kernel clinging to the corner of his mouth. "What's up, bud?"

"You don't believe in all this junk, do you?"

She was getting there. "I believe there are some things we can't explain. Some things we see and hear that don't make any sense with the knowledge that we have."

He rolled his eyes with the authority of a seven-year-old skeptic. "My mom says ghosts aren't real. That God would never let anyone suffer so long between here and heaven."

"Then why are you on the Haunted Cuttersville Tour?" Shelby was considering slapping a PG-13 rating on her tour anyway, and this was confirming it. She spent the two hours talking about philandering men and women, drunks, violent crimes, and psychotics bearing machetes. She didn't want to be responsible for churning out the next serial killer.

"My mom doesn't know. My grandparents brought me." He jerked his thumb back to a couple in their sixties, who had been hanging on her every word since go.

"You know, I just think some things we have to accept we can't explain and move on." Like her lunatic lust for Boston Macnamara. "If ghosts are real or not, it doesn't really matter, does it?"

Except that it was her chosen profession to march people around and tell them they were and where to find them.

"I just think you have to say that so you can take our money." Mr. Wise-beyond-his-years turned and went back to his grandparents.

Shelby herded the group of six back toward the road and fought a sigh. Suddenly what she'd done for the past two years for kicks and to keep herself fed seemed frivolous at best, violating at worst. If there was no such thing as a ghost, then she was fleecing folks, even if they left her tour entertained. And if there were ghosts, well, parading people past them seemed rude. If she were dead and forced to hang around wearing the same clothes for hundreds of years, she wouldn't want anybody staring at her.

Especially the clothes she was wearing now. Glancing down at her khaki shorts, with a stain of unknown origin on the cuff, and her brown tank top, she realized her wardrobe was downright sad. But there was no money to buy anything new, especially not if she was going to start worrying about the ethics of interpersonal relations between the living and the dead.

Who knows, maybe Red-Eyed Rachel had been trying to take a nap or something and there she was with her tour group. That would make anybody cranky.

Though maybe it didn't have anything to do with spirits, but with her, Shelby Tucker, twenty-six years old and no future other than hanging out at the Busy Bee and scraping enough money together every month to eat artery-clogging food. She did not even own a car, and her seventy-year-old grandmother was housing her.

She hadn't meant to be quite so aimless. When she was a little girl, her visions of the future had alternated between being a wife and mother, Wonder Woman with a less slutty outfit, and a vet. The vet would have been the smartest route to take, but she had told Boston the truth when he had questioned why she didn't get a better-paying job.

While she was great with animals and could memorize things, she had been lousy at schoolwork growing up. Sucked raw eggs kind of lousy. By sixth grade they had figured out she was dyslexic, but it had been too hard to catch up, too difficult to retrain her brain to the extent that was required for higher learning.

Now she wished she would have tried harder, as she

walked the group to the Bigleys' barn, where a ghost cow was known to moo for grass he could no longer chew.

Boston was impressed with the Samson Plastics plant. It was clean, efficient, and appeared to be producing at peak productivity right there in the middle of nowhere, sandwiched between a dilapidated barn and a cornfield. Sure, there was a bit of a twang in the voices of the employees, but their T-shirts and jeans looked the same as any of the workers in the Chicago plant, and there was the same level of separation between management and workers on the line.

Unlike back in Chicago, though, he felt no sense of competition. Here, he was clearly top dog, the first VP from Samson ever to do more than pop in for a random visit. It had Bob and Phil spinning in circles trying to alternate between kissing his ass and pumping him for information.

Which he didn't have.

Bob seemed a little more willing to speak frankly, so after milling around the plant introducing himself, studying some output reports, and checking out the makeshift office the guys had created for him in a storage closet, he sought out Bob.

"Hey, Bob, how's it going?" Boston strode into his office and took a seat without waiting for an invitation.

Bob looked up from his computer and shot him a nervous glance. Boston could practically see the sweat forming and pushing out Bob's busy glands. In the past, Boston had always enjoyed moments like this, when he knew that he was in control, that the meeting was his to manipulate however he intended. But watching Bob, Boston felt no such thrill. In fact, he felt something that might be . . . guilt.

Guilt? He straightened his spine. He had no reason to feel guilty. Who gave a shit if he wasn't being completely honest with these guys? This was *business*, and he needed to protect himself, watch his back.

"I realize you weren't expecting me, but the office you've given me doesn't have an outlet. It's a little difficult to conduct business without phone or Internet access."

Bob swallowed. "Sorry, Boston, I didn't notice that, but we'll work something out, don't you worry. If this is going to be long term, we can rearrange some staff."

Boston heard the question in his voice, and he was about to imply that he was going to be watching Bob's and Phil's backs for quite a while, when his gaze fell across a picture on Bob's desk.

It was Bob and a cute, round brunette with their hands on the shoulders of two Bob-looking boys, somewhere in that hazy age range of four to eight. Boston wasn't around kids enough to pin it any closer, but the happy smiles of the family as they posed with a guy in a striped cat costume got to him.

"This your family?" He lifted the wood frame and studied them closer. The whole concept of happily ever after and family vacations was foreign to him and it made him curious.

Was it all an act? Or did people actually enjoy raising their children together? His parents certainly hadn't. When they hadn't been winging Wedgwood china at each other, they had been releasing their frustration in the beds of a staggering array of nannies and tennis coaches.

"Oh, yeah." Bob relaxed a little. "That was this past April. We went to Disney World for a week. We had a great time. My boys, Bryan and James, they're four and six, and they just loved every minute of it."

"Who's the cat?" Boston pointed to the picture before setting it back on the desk.

"It's Tigger." Bob looked at him like he was missing a majority of his brain cells.

"Tigger?" It sounded vaguely familiar but he was having trouble placing it.

"The bouncing tiger from *Winnie the Pooh*."

Boston shook his head. It wasn't ringing any bells.

Bob started moving his finger around and around. "You know, 'Bouncy, trouncy, flouncy, pouncy, fun, fun, fun, fun, fun' . . . no? Must be a parent thing, you get to know all that stuff."

Boston had the annoying feeling that he had missed out on something, and given the look of concern—okay, pity—in Bob's eyes, he thought so too.

Boston was starving, but he couldn't take another red meat–emphasized meal at the Busy Bee. He hadn't seen that much grease since his mother had brought home her latest boyfriend, Fred, the casino owner.

So he entered the back door of the White House, off the gravel driveway where he had been parking his car, anticipating eating an apple for dinner. Despite Shelby's intrusions and getting locked in the parlor on his second day as a renter, he kind of liked the fussy hominess of the house. It wasn't modern or manly, which dominated his apartment back in Chicago, and there was no wine rack, but it was warm and friendly and big, with large rooms, high ceilings, and detailed woodwork that didn't exist anymore.

The kitchen was yellow, which he suspected wasn't an authentic Victorian color, but he didn't care. Especially not when the smell of roasted chicken greeted him.

For a microsecond he wondered if he was in the wrong house. He wasn't, and the chicken wasn't a hallucination.

Neither was it Shelby standing in front of his stove, which he had to admit he had expected for a second. Probably because he didn't know any women in town except for Shelby and Mrs. Stritmeyer and he had a hard time visualizing Jessie slaving over a hot stove in June. Not that he could really picture Shelby doing that either, but it was a nice visual wish, her in those denim shorts and the fantasy heels cooking him chicken.

The kitchen was hotter than he had realized. He pulled at his tie a little.

"Hello," he said to the matronly woman in a shapeless dress working vigorously with a whisk. Definitely not as appealing as Shelby in short shorts, but the woman had cooked chicken, and for that she was his new best friend.

She turned, dark hair pulled back off her face, a kind smile tugging her mouth upward. "You must be Boston."

Wiping her hands on her apron—good God, aprons still existed?—she held her hand out to him. "I'm Mary, your housekeeper. Your supper is almost ready."

Boston found he could love certain things about Cuttersville. The housekeeper who fixed him food was one of them. "You cooked for me?" He wanted to be perfectly clear on that point, because if she removed that chicken and left with it, he was going to cry.

Mary nodded. "I hope you like roasted chicken with

lemon sauce, baby potatoes, and fresh-baked bread. And there's an apple pie for dessert."

Jackpot. His stomach growled. "It sounds wonderful."

"Well, I can't be here every night." Mary turned and adjusted the heat on the stove. "But I'll come by once or twice a week and clean the house for you."

Yes. "I appreciate it."

"And just a little advice . . . you might want to pick up your undergarments in the mornings, since Shelby brings a tour through at eleven."

Oh, nice. He had left his boxers on the floor for Shelby and her tourists to snicker at. Of course, Shelby had already seen him naked with an eyelet spread capping him, so underwear was really incidental in comparison.

"Uh, thanks. I'll keep that in mind."

"The chicken will be ready in five minutes and there's extra sauce here in the bowl." Then Mary gave him a wave and opened the back door. "See you in a few days, Boston."

"Bye, Mary." He watched the door close behind her, then grabbed the pot holders she'd left on the counter and opened the oven, just intending to smell it.

Two minutes later, he was sitting at the table and gorging himself, heartily enjoying the chicken and potatoes.

And if he heard an occasional creaking sound from the parlor directly in front of the kitchen, he convinced himself the house was settling. It definitely wasn't Red-Eyed Rachel's footsteps because ghosts didn't exist.

Five days of traipsing through the man's bedroom and never seeing him was getting to Shelby.

So when she ran into him on the square in front of Hair by Harriet, she couldn't stop a cheesy grin from sliding across her face. "Hey there, Boston Macnamara. What are you up to?"

Boston pushed his sunglasses up his nose with one finger and gave what could pass for a smile or a twitch. "Shelby Tucker. I'm getting a haircut."

Shelby took in his neat black hair, short and trim. "Are you done already?"

"No." He frowned. "I was just about to go in." He threw his thumb toward Harriet's.

Momentarily distracted by the fine picture he made standing on the sidewalk in a gray suit, she didn't take the time to soften her response. "You're going to Harriet's? For a haircut?"

He sighed. "It does say Hair by Harriet. And I see people in there, so it's not a pet-grooming store. What's the problem?"

"Uh . . ." Shelby wasn't quite sure how to tell him that the only men to step foot in Harriet's were Clyde, who was married to Harriet and got his hair cut for free, and Shelby's cousin Brady, who had to go to Harriet to acquire sapphire highlights. "Nothing."

She thought to suggest the barber, but then worried that he would give Boston an army flattop, which would be a damn shame. He looked too good the way he was to ruin himself with acclimation to Cuttersville.

"You between tours?" Boston didn't look in any hurry, despite his hair needs and the oppressive afternoon heat. He leaned against the glass pane of Harriet's front window, not looking the least bit sweaty.

Shelby felt like a goat, sticky and dirty.

"Actually, it's a slow day. No tours at all."

"Maybe you could give me the Haunted Cuttersville Tour sometime."

"Really?" she asked in surprise.

"Sure. A private tour."

The words weren't exactly suggestive, and he wasn't smiling, but Shelby felt the force of his presence clear down to her inner thighs.

"You never did tell me the rest of the story, you know. Like what happened to Rachel's maid and who is the Blond Man."

Not that she thought he gave a hoot about what had happened to the maid, but she nodded slowly. "The maid was smart and took advantage of the situation. She cried that she had been forced by the fiancé, and went on to marry a local lawyer and have three sons."

Boston smiled, though it was distracted. "Everyone's out for what they can get, huh?"

"Not everyone."

"No?"

He studied her, making her once again self-conscious of her raggedy clothes. She had never given a rat's hooey about her clothes before, and here the man had her so tied up in knots she wanted to put a skirt on for him. It was embarrassing.

"And I'd be happy to give you a private tour." Of her naked body.

Shelby was appalled with herself. Never, not once, since puberty had kicked in had she lusted after a man like this, plain and simple.

The door to the salon went flying open and slammed Boston on the shoulder. He gave a grunt and turned.

Shelby sighed. The fat was in the fire now. Harriet was descending on them in full fuchsia sail, a smile on her round face.

"Shelby, honey, you coming in for a cut? I've been dying to get my hands on your mop for years now."

Oh, thank you. Blowing her bangs out of her eyes, Shelby glared at Harriet. She and Boston had been connecting, reaching for that precarious sultry moment in the White House parlor when she had been sure he was going to kiss her, and here was Harriet pointing out that Shelby wasn't exactly a man's wet dream.

"I don't want a haircut, Harriet."

"But you could be a pretty girl if you just took care of yourself." Harriet was all clucking concern, even as the talons dug in.

"Shelby's pretty the way she is."

Shelby wasn't sure who was more surprised, her or Boston. He looked like he'd been flattened with a tractor. She just felt like she had been squashed. But in a good squashed way.

And while she stared at Boston and he stared back, Harriet wiped her hands on her pink billowing blouse and stuck one out at Boston. "I don't believe we've met. I'm Harriet Danforth."

Boston recovered enough to shake her hand. "Boston. Boston Macnamara. And you must be Chevy's mom."

He shot Shelby a look of amusement and she slapped her hand over her mouth so she wouldn't laugh. He remembered what she'd told him about the origin of Chevy Danforth's name. It was a frightening vision, Harriet carried away by passion with Clyde Danforth in the back of a nineteen-seventy Chevy Nova.

"Yes, I am. Have you met him, Boston? Is that your real name? Or is it a stage name?"

Now Shelby did laugh. "He's not a circus act, Harriet. He's a Samson executive."

Boston's hand remained trapped in Harriet's but he shook his head and kept smiling, impressing the hell out of Shelby. "Boston is my real name. And I haven't met Chevy. Shelby just mentioned him to me."

Harriet clasped Boston's hand between both of hers, giving enthusiastic pats and jerks, so that his whole arm was working like a puppet string. "Oh, I see. Well, Shelby's always had a crush on Chevy, so I'm not surprised she mentioned him."

"I do not have a crush on Chevy!" she burst out, mortified in the extreme. Chevy was nice if you liked talking dirt bikes and Budweiser memorabilia, and you didn't mind that his body was the size of a 747, but she had no aspirations to live with a walking beer encyclopedia.

Boston raised an eyebrow.

Harriet leaned forward and whispered in a voice loud enough to ensure that any person within forty feet heard, "I'm sure Shelby would have eventually married Chevy except that she let Danny Tucker knock her up first."

Boston's startled eyes shifted to her, and Shelby felt a hot rush of shame sweep over her. Lord, but she felt like she was eighteen again, with every gaze in Cuttersville condemning and self-righteous. Gran's disappointed silence. Her mother's shrieking hysterics.

Her fear then that she would never make it fly as a wife and mother.

And sadness too, which crept up on her now sometimes flat out of nowhere and reminded her that if she hadn't miscarried, she would have a seven-year-old child now, just about the age of that boy in the cemetery.

"I have to get going," she said, stumbling over her words. "I'll see you around, Boston. Don't let Harriet give you highlights."

She turned, pain in her gut, intent on making a quick getaway. Boston's commanding corporate voice stopped her.

"I still want my tour, Shelby. I'll see you at the house at seven."

It wasn't spoken as a question, but she didn't want to argue it with him in front of Harriet. Nor did she want any of the salon sharks who were plastered to Harriet's front window to see the stupid tears in her eyes.

"Fine. But it's fifty bucks for a private tour."

It was only after he agreed and she walked away that she realized something about that phrasing sounded vaguely like prostitution.

Just her luck, Harriet would be spilling it all over town that Boston Macnamara was pimping out Cuttersville girls and Shelby Tucker was his madam.

Boston stepped out of the shower, feeling his hair to make sure that all of the mousse Harriet had slapped in it had been removed. He should have known better than to get a haircut in Cuttersville. Common sense would have dictated that he wait until the weekend and drive the hour and a half to Cincinnati to get a cut by someone who wasn't still using nineteen-eighties hair products.

But he hadn't, so he'd gotten mousse.

Fortunately, she hadn't messed up the cut. He padded

across the white tile floor, his feet still damp, and looked in the oval mirror hanging over the vanity sink. He had only needed a trim, with those annoying little neck hairs shaved off, and Harriet had managed that, all while extolling the virtues of her unmarried daughter and questioning Boston about his financial status.

If he ever had the misfortune to meet Holly Danforth in person, he was going to run. Harriet made her daughter sound like a cross between Martha Stewart, preconviction, and Pamela Anderson, which was frightening. A woman who could bake a soufflé in a thong bikini was more than he cared to encounter in his kitchen.

Not that he wanted to be thinking about Harriet's daughter when Shelby was coming over in ten minutes. He had a lot of questions for Shelby Tucker, starting with why she had never bothered to mention that she had a child with her ex-husband. It wasn't his business, he supposed, but despite all best efforts, his attraction for her had grown steadily over the week since he'd met her. He was lusting after some poor kid's mother and that just seemed wrong.

The doorbell rang, loud and clear even over the radio he had playing.

"Shit." He was still in just a towel and Shelby was early. But at least the gunk was out of his hair.

Rubbing his body vigorously, he heard the front door open. Jesus, Shelby had used her key, which was not what they had agreed to. Or maybe they had never actually resolved that sticky little issue.

"Boston?"

"I'll be down in a second," he yelled, stepping into his boxers, water still dripping down his chest.

Shelby's feet were on the steps, the boards creaking as

she ascended. What the hell was she doing? The bathroom door was open.

He had one leg in his khaki pants and one leg out when she appeared in the hall.

"Oh! God, sorry, Boston." Her cheeks flushed beneath her golden tan, and those soft brown eyes were pained. "It's just, I didn't want to be alone downstairs."

Her teeth dug into her bottom lip. "I got a little freaked out standing on the porch. Stupid, huh?"

He dropped his pants so he'd look like less of an ass. "It's okay. But I've been here all week and nothing even remotely weird has happened."

"Can I wait up here while you . . ."

She dropped her eyes below his waist, a little blush on her cheeks, and he was amused. He didn't recall Shelby being shy about the whole thing the first time they'd met.

"While I put my pants on?" Boston ran his hand through his wet hair, pushing it back so it would stop dripping on his forehead. "Are you going to watch? Or are you embarrassed?"

Eyes snapped up and she snorted. "I've seen you in less than that, remember."

He remembered. He just wished circumstances had been different. Like that she had been witnessing his penis willingly and with sexual appreciation, not gaping in horror at it like it was a car accident victim.

Given another chance to be seen naked by Shelby, he wanted to put his best face forward. He really wanted to toss off a suggestive comment now—that maybe she repeat the experience with better results—but it came to him again that Harriet had said she'd been pregnant with Danny Tucker's child, and he stayed silent. He'd never come on to a mother before, and the idea wasn't appealing now.

As he grabbed his pants back off the floor, Shelby leaned against the bathroom door and stuck her hands in the pockets of her olive green shorts. "Listen, Boston, I wanted to let you know something. Obviously I heard what Harriet said to you about me and Danny, and I wanted you to know she didn't tell you everything. I don't have a child. Two weeks after Danny and I got married, I had a miscarriage."

Ouch. That made him feel like hell. He didn't want her to have a kid, but he hadn't meant for her to miscarry. And he hadn't wanted her to share something so personal that obviously made her uncomfortable when he was just a passing interest, a guy renting her grandmother's house. That was all he could be, since he was leaving in a few months.

But that didn't stop him from reaching out, pants dropping back to the floor, and pulling her closer to him. "I'm so sorry, Shelby. You didn't have to tell me that."

She shrugged. "I felt like it made me sound like a bad mother, not mentioning having a child, and I didn't want you to think that, or that I wasn't responsible enough to take financial care of my child."

Since the thought had crossed his mind, he wisely kept quiet. "So I guess everyone in town knew why you got married, huh? That must have been hard, especially being so young."

Shelby blinked those soulful brown eyes at him and gently tried to pull her hand out of his. He didn't let her.

"It didn't matter, I guess. And I would have married Danny in a year or two anyway. Getting pregnant just sped things up. We'd been dating since I was fifteen."

He didn't know Shelby Tucker, and though he'd contemplated exploring a brief affair with her, he had never intended to get personal with her. But with Shelby a foot in front of him, smelling like summer flowers and looking soft and vulnerable, he couldn't stay uninvolved.

"I can't imagine losing a baby, Shelby. I'm not sure I'd ever get over something like that."

"I don't think I have," she whispered.

Then his lips were moving toward her, and he anticipated the sweet taste of her mouth. All week she'd been rolling around in the back of his head, an unlikely and undeniable temptation, a curiosity that he had to investigate.

Now he was going to kiss her deeply and fully.

Until she jerked back away from him when the music on his radio cut off. Boston turned to the radio, wondering what the hell was the matter with it. Then the lights flickered on and off, on and off.

"I'm going to pretend that didn't happen," he said carefully, standing very still.

Shelby looked around the bathroom, hands airplaning out in front of her. "But it did! And I feel something cold, do you feel that?"

Oh, shit, he did, like a big wet fan was blowing on his stomach and he was suddenly reaching for the door, kicking it open with his foot. "Get the door so it doesn't shut."

Shelby gasped. "Oh, good gravy, I don't want to get trapped in the bathroom with you!"

Boston managed to laugh, despite having to prop the door open with his back, his feet, and his hands, all still wearing nothing more than boxer shorts. "I can definitely think of better rooms to get trapped in with you."

"Like what?" Shelby stepped over him into the hall. "The kitchen? We'd have food."

"Or the bedroom," he said, than decided the bizarre stress of the moment had been responsible for that leaving his mouth.

Which could also explain why Shelby grabbed his arm and pulled him roughly. "I agree, that would be better."

He let her drag him into the hall, and they both watched in shock as the bathroom door slammed shut behind him.

The lock clicked into place.

Shelby put her hand on her heaving chest. "You know, this never happened before you showed up. Never saw a damn thing. Nothing. Not a cold spot, or a flicker of a light, or a vision or a single stinking creaking sound. And now I'm seeing all kinds of crazy things."

Boston started toward his bedroom, wanting more clothes on before he either continued this discussion or his body got confused as to why he was half naked around Shelby and not acting on it. He also thought it might be a good idea to get the hell out of the White House for a little while.

"So, it's my fault?"

"Yes! It has to be." Her voice followed him, high-pitched, this side of hysterical.

"It's just a coincidence." Reaching in his dresser, he pulled out a pair of shorts that had been washed, ironed, and put away by Mary.

"Aren't you afraid?"

He checked. Fear, no. Annoyed, sort of. Turned on, yes. "No, I'm not afraid."

Then he realized Shelby was standing in the room with him. "Shelby, back up, get out of the . . ."

The door to his bedroom was rolling shut with no sound, but efficient speed, and there was no time to do anything but swear as it clicked in place. He knew as surely as his name was Boston Macnamara that they were stuck.

In his bedroom. Together. With no cell phone.

And sexual tension so thick they'd need Danny's tractor to knock through it.

Chapter Six

Shelby tried the door, shaking the knob violently. "Did you do this, Boston? Are you psychic or something?"

She did not want to be stuck with Boston again, in his bedroom, of all places. Where that eyelet spread was conjuring up all kinds of memories.

Boston scratched his bare chest and stared at her. "No, I'm not psychic. I'm a wizard, like Harry Potter."

Shelby licked her lips. It took her a full ten seconds to decide that he was kidding, which meant she needed to get a grip.

"No reason to get smart with me."

Boston gave a little laugh. "Come on, Shelby. If I had paranormal powers, I wouldn't flicker the lights. I'd vaporize your clothes or something."

She was too frightened to even feel the kick of lust

Boston's words should have given. Not as big a kick as usual anyway. "That's not funny!"

And why the hell was he always strutting around without a shirt? Didn't he know it was a bad idea to start anything between them? That any flirtation they engaged in had nowhere to go since he was hightailing it out of town as soon as he could and she'd be here until the day she died? And maybe beyond, knowing Cuttersville.

Nope, any sort of . . . thingy between them had nowhere to go. Except to Boston's big four-poster bed with the antique eyelet spread. Just three feet away from them. Where she'd already witnessed how impressive he could be, and that had been without any provocation.

"Where's your cell phone?" she demanded, ready to pat down the pockets of his shorts to find it. She had to get out of this house *now,* and she wasn't sure which was scarier—that ghosts were picking on her, or that she suddenly knew if she stayed with Boston, she would leap on him and beg for sex.

"It's downstairs in the kitchen by my laptop."

"Why isn't it with you? Someone could be trying to reach you!" Shelby paced back and forth, her breathing ragged.

Why after never once showing their pale dead faces in three years were the White House ghosts suddenly slamming doors left and right? It wasn't right. It was rude just to leap out of the afterworld like that and start fiddling with people's property.

Of course, Rachel had lived in this house first.

"I was in the shower, Shelby. I don't answer my phone when I'm in the shower."

"Did you see ghosts in Chicago?" Rubbing her elbows, Shelby went over to the window and undid the latch.

It was a long drop down, but maybe if they got it open, they could yell like loons until someone heard them.

"No. And I'm still not seeing ghosts."

Shelby stopped tugging on the window, which was stuck shut, and thought that through. Boston had a point. They weren't actually seeing anything and she ought to be grateful for that, especially since Gran had told her about the Old Colonel traipsing around naked.

"You're right. I'm panicking and I don't really know why."

But she was getting an idea. It had to do with the realization that for the first time in her adult life she was so physically attracted to a man it was making her nuts.

Boston came up behind her and put his hands on her arms, rubbing up and down softly. "It's okay, everything is fine."

That was not helping.

Shelby stepped away from him and pushed her hair out of her eyes. "It's not fine. We're trapped! Again."

"Don't tell me you have to go to the bathroom again."

"No."

"So what's the big deal?" Boston sat down on the bed. Then he lay down, sticking his hands behind his head, like he didn't have a ding-dong care in the world.

Shelby watched his broad chest rise and fall, and tried not to think about the fact that his shorts were loose enough for her to slip a hand inside, right below his washboard stomach. His skin still looked warm and damp from the shower, and the unmistakable feeling of a hot blush stole over her face.

If he noticed, he didn't say anything. "Did you tell anyone you were coming over here?"

"Well, Harriet Danforth knew, which means the whole town knows."

He nodded. "See? So when you don't come home tonight, your gran will come looking for you, or send someone over to find you. Especially after what happened last time in the parlor."

Shelby took a deep breath. "You're right. That's a good point. Dang, I don't know what's the matter with me. Of course someone will come looking for me."

Jessie Stritmeyer was strolling down Main Street at half past seven, looking to get herself some peach ice cream, when Harriet Danforth flagged her down.

Harriet got on her nerves, with all that teased-up hair and big earrings that matched her too-bright blouse. Jessie paused on the sidewalk, stifling a sigh, and leaned against the old metal parking meter that nobody had bothered to stick a nickel in for about twenty years.

"Now, Jessie, I'm sure you've warned her, but I just don't think it's a good idea for Shelby to be running around with that city boy, Mac Boston."

"Boston Macnamara."

"That's what I said." Harriet looked perplexed. "And don't you think it's unsafe for Shelby to be alone with him?"

Jessie couldn't resist a snort. If Shelby was in danger from Boston, Jessie would eat her petunias. "He's not a serial killer, Harriet, just a Samson executive."

"But you know how Shelby is." Harriet pursed her lips, and those wide-set eyes held a vicious gleam. "And if she finds herself pregnant this time, I highly doubt a Chicago businessman will want to marry her."

That was below the belt, implying that Shelby was a hussy, and Jessie was about to tell Harriet she could shove her fuchsia earrings where the sun don't shine, when she thought of something. "So, are you saying Shelby's with Boston right now? They're off alone somewhere?"

"Boston inquired about a *private* Haunted Cuttersville Tour. Shelby said she'd meet him at the White House at seven tonight."

Jessie grinned. That boy was finally getting the lead out. Private tour, indeed.

"I still don't see why Shelby left poor Danny Tucker after he did the right thing and married her when she was in trouble."

Trouble that Danny had gotten her into, if Jessie remembered correctly. She didn't even bother to hold back an eye roll. "They were young and stupid, Harriet, and got carried away one night. Sort of like you and Clyde, if my memory serves."

Harriet blustered and Jessie chortled. That was the fun thing about sanctimonious busybodies. They were so much fun to rankle. "Shelby leaving Danny isn't any of your damn business, and it's nearly three years ago now anyway. And if Shelby wants to give Mr. Moneybags a haunted house tour, that's not any of your or my business either."

That was stretching it a bit. Jessie did think it was her business, but not in the way Harriet intended.

Harriet waved a fly away from her nose. "How modern of you, Jessie. But you mark my words, Shelby won't be coming home tonight. If she were my daughter, I'd send Clyde around to haul her home."

Sticking her nose in the air, Jessie pulled out her own

righteous voice. "I have no intention of butting into my grown granddaughter's life. If she wants to spend the night with Boston, then that is her decision and I completely respect that."

After all, Shelby sleeping with Boston had been Jessie's plan from the get-go.

After thirty minutes of watching Shelby pace, Boston figured he had another two hours max before someone came around looking for her. He meant to take advantage of every single remaining second.

Lying on the bed had been a good move. Shelby's face had turned as red as a traffic light when he'd stretched out across the ridiculous bedspread that had nearly maimed him. He had been so irritated with the sight of the spread the week before, he had balled it up and tossed it over the rocking chair in the corner to prevent any future incidents. But then Mary the housekeeper had come along and put it right back on the bed.

Normally he approved of efficiency, but in this case he would have preferred if she'd left his bed rumpled and unmade.

Not talking to Shelby had been a smart move too. She looked irritated with him, which was a big improvement over scared silly. As he'd lain on the bed, eyes half closed, he'd noticed her glance over at him a half-dozen times, occasionally muttering under her breath.

When she did it again, he asked, "Did you say something, Shelby?"

"No," came the petulant reply.

Boston patted the bed next to him. "There's nothing to

Erin McCarthy

worry about, you know. Just have a seat over here and keep me company while we wait." He gave her a smile. "Maybe you can tell me all about the Blond Man this time."

It occurred to him maybe he should be focusing less energy on coaxing Shelby to relax, and more energy on getting them out of there first, and worrying about the paranormal invasion in his house second.

After all, he wasn't supposed to even like Shelby Tucker. But he did, which was why he had avoided her for the last five days. He had recognized his feelings for what they were, and they had scared him far more than any door-slamming spirit.

He liked her. Her quick mind, her direct way of speaking, her loyalty to her family, her robust deep-from-the-gut laugh. And her body. Oh, yeah. He liked that.

Shelby blew her hair out of her eyes. "You really aren't scared, are you?"

"No, and I'm surprised you are. I'm sure there is a completely logical explanation for all of this, like drafts or electrical surges or something. And even if there isn't, it has no bearing on my life. Inconvenient, maybe, but that can be dealt with."

"You like everything neat and tidy, don't you?"

Though she made it sound like a flaw, he nodded. "I control my life, not the other way around."

Except for this little detour to Cuttersville. But he would get himself back out of here, he was sure of it.

"So it doesn't bother you that we're stuck in your ten-by-fourteen bedroom, with the window stuck shut, the door locked, and the sun about to set in an hour?"

"Nope." Hell, when put like that, it sounded even better. A sunset, dusky lamplight spilling across the old Victorian bed, Shelby underneath him. Yes, it was sounding better and better.

Because he wanted Shelby Tucker, despite the complications that could ensue. The opportunity was just too convenient to pass up. And if he was upfront with Shelby about the fact that he was leaving as soon as Brett gave the word, they could enjoy a few weeks of dating and whatever naked pleasure that might bring.

Shelby sat down in the rocking chair, all the way across the room from him. Too far away for him to touch. "So what do you do at Samson, Boston? And how'd you end up in Cuttersville? I don't think you're here by choice."

He laughed. "What gave it away?"

Shelby grinned back at him, setting the chair in motion before tucking her feet up under her knees. "Oh, I don't know. The shoes, the clothes, the look of horror on your face."

"And here I thought I was hiding my feelings." He propped himself up with one hand. "It's just part of my job to check out various Samson holdings." Though he'd never been banished before. That still infuriated him, the why of Brett's decision.

He had started to wonder if there was someone else working on Brett, influencing him. A rival of Boston's for the position as Brett's right-hand man.

"This town needs Samson, you know. Half the people here work at the factory, and they'll starve if it were to ever close down."

Boston saw the concern in Shelby's eyes, felt her anxiety for her friends and neighbors, and he didn't have the heart to play the game with her. He didn't want to hide his cards from her the way he had with Phil and Bob. "I'm not here to close the factory, Shelby, even though it does have slightly lower productivity than some of the other plants."

She leaned against the back of the rocker. "Well, you can fix that, then. Get everyone here to speed up so the factory stays."

He supposed he could, though until that moment his concern had been strictly with getting himself out, not ensuring the plant's viability.

"Part of my job is to assess the plant's weaknesses, that's true."

"Did you grow up in Chicago?"

"Yes. In a sleek modern condo downtown." It had been cold and empty most of the time except for the revolving door of nannies and housekeepers. The one constant from his childhood had been Al, the doorman.

"You must hate this creaky fussy old house." Shelby waved her hand at the robin's-egg blue bedroom wall.

"Actually, I like it, believe it or not. It's solid, a home. My parents' condo was sterile."

Shelby smiled at him, a genuine flashing of teeth that settled all over him like a caress. He went half hard, which was ridiculously inappropriate for the conversation they were having.

"Do they still live there? Your parents?"

The thought was almost laughable. "No. My mom sold the condo a few years after my dad strolled off with my babysitter. Now she lives in Boca Raton. I have no idea where my dad is, and don't care to find out."

Boston wasn't sure why he had just told Shelby about his father running off, or why he suddenly felt those old painful feelings of jealousy about his friends who had a stabler home life. Shelby was one of those, with this quiet town of pretty little houses, and family that would do just about anything for her, including her oversized ex-husband. He'd stopped feeling sorry for himself years ago and had accepted his life for what it was. He had his career, his success, and that was what was important.

Which didn't explain why he felt almost, well, lonely.

"I don't know where my dad is either. Mine ran off with one of my mother's closest friends, and everything in my parents' joint bank account."

Boston almost laughed. What a sad coincidence. "My dad didn't settle for joint assets. He took an extra ten million from his employer that didn't belong to him and fled the country with Carrie, my babysitter, who at the time was all of eighteen years old."

He had never told that to a living soul. But for some reason, it wasn't painful to tell Shelby. It was almost a relief to air his dirty laundry to someone who wouldn't use it against him.

Shelby's mouth dropped. "That's awful! It's hard to find a good babysitter, you know."

Now he did laugh. "Actually, I never really liked Carrie. When she would wash my hair, she'd rub really hard with these clawlike nails. And she couldn't push me on the swings because her jeans were too tight."

Occasionally he'd wondered how long Carrie and his father had stayed together. He was betting not much more than a year or two.

"Why was your babysitter washing your hair? That's a mother's job."

Shelby looked downright indignant. On his behalf. He felt flattered. "Not when your mother was a busy attorney who spent what little free time she had on the tennis courts."

A definite snort came from the rocker. "Playing with fuzzy balls is more important than taking care of her child?"

Boston grinned and waited for Shelby to catch the humorous double meaning of what she'd just said. "My mom really liked playing with a wide variety of balls, especially from different manufacturers."

It took her a good long second, but when she realized what he meant, her brown eyes went wide, her feet dropped to the floor, stopping the rocker, and her tongue slipped out to nervously wet her lips. "Oh. *Oh.* Well, shoot, we both come from a couple of oversexed parents, don't we? My mom's a pretty decent mother, but she's a serial dater. I think it's a self-esteem thing since my dad left her."

Boston had often thought the same thing about his mother. She had a compulsive need to prove she was desirable to men.

"And last I heard, my dad had taken up with Sissy Blancher, who as a senior was head majorette of the Cuttersville Cougar Marching Band the same year I was a sophomore." She shook her head, lips curved up. "That's why I've never bothered to change back to my maiden name. I'd rather keep Danny's name than my father's."

And while they were on the subject of Farmer Danny, Boston had a question or two about him. "So why did you and Danny split up? You certainly seem to have retained a friendship."

If Danny's sucking her fingers could be classified as friendship.

Shelby shot out of the rocker and started pacing back and forth again, her white gym shoes squeaking on the hardwood floor. She paused in the middle of the plum-colored rug and put her hands on her hips. A shrug followed. "No big mystery. We just figured out we were better off as friends than being married."

That didn't tell him a damn thing.

"Have you ever been married, Boston?"

He shook his head. "No."

Shelby sat at the foot of the bed and frowned. "Well, you're leaving, right? I mean, you're here until the company says you can leave and then you're gone, right?"

"Yes." She had totally lost him, but that point wasn't in dispute. He was definitely leaving the first opportunity he was given, even if that meant going somewhere other than Chicago. He'd go anywhere that had a sushi bar and a theater.

"So, if I tell you things, it doesn't matter, does it? You won't tell anyone, and you're not staying."

Now he understood. Here, trapped in the stuffy blue bedroom with a person who was virtually a stranger, it was easy to say things you wouldn't normally imagine speaking out loud. Hadn't he confessed about his father? "I won't tell anyone anything you say. And truthfully, I'd appreciate it if you didn't pass along those little anecdotes about my father either. Not many people know that about me."

"Done." Shelby pulled a leg onto the bed, seemingly unaware that the movement drew her shorts up to her panty line.

Boston was aware. Aware and overcome with the urge to lick that spot.

"I want to have sex with you, Boston."

His head snapped up. "What?" His cock went fully

hard, ready for action. She just needed to say go and he was there.

He sat up, reaching for her.

"But I can't."

He fell back onto the bed.

Damn it, that was cruel.

"And maybe you don't even want to have sex with me, and I've totally humiliated myself. But since you came to town, I've been thinking I might enjoy that, but it's just not a good idea. So if you were thinking about it, stop."

And this conversation had shown such promise.

Boston sat fully up, since lying down wasn't helping him think about anything but Shelby climbing onto his lap. "Why can't we sleep together if we want to? We're mature adults. We're trapped in a room together. No one will get hurt and no one in Cuttersville needs to know."

He certainly hadn't planned on having an affair with Shelby Tucker, but the idea was growing on him. Quickly. It was the best possible way he could think of to pass the time in exile in Cuttersville.

Shelby watched Boston, who looked ready to pounce on her any second now. For a minute, she was worried she'd spoken too directly and that he would laugh at the notion that he could be attracted to her. But her fears had been misplaced, given the look on his face and the way his fingers twitched in her direction. If he had those paranormal powers he'd talked about earlier, she suspected her clothes would be a thing of the past.

It was her nature to be honest, which was why she'd spoken up in the first place, but now she was left trying to figure out how to explain to Boston that she was a cold fish, incapable of pleasing herself or a man. There was no way to say it without making herself sound like a freak, or without being disloyal to Danny. She wouldn't embarrass or hurt Danny for the world.

"I have to live here. People are going to know." Shelby played with the edge of the eyelet spread, nervously sticking her finger through one of the holes and pulling it back out again.

"Not if we're discreet. Don't people here date?"

"Not me." She stuck her finger in the hole a second time, sorry she'd started this conversation. "I haven't dated at all since I left Danny." In and out went her finger.

Boston grabbed her hand. "Stop that." His voice was tight.

Startled, Shelby glanced at him, immediately taking in the tent his shorts were making. Oh, Lord, she'd gone and turned him on. Now what was she supposed to do? She knew from experience he didn't give up a stiffy easily.

"So you're saying that you haven't slept with any man since Danny and you're nervous."

No, but that sounded good. "Exactly."

The seconds ticked by and Boston didn't say anything. He just stared at her, his jaw locked and his eyes narrowed. He was close enough that she could smell the shampoo from his shower, see the muscles in his arms flex. She was about to bolt off the bed or scream when he finally spoke.

"Do you know who Tigger is?"

Now it was her turn to stare. That just confirmed that city folks were missing some marbles. Too much pollution and radioactive wires hanging over their heads. "What?"

He repeated the question, but it didn't make any more sense the second time than it had the first. "You mean the bouncing tiger from *Winnie the Pooh*?"

"Yes." He leaned toward her. "I thought so."

Shelby scooted back. "What are you talking about?"

"Doesn't matter." He put his hand on her chin and moved in so close she about went cross-eyed trying to watch him. "And it doesn't matter if you're feeling nervous or inexperienced. All I want is a little kiss, Shelby. Just one. And no one is going to interrupt me this time."

Chapter Seven

Boston saw Shelby Tucker's coffee-colored eyes go round right before he closed his own and kissed her.

A deep, reaching, full-mouth kiss that left any thoughts of holding back eradicated.

She tasted sweet and warm, with moist plump lips that gave just the right amount of pressure back. Not too hard and not too soft, but just right, and he leaned in closer, wanting more, wanting to keep her there. Her thick hair brushed across his forehead, and her fluttering fingers teased over his bare chest, shifting his curious desire to edgy lust.

Shelby's breathing was heavy, her lips open, and Boston never hesitated. He went in with his tongue, one hand creeping down her back to drift over the top of her firm ass, realizing the upside of Shelby dressing in sloppy clothes. The shorts she had on were loose enough that he had a clear path down them, should he choose to pursue it.

She raked her nails down his chest, settling in right at his navel, so close to his fly his cock twitched. He choose to take the path down her pants, cupping that smooth behind while kissing her with a reckless and unskilled abandon that would have appalled him had he been thinking clearly.

He wasn't. He was just touching and feeling and sliding into a haze of sweet desire, Shelby's tongue making a tentative taste of his bottom lip, her nails digging into his flesh right above his waistband.

A little shift and he was lowering her to the bed with the hand that wasn't down her pants. His mouth fell off hers. Taking in her flushed cheeks, sun-kissed hair starting to spill out of her lopsided ponytail, and shiny wet lips, Boston bent over to kiss her again.

He wanted to make love to her, right here on this four-poster bed, to fit himself inside her and watch her come apart under him at his gentle strokes.

Nibbling on her bottom lip, the full cherry flesh smooth, Boston worked on shifting her bulky T-shirt up over her ribs so he could duck under.

"Boston," she said, her breath tickling him.

"What?" he asked, distracted, her shirt resisting his tugging. It gave, and he slipped a hand over her breast, cupping the warm fullness and brushing over her nipple.

"Never mind."

He kissed her chin, he kissed her neck, he spent some serious time and attention on that sexy little dip under her collarbone, while his fingers explored and pursued and teased. Shelby's fingers fell off him to lie still at her sides.

Her head arched and she gave a series of very arousing moans that stroked both his ego and his cock.

"Boston?"

"Yes?" He found his way under the stretchy fabric of her bra.

"Forget it."

Okay. He pulled down the neck of her shirt until his tongue and his finger met at the swell of her breast. He sucked.

"I . . ."

"What, Shelby?" Boston flipped the bra down so it exposed her whole breast and one firm, rosy nipple.

He leaned back to give himself a better view. Damn. She was just hot. Totally different from all those fashionable women he had dated, whose moves in the bedroom were orchestrated and designed to show their bodies off to their best advantage. They had been successful at satisfying him, that was true. And in fact, he had always gotten the feeling that being successful in the bedroom was just as important to them as success in the boardroom.

It was easy for him to understand. He'd been doing the same, always aware of how he was presenting himself to a lover, concerned with ensuring her pleasure. The satisfaction when he knew he'd been successful and she'd had an orgasm. Success-driven sex.

But in all of those encounters, there was that element of *real* missing.

With Shelby, everything was real, unplanned, just reaching out and doing what felt good, and he didn't think he could predict one second to the next. Didn't want to. Didn't want to think or plan or strategize, just touch and taste and revel in her.

He covered her nipple with his mouth.

"Nothing," Shelby said, the word falling out on a gasp. "Forget I said anything. Just stick a sock in my mouth so I shut up."

Boston could think of something better than a sock to put in her mouth.

But he was starting to get the feeling something was wrong. He gave one last greedy pull on her nipple before releasing it with a sigh. Reluctantly, he withdrew from her shorts.

"Is something wrong?" It was too much to hope for that there wasn't, given the look on her face.

Instead of aroused, she looked worried.

"No, not really."

How reassuring. "If you're not enjoying this, just tell me to stop."

She swallowed. "But I am. Enjoying it."

It was something. Boston perched awkwardly, one foot on the floor, his other on the bed, knee pressed into a spring. It was an uncomfortable way to be coaxing Shelby into confessing what was wrong.

He stood up. Shelby looked a little bit disappointed. But only a little.

Immediately she pulled her shirt back down, covering her bare breast. "I don't mean to be a tease or anything, but I just can't do this."

So much for his fabulous plans of spending their lockup in bed, drenched in naked pleasure.

"I swear, Boston, you'll thank me in the long run."

Please. That was what people said when they took away from you something really, really good.

*　　*　　*

Shelby watched Boston take a deep breath and walk with slow steps, hands on hips, over to the window. "I don't want to do anything you don't want to do, Shelby," he said to the glass.

"But you're not." Oh, Lord, she was acting like a total fool. But what if she let Boston keep on the way he was going and nothing happened? She was out of practice faking orgasms.

And she didn't want to fake one. She wanted a real one. But how could she explain to Boston that only on rare occasions and during a full moon did she manage to come with Danny and that it wasn't Danny, it was absolutely, most definitely her. There was no polite way to say she couldn't get off.

Boston was staring out the window and attempting to pry it open. Apparently he'd had enough of her and her indecisive meanderings. "I'm at a loss here, Shelby," he said over his shoulder. "So after I figure out that this damn window really won't open, I'm going to sit down in the rocking chair and we can just have a friendly conversation to pass the time. I'm going to stay away from the bed so I'm not tempted by you, because I really don't want to do anything you're not completely ready for."

Shelby thought that sounded like an okay plan, except when she looked over at the rocking chair he was referring to, to gauge how far away from her it was, her jaw dropped. Good gravy, that thing was *rocking*. By itself.

Back and forth, faster and faster, like a very agitated person was sitting in it. Only there wasn't anything but a rose-colored cushion on it, and as far as she knew, cushions couldn't push rocking chairs.

"Uh . . . Boston?"

"What?" Sounding surly, Boston abandoned the window and turned around, brushing his hands on his shorts.

She pointed to the rocker. "That chair is rocking."

Boston frowned. Shelby inched farther back on the bed, grabbing a bed pillow. She wasn't sure that beating a ghost with an eyelet pillow would be very effective, but it gave her a small measure of comfort.

"It's probably just the draft from the hall or a breeze I created by jerking on the window."

If he wanted to be dense, that was his business, but she knew what she was seeing and it wasn't any piddling breeze. "It's Nanny Baskins."

The chair rocked faster.

And Boston, that idiot, went over to the chair and tentatively touched the arm.

"What are you doing?!" Did he want to be slapped into the light or sucked over to the other side? Geez Louise, the man didn't show a lick of sense.

"I don't feel anything. Not a cold spot, not a warm spot."

The chair kept rocking, and he made like he was going to sit in it.

Shelby leaped off the bed. "Stop! You can't *sit* on the woman, for crying out loud!"

Boston hesitated, then let out a cry of surprise. Jerking forward, he reached down and rubbed his leg. "Something slapped my thigh!"

Shelby rolled her eyes. Really, what did he expect? "Well, she's a nanny. She was just disciplining you for your rudeness."

Still rubbing his leg, he shot her a disbelieving look. "I am thirty-two years old. I do not need to be disciplined by a dead nanny."

"She thinks you do, apparently." Shelby crossed her arms in front of her chest and shivered. The chair had stopped rocking.

"She couldn't have children, you know," she whispered.

"Who?" Boston sat down on the foot of the bed and rubbed his hands over his face.

"Nanny Baskins. Her husband left her when he decided she wasn't fertile, though for the longest time the town thought he'd died in an accident down in Cincinnati." Shelby, still clutching the pillow, sprawled across the head of the bed, on her stomach.

"Another vengeful spirit?" Boston cast another look at the still rocker.

"No, not at all. Once her husband left, Emma Baskins became a nanny, and they say she was never the least bit bitter. She got what she wanted after all. Children to raise, and she loved them like her own. Two generations of children she raised here in the White House, and did a fine job of it too. One of her charges became mayor, another a doctor, yet a third was the first woman in Cuttersville to go to college." Shelby had always imagined Nanny Baskins to be something like her own gran, loving but firm.

"She sounds better than Carrie." Boston grinned at her.

Shelby laughed. "Much better. And they say she stays on, watching over each subsequent generation of kids living here, just to make sure everything's alright. But there haven't been any kids here in twenty years or so. She must be lonely."

The thought made her melancholy. How many times had she given that speech and she'd never once thought about how sad it was for a woman who loved children to be waiting for more to take care of. And how burdensome it must be to be stuck in the same place for eternity, if there really was such a thing as ghosts. Which she was rapidly coming to conclude either there was, or she was as cracked as a nut.

"Well, Nanny Baskins, I apologize for almost sitting on you," Boston said to the room.

Nothing happened.

"Maybe she doesn't forgive me." Boston rolled onto his side, and Shelby immediately wished he hadn't.

They were right back on his bed again, and he still wasn't wearing a shirt, and he still was as sexy as all get-out, and she still hadn't had sex in three years.

But he kept his promise. Boston started talking to her, just idle chitchat, mildly complaining that he was hungry, and telling her about all the great restaurants in Chicago.

She liked listening to him talk, and he had her laughing with his descriptions of the trauma his arteries were suffering under the greasy diet the Busy Bee Diner had him on. Shelby figured her arteries were immune. If she ate salmon, her arteries would likely shrivel up in horror and die.

Somehow or another, as they talked and the minutes ticked by, they wound up lying next to each other on the bed, Boston flat on his back staring up at the ceiling. Shelby was closer to him than she'd intended, relaxed and enjoying his company. The room was darkening, the sun just about gone, and it had to be past nine.

Sleepiness started to steal over her. She turned on her side, her nose next to Boston's very nice biceps muscle. She yawned. "It's been twenty minutes since you checked the door. Shouldn't we check again?"

Instead of rushing over to the door, Boston lifted his arm and wrapped it around her, pulling her into his chest.

Hello. Big sexy solid chest touching her.

"We're stuck, Shelby, face it."

Her lips quivered. She just wanted to plant a little teeny kiss right there on his nipple, just to see what it felt like, how he tasted. But if she did, she'd land flat on her back, she was sure. Which suddenly sounded like such a good idea.

What was she afraid of? Being embarrassed? Dying of pleasure? They were trapped in a house with mischievous dead people; she shouldn't be worried about how her sexual performance compared to Chicago career women.

She should just go for it. Have one night of passion before she spent the remainder of her days shuttling tours through Cuttersville, before she wound up old and childless and eccentric, caring for seventy-two cats and wearing men's clothes.

The image was enough to embolden her. Shelby pressed her lips onto his chest, while simultaneously reaching down and stroking the front of his shorts.

He jerked beneath her touch. "Uh. Shelby?"

Shelby traced her tongue across his flesh, enjoying the hitch his breath gave. He was warm and hard and . . . and lacking in a penis? Shelby paused with her mouth on his pectoral, preoccupied. She was feeling all over kingdom come down there and was empty-handed. Ignoring his strangled groan, she kept moving around, determined now.

Where was the damn thing?

Then it occurred to her maybe she couldn't find it because it was . . . not interested.

She froze, eyes fixed on his chest, her hand over his zipper. She gave a few desperate pats around, not willing to look up and face Boston.

"To the left," he said, his voice low and rough.

She shifted and encountered a solid wall of hard-on. "Oh!" Whew. That was better.

Splaying her fingers over it eagerly, she went back to her earlier exploration of his chest. Hard hands gripped her shoulders.

"What exactly are you doing?"

"I thought it was obvious." She chanced a glance up the length of his chest. He stared down at her over his chin, dark eyes aroused and yet disapproving.

Shelby smiled at him. "I'm ready now."

He frowned. "And you're not going to change your mind this time?" he asked suspiciously.

It was a fair question, given her earlier waffling. "No, I swear to you, I will not change my mind."

He studied her for a minute, then he sat up, pushing her up with him and stripping her T-shirt off before she could say monkey's uncle. The shirt fell on the eyelet spread while his mouth went straight for her breasts.

They moaned together when his lips made contact with the rounded flesh popping out of her bra. Shelby went for the button on his shorts, figuring if she had him naked, she couldn't miss this time.

Her own shorts were so loose that Boston had them half down her thighs without even undoing the button. On their knees, he kissed her, taking her tongue and sending a rush of desire through every inch of her body. Lack of passion didn't seem to be a problem when she was with Boston.

Gran's potbelly stove burning full blast was cooler than her inner thighs were. She was throbbing, clenching, aching. Her nipples pushed painfully against the bra, and her hips rocked forward against him.

Boston didn't know where to touch first, so he went for a little of everything. He ate at Shelby's mouth, loving the ragged sound of her breathing, while he slipped a hand over the front of her panties. She was hot, and when he stroked, nudging her panties a little between her folds, the fabric came back damp.

Shelby hadn't been able to get his shorts and boxers all the way down since he was on his knees, and he used one hand to shove at them, lifting one knee at a time. Holding her and his pants, and leaning at the same time, proved to be his downfall. They both tipped over and landed on their sides on the bed, which was a beneficial thing. Even though their mouths separated in the fall, his hands were free to dispose of his shorts, and quickly move to Shelby's.

"Are you sure you want to get naked on this spread?" Shelby asked. "It might be dangerous."

She was wearing an unholy grin. He was willing to forgive her since her nipples had tumbled out of the top of her bra in the fall.

"Very funny." Boston pulled one pink plump nipple into his mouth and sucked. It shut her laughter up quickly.

He was still wearing his boxers, and she had on her panties, but when he pressed against her, it felt delicious and hot, an arousing tease of what it would feel like to sink inside Shelby's firm thighs.

Still moving his tongue over her nipple, Boston gripped the wet cotton of her panties and pulled them to the side. He swirled his thumb over her, finding her clitoris and brushing it.

Shelby arched her back. She made delightful little whimpers that had him sinking his finger into her damp heat, deeper and deeper, then back out. Damn, she felt good, tight and pulsing, and her thighs spread wider for him.

"Yes!" she shouted suddenly, her hand slapping him on the back.

Startled, Boston kept stroking and her voice rose in excitement. "Yes, yes, yes!"

Was she coming already? He'd barely touched her, but she really sounded like she was in the throes of an orgasm. Feeling a little confused but pleased, Boston kept a steady rhythm, not wanting to interrupt her pleasure. And she'd been worried about her lack of experience. Clearly she hadn't counted on his skill.

Shelby slapped at him again, harder this time. "No, no, no!"

What? What the hell had he done? Boston looked up and saw she was struggling to get out from under him, excitement on her face. Excitement was good, struggling was wrong.

"Get off me! The door's open."

That wasn't on his list of things he'd like her to say.

"Yes, yes, yes" was a good start. "Oh, Boston, that's perfect" was a good follow-up. And "Take me again, you're the best I've ever had" would be a great finish. Nowhere did that list include her saying "Get off me."

Shelby jumped up with the dexterity of a circus acrobat, leaving him lying on the bed in his boxers alone. Staring at the open door. Damn. When had that happened? Sometime between her groping for his cock and him shifting her panties aside.

She had her shorts up and buttoned, her shirt down, and the door propped open with her back before he could even lift himself up.

"What's the matter? You should be relieved." Shelby hooked the rocker with her foot and dragged it over to the door. She propped it under the doorknob and said, "You should get bricks for all the doors to keep them open."

Did she not notice something? That they had been just about naked, on the verge of some very hot and sweaty sex, and now they were . . . vergeless? "I'll do that," he said wryly, forgoing his shorts and heading to the door in his boxers.

Not that Shelby noticed. She was already halfway down the stairs. "Oh Lord, it's quarter after ten! Gran will be wondering where I am since I didn't even take the car."

"You're going to walk home?"

"Sure." She shrugged and stopped in the front hall.

"Absolutely not. I'll drive you. Just let me get my pants on." He turned back toward his bedroom.

"I'll be fine. This is Cuttersville, not Chicago."

"Serial killers and rapists live everywhere. Don't you dare leave this house." Boston had no problem picturing her strolling off without him. He shoved a leg in his shorts and hopped back into the hall.

"Alright." She cocked her head at him from the bottom of the steps. "Why are you so grumpy?"

He buttoned his fly and jogged down the steps, feeling beyond grumpy. He felt downright pissed off. "How can you ask that? We were interrupted in the middle of something I was enjoying quite a lot, if you hadn't noticed, and you don't look the least bit bothered by the fact that we had to stop."

Shelby flushed. "Oh, well, I am. It's just I thought it might be our only chance to get out of that room for who knows how long, so I had to act and grab the door before it shut again." She patted his arm. "But we can start back up where we left off."

It felt suspiciously like she was consoling him. But he'd take what he could get. "Where?"

"Anywhere without a door. Like here in the hall," she suggested innocently. "Of course, the front door could lock, so I suppose we'd have to prop that open."

Boston sighed, all horny hope evaporating. "Shelby, I am not going to make love to you standing in the foyer with the front door open for anyone to walk by."

"We could turn the light off. And nobody walks by here anyway except Mrs. Caruthers and her blind dachshund."

Well, terrific. At least the dog wouldn't see them. "No."

"Then how about your car?"

An image of Harriet and Clyde Danforth in a rocking Chevy Nova leaped to mind. An involuntary shudder passed through him. "Absolutely not."

Shelby pulled on the rubber band holding her hair back, adjusting it so her heavy hair lifted higher on her head. "I guess we'll just have to wait, then. We'll be better prepared next time with a cell phone, food, and a means to escape if it happens again. Stuff like that."

"It's not going to happen again."

Disappointment crossed her face. "You don't want to try again?"

It was gratifying to see she was finally acting like she'd enjoyed their time on the bed at least a little. "No, I mean we're not going to get locked in again. It was just a coincidence that it happened twice."

Shelby raised an eyebrow and pursed her lips like he was an alcoholic in denial. "Alrighty, then, if you say so. But I'm not setting foot in this house anymore without a cell phone, a bag of snacks, and a big old brick for emergency purposes."

"We could go to your place."

Her jaw dropped. "I live with my *grandmother*!"

It was on his tongue to suggest he could sneak in her window when he stopped himself. He was not a sex-driven teenager. He was only eight years away from forty and surely he could control himself.

Shelby reached up to fuss with her hair again, and her shirt slid past her waistband. That sliver of golden flesh had him doubting his control.

"Aren't you going to put on a shirt?"

"No." And while he took her elbow protectively and shuttled her into his BMW gently, he couldn't bring himself to say anything else.

It didn't matter. Shelby chattered the whole way to her grandmother's, which was all of three minutes away. She hopped out of the car and waved him off, but he left his car running and got out, following her onto the porch.

After she had unlocked the door and opened it, she turned to smile at him. So sweet, so honest, so lacking in guile.

He was on her, moving so fast she let out a cry of surprise that he stifled with his mouth. He kissed her over and over again, until her hands fell slack and together they stumbled back against the front door, slamming the doorknob into the interior wall.

Somehow he'd inserted himself down her shorts, cupping her firm cheeks and grinding her against him.

The porch light went on, blinding him and sending him leaping back, feeling and probably looking guilty as hell.

"Sorry."

Shelby clung to the door and pressed her wet lips closed. The bright fluorescent glow of the bulb over her head sent shadows across her pretty face. "Don't be sorry. I'm not."

"Well, good night," he said, feeling confused and aroused and stupid. What the hell was he doing?

"G'night."

Boston wasn't behaving at all the way he did normally, he realized as he got back into his car. Forcing himself not to glance back at Shelby standing vulnerable and beautiful on the old white porch, he backed out of the drive. He was professional, driven, reserved. He held his personal feelings back. For the most part, he lived for his job and was solitary outside of work.

It had always suited him just fine.

But now he was distracted, his mind shifting away from work the minute he walked out of that plant. And right on to Shelby.

It didn't make sense. She wasn't anything special, just a little dust-covered unambitious local girl who needed a stylist to hack away half that hair.

But she was real, and honest, and giving, and the sexiest woman he had ever encountered in his life, and he was starting to think that he could tell himself otherwise, but deep down he knew she was very special.

Which meant he could not take advantage of her. He couldn't offer her anything beyond a quick hot affair, and that wasn't fair to Shelby. She deserved better. She deserved love, and he wasn't capable of giving that.

Not to mention that this was her town, and if they fooled around, everyone would know. He would leave and it wouldn't matter to him, but it would matter to her. People would talk about it here for a long time, and that was something he just didn't want Shelby to have to endure.

No, he couldn't sleep with her. It was probably a good thing they'd been interrupted.

He nearly groaned at the thought, suddenly exhausted and wanting nothing more than to just tumble into his bed and sleep for about twelve hours. Except that he had to get up early tomorrow and go buy bricks to use as doorstops. He didn't even know where one went about buying bricks.

In his experience, they just showed up on the side of buildings.

Boston sighed as he parked the car back at the White House. Maybe it was time to call Brett again and try and get himself the hell out of there.

Chapter Eight

Sleep would have to wait, Boston decided, when he walked around the back of the house and found a teenage boy with blue hair sitting on the back step, smoking a cigarette.

Shelby's cousin.

"Hey, what's up?" Brady said, blowing smoke to the side.

"Nothing. What's up with you?" Boston debated lecturing him on the effects of tobacco, then realized he was too tired to be properly firm.

"I'm just looking for Shel. She around? Mrs. Danforth said she was giving you a tour."

"I just took her home."

Brady grinned in the dark, his white teeth flashing. "That was a helluva long tour, huh? She must have shown you just about everything."

He would have to be an idiot not to catch Brady's raunchy tone of voice, but he chose to ignore it. Putting his key in the door, he opened it and stepped around Brady. "Just the usual."

Brady crushed out his cigarette on the stoop and scrambled to his feet. "I think it's cool if you hook up with Shel. She deserves someone paying a little attention to her. This town treats her like Cinderella or something, man."

Boston flipped on the kitchen light and looked at Brady curiously. "And that bothers you?"

"Hell, yeah. Pisses me off. I wish she'd leave this place and go somewhere new, then people would have to see her for who she is, not what they think she is."

Boston liked Brady's emotional and protective tone. He sensed Brady was also in a talkative mood, and Boston decided it was worth a little lost sleep to hear what the kid might be able to tell him about Shelby.

"And what is Shelby?" A giant moth flew past Brady's blue head, attracted to the kitchen light, and Boston added, "Get in here and shut the door."

Brady did, spinning the earring in his eyebrow as he moved. Watching the skin pull out made Boston a little nauseous, but he decided that was probably due to lack of nourishment. He hadn't eaten since lunch.

"Shelby's smart. She's loyal. She doesn't talk down to anyone and she doesn't need fancy clothes and a house to be happy." Then Brady shrugged like he'd gotten too sentimental. "She's cool, that's all."

Boston pulled open the refrigerator and stared at its sparse contents. Brady's assessment of Shelby was exactly what he'd thought of her. Too good for him.

He stood up so fast he nailed his head on the freezer door. Where the hell had that thought come from? Shelby was not too good for him. No one was too good for him, and he wasn't that little kid anymore who just desperately wanted his parents to love him.

Irritated, he grabbed a drinkable yogurt and ripped the top off. He took a swig, then turned to Brady, realizing a second too late that he shouldn't be eating in front of him. "Want one?"

Brady shook his head, lip curling up. "No way. That's like girl food."

"What do you want? A bloody steak and greasy eggs?"

Brady grinned. "That sounds good. With a beer."

Boston found himself amused. "Yeah, in about five years." He pulled open the deli drawer. "Best I can do is a ham sandwich."

"Cool." Brady vaulted himself onto the counter and leaned over, reaching into the drawer between his legs. "Here's a knife for the mustard."

Boston pulled out the sandwich fixings and set them on the counter. He went for a couple of plates. "So where's your girlfriend tonight?" He'd never got a glimpse of Brady's girlfriend, but he remembered her indignant squawk from behind the closed door.

"Dude, she has like the most unreasonable curfew you've ever heard of in your life. She has to be home by ten-thirty. I mean, what's up with that?"

Taking in Brady's blue hair sticking up in spikes, his eyebrow ring, the silver tongue stud that flashed from time to time when he spoke, and the spiked bracelet, Boston wasn't surprised. Brady's T-shirt had what looked like a bleeding head on it. "Maybe they're protective."

As he started to assemble sandwiches, Brady snorted, kicking his legs against the cabinets. "There's overprotective and then there's a fucking bubble, man."

Brady swiped a piece of ham from one of the open-faced sandwiches and tossed it into his mouth. "And here's a little warning for you. The chicks in this town want commitment. We're talking a ring, the wedding, the whole forever bullshit. So you just watch your back."

"All of them?" Shelby didn't strike him as eager to jump into marriage again.

"All the ones I ever met. Joelle wants to get engaged. Isn't that *nuts*? We're like fifteen. She's cool and all, but man, I want to see what's out there. Shop around."

Boston couldn't disagree with that. He'd done quite a bit of shopping himself. He cut their sandwiches in half and handed a plate to Brady.

"Thanks. I mean, look at you. You're like, what, forty?"

Boston paused with his sandwich half to his mouth. "I'm only thirty-two."

"See, that's still pretty old. And you're not married. What's the rush?"

None, as far as he could tell. It wasn't like he had any ambitious hopes for a happily ever after anyway. "I've been building my career."

A ham sandwich waved in front of him. "See? Exactly."

"So, why did Shelby divorce Danny?" That bothered him. It had since he'd first seen her with Danny outside the diner, looking way too friendly for exes.

Brady shrugged, downing the last bite of his sandwich. "Hey, got anything to drink? And I don't know, Shelby never tells me personal stuff like that, and I was just a kid anyway. Eleven or twelve when she left him. I thought my aunt Susan was going to have a stroke, though. Man, I remember that. She screamed herself hoarse."

Boston dug two soft drinks out of the fridge and arched one through the air to Brady. "Why?"

"They didn't want Shelby to leave him, thought she was making a mistake. My aunt thought Danny took good care of her."

He popped the top on his drink and took a sip. Something about Brady's comment bothered him. "What do you think of Danny?"

Another shrug. "He's cool. But hey, if Shelby doesn't want to be married to him, I don't see that it's any of Aunt Susan's business, you know? And Shelby doesn't need anyone to take care of her. What is this? Like the fifties, man? Come on."

Boston was liking Brady more and more with each passing minute. But he was left even more with the impression that he needed to stay away from Shelby Tucker. He couldn't get involved with her, no matter how appealing she was. Brady had said that women here wanted commitment, and he couldn't give that. Not even close.

"It's because she's dyslexic, you know."

Those words brought him back to attention. Shelby had a learning disorder? "She is?"

"Yeah. She's real smart, but being dyslexic messed her up in school." Brady scowled at him. "She can read, though, I don't mean that, it's just stuff is harder for her and her mom was a total freak about it, acting like she's disabled or something."

Which was probably how she'd tumbled into marriage and now haunted house tour guide. Nobody had encouraged Shelby to aim higher. The thought made him feel anger and sadness and a few other emotions, all of which were inappropriate for a woman he planned to stay the hell away from.

They finished eating in silence until Brady cocked his head and pinned him with a stare. "What is up with your hair tonight? You're always like Mister *GQ*, but tonight you look like shit."

Boston glanced at his reflection in the microwave. Nice. He looked as if a wool sweater had landed on his head. He'd taken the mousse out of his hair during the shower, but hadn't had a chance to put his regular products back in. All night he'd been with Shelby, fuzzy-headed and deodorant-free. That must have made quite an impression.

"I didn't have time to put my hair stuff on."

"What do you use?" Brady touched his own hair. "I'm not getting a good hold with what I'm using."

"It's forming cream. Twenty-five bucks a jar, but it does the job without looking shiny."

"What brand?"

"I don't know. Want me to go up and get it?"

"If you don't mind."

"No." Boston took the steps two at a time and laughed to himself. Brady had thought yogurt was feminine. What did discussing hair products qualify as?

A minute later, he slapped the jar in Brady's hand, who had slid off the counter.

"We can't buy anything like this here," Brady said, inspecting the jar. "It sucks to live in the sticks."

"You can order it online."

"No computer."

"You can use mine."

"Seriously?" Brady looked up at him as he unscrewed the lid, surprise on his face.

"Sure. You can come here and use it some night."

"Thanks, man." Brady smiled, then frowned when he looked at the forming cream. "This stuff is nasty looking. No offense or anything, but it looks like you shot your wad into the jar."

It took Boston a second to infer Brady's meaning, and when he did, he couldn't help laughing. "It does not."

"Yes, it does." Brady stuck a finger in and pulled out a dripping white glob of forming cream.

Boston saw the resemblance immediately and decided he would be switching to clear-colored pomade.

Brady put down the jar, then rinsed his dirty plate under the faucet and set it in the dish rack.

"Well, I've gotta head out, but I might help Shelby out tomorrow with the tour if it gets out of hand, so I'll see you then."

Boston felt a touch of alarm. "Out of hand? Why?"

"Word's out that the spirits are talking, locking doors and shit. People want to see. I'd expect double to triple the number of gawkers tomorrow."

Oh, wonderful. And he couldn't even bitch about it because he knew how much Shelby needed the money.

Brady left with a wave, leaving the back door open behind him.

Boston went to close it, but it glided shut on its own before he even got there.

Stopping in the middle of the sunny yellow kitchen, Boston glanced around suspiciously before deciding to head to bed. "Thank you," he said to the empty room as he passed through to the hallway.

The only answer was the click as the kitchen light turned off behind him.

He was avoiding her. Shelby sighed, standing on the front porch of the White House, pulling the door closed behind her. Seven days, a whole blinking week, and she hadn't seen him once.

Not since she'd interrupted him on the verge of giving her an orgasm and had leaped out of his bedroom.

What kind of a woman was dumb enough to do that?

She was, apparently. And all week she'd been feeling like someone must have whacked her with a stupid stick. A really big stupid stick.

It was an understatement to say she was regretting her actions. But she'd been in the middle of feeling all kinds of strange swirling emotions about Boston, confusion and embarrassment and a panicked sort of anxiety that he'd find her about as sexy as a block of ice, when she'd looked up and seen that door roll open.

An escape route from a man who had her feeling like she was way too old to be acting so ridiculous.

Only seven days and seven long frustrating nights later, she was rethinking things a bit. At night she dreamed about him.

During the day she traipsed her way through his house twice on the tour, smelling his aftershave lingering in the hall and seeing his bed neatly made, his coffee mug un-rinsed on the counter. Not to mention she was constantly having to talk about him, explaining to the tour-goers what exactly had happened the times they'd been locked in rooms together by unruly spirits. Well, she left out the bit about her springing off the bed half naked, and the actions immediately preceding it.

Gran nudged her. "You're supposed to be the guide. Tour's leaving without you, Shelby."

A serious lack of energy left her shoulders sagging and her wondering if she needed a multivitamin. And she could actually afford a ten-dollar bottle of pills now that her tour was just about busting at the seams every day. Everyone wanted a chance to see the White House's increased paranormal activity.

Shelby stepped onto the lawn and tried to put some enthusiasm into her actions. "Thanks for helping out, Gran."

"Oh, I'm enjoying it, hon. Having all these people swarm around is more excitement than I usually get."

Glancing at Gran, wearing a tennis visor, Shelby tried to smile but wasn't quite successful. The twenty tour-goers were heading down the road, impatient to get to the next stop, the spot on Miller Road where a long-dead jilted groom was known to pop out at couples getting amorous and rock their cars.

"They're starting to get mad, Gran. Since Boston and I got locked in his room, no one's seen a darn thing. They all wanted to see something, and nothing's happened, and they're liable to turn on me any day now. I could be out of business by next week."

Maybe she was exaggerating, but she was starting to get nervous. Normally, people *thought* they saw or felt or heard something, and the tour really only promised the possibility of ghosts. But since word had flown around town about the incidents with Boston, people took the tour expecting to see something obvious. Lights flashing, objects moving, doors slamming, cold winds, the whole kit and kaboodle.

Gran huffed a little as she walked faster to keep up with the mob. The road was pitted and gravel strewn, so Shelby put her hand on Gran's elbow to keep her steady.

"Shelby, I've been thinking that maybe it's Boston who's causing all the activity in the house."

"Like he's a psychic or something?" God, that was a horrible thought. If he could conjure up dead people, she was really going to have a hard time relaxing around him. Imagining a spectral vision hanging over her shoulder while they were getting intimate was definitely going to cause performance anxiety.

Not that it appeared he wanted to get intimate with her anymore, given the fact that he was as absent as the ghosts.

"I just think maybe he's agitating the house somehow, without meaning to. I think maybe you should ask Boston to help you out with the tour."

Shelby actually laughed out loud. "Gran, he hates the tour. He's not going to join me as cohost."

"Well, just ask him to be in the house for the later tour. He's a nice man, honey, he'll help you out if he thinks you might lose business. If it's one thing that man understands, it's the bottom line." Gran gave her a sharp look. "Besides, if a man's going to stick his hands down your pants, the least he can do is help you out now and again."

Stumbling on a rock, Shelby felt her face heat. "Uh . . ." She'd suspected Gran had seen her with Boston on the porch, but she had never wanted to *talk* about it.

Gran smirked. "Now don't be embarrassed. I know all about the birds and the bees, Shelby Louise. And I was thinking you might want to run to that new CVS and buy yourself some condoms."

Even better. Her grandmother was recommending birth

control. Shelby just nodded, not sure what the right thing to say was when discussing your sex life with a geriatric relative.

"Now, are you going to be home for dinner tonight? I was thinking of having you pick up some chicken."

"Actually, I'm having dinner out at the farm with Danny. He called me yesterday."

Thoughts racing ahead to the fact that she should probably pick up some dessert to take, she was only half listening to Gran.

"Smart idea. Play one off against the other."

When the words finally filtered through, she stared at her grandmother. "What do you mean?"

"Nothing." She smiled with a smugness that wasn't all proper for an old lady, in Shelby's opinion.

Gran's old Pontiac took all the bumps in the dirt road with a loud rattle, a heaving bounce, and the threat of just dying altogether. Shelby figured if the car quit, it wouldn't matter at this point. She could walk the rest of the way up the road to Danny's house.

The farm lay silent, baking in the summer sun, the soybeans pushing toward the sky, looking hearty and hale. She drove past the big farmhouse where Danny's parents lived and waved to Mr. Tucker on his tractor. She'd always loved her in-laws, the warm stable way they ran their lives, unlike her flighty mother and never-to-be-seen-again father.

In fact, she'd loved a lot of things about her years as Danny's wife. She had been young, and more than a little frightened, but she'd wound up enjoying her role as housekeeper, cook, and occasional beer-fetcher. She'd figured that if she was happy, what did it matter that she didn't have a thriving career?

Sure, she worked hard around the house, but Danny also worked hard in the fields, and at the end of the day it had all been equal.

It wasn't monotony, or drudgery, or hatred of the farm that had driven her to a divorce. And if she hadn't miscarried, she was certain she never would have left him. But she didn't have a child, and had put off Danny every time he'd suggested later in their marriage that they give parenthood another go. Because she had known if she had a child, she couldn't leave.

And while she loved Danny and the farm, she had just known something was missing. He didn't make her toes curl, never did, and didn't a girl deserve a shot at some toe-curling before she died?

It had seemed fair enough, but as Shelby let the car wheeze to a halt in front of the smaller ranch-style house Danny lived in, she wondered if she was just a fool. It had been three years and her toes hadn't even so much as wiggled until Boston had come to town. And while he could curl her toes clear back to her heels, he couldn't give her much more than that.

With a sigh, she hauled her melancholy self out of the car, cherry pie in hand, and went to the door.

Danny let her in with a grin and a hug, and she forced a smile back. It wasn't his fault she was a wreck.

Sniffing the pie, Danny took it from her. "Cherry? Man, that smells good. Did you bake it yourself, sugar? You always had a way with pies."

"No, no time. I bought it." Though his offhand compliment made her suddenly want to cry. As did the familiar furnishings and knickknacks around the little house.

They'd picked out those plaid sofas together at a going-out-of-business sale in Wilmington. Moving into the L-shaped kitchen, she saw he'd never taken down the green gingham curtains she'd hung, and the little rooster painting she'd found at a garage sale still perched over the two-person table. It had been well over a year since she'd been in the house, and at the time she hadn't even noticed he hadn't changed a thing, but for some reason now it landed on her like a tipped cow.

"Want anything to drink?"

"Just some water." Shelby peeked out the back door window and saw that the garden was full of weeds and hadn't been planted that year. She'd spent many pleasant days fending off dandelions and slugs in that plot of land. "No garden?"

"No time to keep up with it. My mom still has hers and I snag some fresh stuff from her."

Shelby opened the back door and stepped out onto the deck. Danny already had the grill fired up, smoke pouring out from under the lid. She smiled at him, taking in the view of the endless acres of fields, alternating between fallow and thriving with soybeans. "So, what's on the menu?"

Plopping herself down on a plastic lawn chair, she listened to the steady mechanical spray of the irrigation system watering the crops, and the underlying hum of insects.

"Steak and potatoes. And a salad, but I mangled the tomatoes trying to cut them, so it doesn't look pretty."

Shelby laughed. "If it's edible, what do I care what it looks like? Let me help you, though."

When she went to stand back up, his hand fell on her shoulder. "No, you sit. I've got it."

Something about the tone of his voice made her look closer at him. Danny had actually never invited her to dinner before. He wasn't much of a cook. Plus he was wearing a green polo shirt stretched a little tight across his broad chest, with nice khaki shorts. Danny almost never wore anything above the waist but a T-shirt or his bare skin.

The picnic table was set too, with a cheerful yellow plastic tablecloth, held down by plates and a pitcher of lemonade. The paper napkins sported little red cherries on them. Alarm rushed through her. Either Danny had been watching *Martha Stewart Living* during his free time, or he wanted to tell her something.

Like maybe he was getting remarried.

Alarm kicked up a notch to extreme agitation, which didn't make sense, but she didn't stop to dissect her reaction. Who would Danny marry? As far as she knew, he hadn't dated anyone in six months or so, and he didn't really have the opportunity to meet women outside of Cuttersville.

Was he dying? No, he looked just as healthy as always. She sipped the water he gave her and pondered the possibility of him selling his house and clearing out, heading off to Vegas to be a blackjack dealer or something.

That was probably what Brady would be doing in a couple years, but it wasn't Danny. He loved the farm, and wouldn't leave it.

They talked about the weather and the crops and Shelby's tour while Danny cooked the steaks, and the whole while she was thinking, worrying, wondering.

Finally he sat down across from her, a full plate of food in front of each of them. Shelby took a bite of her juicy steak and started to chew.

"Shel, what would you think about getting back together? I really want you to come home."

The meat stuck in her cheek, and Shelby stared at Danny. That was absolutely the one possibility she hadn't considered. "I'm so glad you're not dying!" she blurted out. Not to mention she was secretly a little bit thrilled he didn't want to marry someone else, which was just tacky of her.

His brow wrinkled. "Dying? Why would you think I'm dying? Shoot, I haven't even had a cold in over two years."

Looking at his brawny, sunburned body, she thought death did seem a little far-fetched. "Well, you invited me over for dinner, and here you are, wearing a nice shirt that looks like you even ironed it. There's cute little napkins and steak. I figured you had to tell me something."

Danny's face turned pink like the inside of her filet. "Damn, I'm that obvious, huh?"

"Not totally, since I thought you wanted me to help you plan your funeral, and it doesn't seem that's what you had in mind." The whole impact of what he'd said finally hit her. Get back together with Danny.

Oh God. She didn't want that.

Her cheerful gingham curtains fluttered at the window behind Danny's head. Or did she?

Shelby tried to evict the obnoxious little doubts. Of course she didn't. Nothing had changed in three years. She loved Danny like a brother, and coveting comfort and drapery was not a reason to remarry him. There still wouldn't be any passion between them.

"No." Danny reached over the table and lifted her hand into his. "I want you to come back, Shel."

"It's been three years," she said weakly, her thoughts as mucked up as her old garden.

"So? It's no secret between us I never wanted you to leave in the first place. I was hoping that now that you've been on your own, you'll see that there wasn't anything wrong with what we had."

She started to open her mouth, to what purpose she didn't know, since she couldn't think of a thing to say, but Danny stopped her by holding up his hand.

"Hear me out, honey. Look, we dated in high school, got married right after, and I can understand that maybe you never had a chance to be on your own, look after yourself, and I respected your wanting to do that. But sometimes being on your own is just lonely."

Shelby tried to remove her hand from his. She wasn't lonely. She was perfectly fine living with Gran and running a two-bit tour.

"I'm lonely, and I think you are too. You loved being here on the farm, I know that, and I think you still care about me."

She stopped tugging and said softly, "I do, Danny. You know that."

He nodded. "I know. And I also know you've got the hots for that city boy."

Pinned in his grip, she sank into her chair and glanced back down at her plate. This was surely embarrassing. If Danny was on to her feelings about Boston, who else knew? "What do you mean?"

"Oh, come on, I see him sniffing around you, and the way you look at him. You get all nervous and giggly."

What? "I do not giggle!"

"Yes, you do. And it doesn't matter. Because you know and I know and he knows that anything between the two of you is just about sex. He's leaving in just a couple months and men like him don't marry girls like you."

That sounded insulting.

"With you and me, it's never been about sex."

Hah. That was the whole damn problem. She wanted it to be about sex.

"We're about building a home together, a life, a family. I can't think of anyone I'd rather have as the mother of my children."

Dang it. Just when she was all set to be mad at him and tell him to shove it, he had to go and be sweet. "Oh, Danny."

"So here's what I'm thinking. You go and have your little summer affair with Fancy Pants, get it out of your system, and then when he dumps you, we'll talk again."

Shelby was surprised when her jaw didn't actually make contact with her plate. It certainly felt like it had free-fallen. "Danny Tucker!"

"What? It's a good plan." He used his free hand, the one that wasn't holding her hostage, to unbutton his top shirt button. "Damn thing's strangling me."

Better his shirt than her. "So you're saying you don't mind if I go off and have a wild sexually experimental affair with a Samson executive." Shelby didn't bother to contain the sarcasm in her voice, but Danny didn't seem to notice.

His eyebrow twitched a little, and his jaw locked, but he shook his head. "I don't like the idea, but I can live with it, if we get back together in the end. I'm trying to be mature about the whole thing, and I don't want you to feel stifled or have any regrets. Especially since I'd like to work on getting you pregnant right away."

Mature wasn't what she called the whole idea. It was preposterous, insulting, bizarre, doomed to failure. And on some level, appealing.

Shelby stuffed a forkful of potato into her mouth so she wouldn't voice that little psychotic thought out loud. What was the matter with her? Sane women didn't go around contemplating reuniting with the husband they'd left. Certainly not after indulging in a decadent sexual fling with a man all wrong for them, allowing them to cling to the memories for the rest of their long, happy, loving, calm, and sexless lives.

Obviously she wasn't sane, because she was considering just that.

Danny raised some good points, damn him. She could never have a relationship with Boston, wasn't even sure she wanted one. He was a controlling workaholic who'd rather be anywhere than Cuttersville. Even if he did suddenly lose his mind and decide she was more interesting than all the skinny career women he knew, she couldn't leave Cuttersville.

But if she had an affair with him, and he left, she'd be worse off than before. Alone and sexually awakened, to boot. Unless she fell in with Danny's nuttier-than-a-fruit-cake plan and married him again. Hadn't she just been feeling nostalgic for the farm?

It was a great place to raise kids . . .

"Oh, Lord, I need some time to myself to think about this. I've gotta go." Shelby stood up so fast she knocked over her white chair, and the plastic bounced on the deck.

"Shelby." Danny came around the table but she was already cutting through the kitchen, desperate to escape.

"I'll call you." Right now she needed to go be alone in a dark room.

Chapter Nine

Except Gran's car wouldn't start.

Danny ended up having to drive her back to town, promising he'd have the Pontiac towed.

Shelby sat in the passenger seat of his pickup and tried not to feel like the Almighty was laughing at her.

Danny was using her silence to further his campaign.

"If you want to keep the Haunted Cuttersville Tour going, you could just do it on Saturdays, at least until you have a baby."

Shelby wanted to ask if Danny had names picked out for this fictitious baby, but she didn't. She had the funny feeling that he would take her seriously and start rolling out Abby and Adam before moving on to the *B*'s. So instead she asked him what had been in the back of her mind since her miscarriage at eighteen. "What if I can't have children?"

Danny ran the truck off the edge of the road a foot before recovering. "What? You can't have kids?"

He looked so appalled, she actually felt a little sick. Did Danny want her or a family? "Well, I did have a miscarriage. What if it happened again?"

His shoulders relaxed. "Oh, is that what you're worried about? Hell, lots of women miscarry. You don't know that you would again. I thought you meant the doctor had told you something."

"No."

"That's alright then."

Danny just had it all figured out as far as she could tell. Shelby leaned her head on the window and sighed. She didn't know what she wanted.

"Just say you'll think about it, Shel."

"I will." In fact, it would probably remove any possibility of getting a good night's sleep.

"If you want to fool around with that city slicker, I'm just asking that you don't flaunt it in public. People are going to talk anyway, but don't make it worse."

Shelby almost laughed at the idea of her engaging in a wild affair that the whole town was talking about. She could only hope for that much excitement. "Danny Tucker, you are not helping your case."

"What?" He was clearly puzzled.

"Oh, never mind," she said in irritation as they pulled down Main Street, passing the odd sight of a taxi in front of the Busy Bee.

She and Danny both looked, wondering who had paid the big bucks in cab fare for a taxi from the city. The last cab to drive into Cuttersville had probably been twenty years ago when Paxton Smith had come back to town after landing a part in a soap opera. He'd come back to brag he'd made it big, then had returned to New York and promptly gotten poisoned by his on-screen wife and bumped off the show.

A woman was emerging from the cab, all long blond hair, tanned legs, and designer sunglasses tinted pink.

"Who the hell is that?" Danny asked in astonishment as they drove past.

Shelby strained her neck, turning full around to get another look. The blonde tossed back her abundant straight hair and adjusted an enormous hot pink bag on her shoulder. She was wearing a white . . . something. Shelby guessed you could call it a dress, but it was a clingy fabric and looked something like she'd wrapped herself in a dryer sheet, or had confused her tube top with a dress.

Over the taxi, across the street, and all the way into Danny's pickup Shelby could smell the cold hard scent of money. Lots of it.

She had no idea who that woman was.

But she was betting Boston Macnamara did.

Boston thought that on a scale of one to ten, his stay in Cuttersville was ranking about a four, which was a serious improvement over the negative twelve he'd expected. He was actually enjoying himself at the plant, and once he had approached Bob and Phil as a peer instead of an evil overseer, communication had opened up between them and they'd been receptive to some of his suggestions.

Heading out for the day after checking the clock to assure himself that he'd missed Shelby's five o'clock tour at the White House, Boston waved to Bob. "See you, Bob. Have a good weekend."

"Thanks, Mac."

The nickname was an unhappy result of their newfound familiarity. Everyone in this town seemed compelled to call him Mac, which was slowly driving him to insanity. The only person who called him Boston was Shelby, and he was avoiding her like vending machine food.

"I'm having a picnic at the house tomorrow after the Fourth of July parade. We'd love to have you stop by," Bob added.

Boston paused in the doorway. "A picnic?" He didn't think he'd ever been to an actual authentic picnic before. "Sure, I'd like that."

"Good. The wife's looking forward to meeting you. We're at 1532 Turkey Trail. White house with gray shutters. Noon is when everyone's coming by."

"Turkey Trail?" Boston asked. "What the hell kind of a street name is that?"

Bob rolled his eyes. "The development is called Hunting Valley, so all the streets have wildlife themes. It's better than Phil's neighborhood, though. They have a Dutch theme, so he lives on Wooden Shoe Drive."

Boston laughed.

"They're the only two developments in Cuttersville, so if you want a house less than forty years old, you don't have a lot of choices."

Boston thought he'd prefer the eccentric White House to living on Turkey Trail, but he kept his mouth shut. "Thanks for the invite, I'll see you tomorrow."

Bob waved and Boston headed for the parking lot to retrieve his BMW. It was hot outside, a sweltering ninety degrees, and he undid his tie immediately and threw it on the passenger seat. He cranked on the air-conditioning for the ten-minute drive home.

After two and a half weeks, Cuttersville was definitely tolerable, with the goal of trying to run the Samson Plastics plant at top efficiency challenging and interesting. He liked his job, even under these hazy circumstances, and in the past had always been happier problem solving at work than doing just about anything else.

He felt the same in Cuttersville, except for one glaring exception. He enjoyed spending time with Shelby, and staying away from her all week had been difficult but necessary. There was a whole list of reasons he shouldn't get involved with Shelby, enough to fill a spreadsheet, but that didn't stop him from wanting her.

There was just something about her golden skin, her soft brown eyes, and that unruly hair that did things to him. Things that resulted in an erection. He wanted her, to touch and taste and hold her, and he wanted to force her attention solely on him, so she'd be so turned on that the house could burn down and she wouldn't even notice.

He wanted her, and he couldn't have her, and she was standing on his porch.

Looking hot in a pair of denim shorts that hovered just above her hips and a little tiny white top that tied behind her neck and showed off her smooth stomach. There was no way she could be wearing a bra with that thing, and as she leaned against the porch post, her breasts thrust out seductively, beckoning him.

He wanted to answer the call, to walk up to that porch and escort her straight to his bedroom, but Boston contained himself. Barely. Adjusting his too-full pants, he got out of the car and waved to her.

"Hi, Shelby. How are you?"

She smiled, and Boston almost stopped walking and got back in his car. Her smile was *inviting*, and it turned him on so bad he was scared.

"I'm fine. Hot." She pulled her shirt out and fanned air up her cleavage. "How 'bout yourself?"

"I'm good." Never bigger. Better, never better.

"Am I interrupting anything? Are you expecting someone—maybe a friend from Chicago?" She searched his face, leaning forward and studying him like the answer was really important.

Boston wasn't sure what she was digging for, so he shrugged. "No." None of his friends in Chicago would come to Cuttersville unless they were threatened with bodily harm and financial ruin. And even if one of his friends were to show up right at that moment, he'd tell them to turn around and go home because he wanted to be with Shelby.

She was gorgeous, absolutely delicious. Her skin was dewy from the heat, and her hands were digging into the back pockets of her tight shorts, making her look like a pinup for a farmers' daughters calendar. She wasn't wearing his Daisy Duke fantasy high heels, but almost as good, she was barefoot.

He was so hard he decided he couldn't walk.

Pausing at the bottom of the steps, he gave her a smile, grateful he'd just undergone a bleaching treatment a month ago. Maybe his blinding white smile would draw her attention away from the pointed gun in his pants aimed at her.

"Then you don't mind my stopping by?" Shelby rolled

her shoulder on the post so she was now turned to him. Her head still lolled back, and she looked relaxed and sexy, her breasts dangerously close to his mouth.

She definitely wasn't wearing a bra. The outline of her nipple nudged through the cotton top and his mouth watered. "Oh, no, I don't mind you stopping by. Want to come in?" *And let me suck your nipples?*

"I really just wanted to ask you something." Her tongue came out and wet her bottom lip, eye level to him since he was three steps down from her.

He wanted to follow her tongue with his and nudge past those plump lips into her moist mouth. To grind her tight little denim shorts against him while his fingers floated up under that deceptively innocent top. "Sure, ask away."

"It's kind of a favor." She sucked in her breath nervously, her chest rising temptingly in front of him.

"Ask me." He was liable to agree to just about anything while mesmerized by her breasts.

"I was hoping you could agree to be here for the five o'clock tour every day."

His head snapped up.

She rushed on. "My numbers have been really good, and I'm making money hand over fist this week, but people want to see something and nothing's happening. Gran and I think the house reacts to you, and if you're there, the tour-goers might see something to get their money's worth."

The argument wasn't winning him over. He had no interest in being a sideshow freak, having bitter dead chicks heaving lamps at him for people's entertainment. If ghosts really even existed in the first place and it wasn't all some explainable coincidence.

He opened his mouth.

"Please," Shelby said, eyes darting to the ground. "If people don't see anything, they'll talk the tour down. I'll be out of business, and . . . and, I'm broke. I need the job."

His mouth closed again. He was screwed, plain and simple. How could he be a total prick and deny her the opportunity to save her livelihood? He couldn't. It would be annoying, but he'd live, and if it didn't work, at least he would have a clean conscience.

The worst part probably wouldn't be the gawking tourists, but his personal struggle to keep his hands off Shelby.

"Alright. One week, Shelby. Then if it doesn't work, if nothing happens, I'm off the hook."

Her brown eyes widened, and she finally pulled her head off the porch post. "You'll do it? Really?"

He nodded. "I'll do it."

Then she made him regret it immediately by throwing her arms around him and giving him a squeezy hug, pressing those perky breasts up against his chest and smothering his nose with her sun-kissed hair. Maybe *regret* wasn't the right word. He was definitely enjoying himself, but he knew he shouldn't be. Too much enjoyment would get him in trouble.

Shelby pulled back a little, but didn't let go, and since she was a little higher than him, his arms wrapped around her to hold her steady. "Thanks, Boston. I appreciate it."

And she leaned down and kissed him, a soft nothing little kiss that made his blood pound and his cock throb and a buzzing roll past his ears, and any good intentions he'd had all week disappear.

When Shelby smiled at him and tried to back up out of

his reach, he held her still. "Just one thing, though. I still want my private tour. Tonight." The tour wasn't all he wanted, and he planned to investigate every inch of Shelby Tucker before the night was over. He shouldn't demand the tour, shouldn't give in to his hormone-driven need to take Shelby, but he couldn't resist. Even to his own ears his voice sounded rude and demanding.

Shelby didn't try and shove her way out of his arms. She raised a brow. "You know, Boston, sometimes you're just this side of bossy."

He figured that wasn't news. Early on he'd learned that if he wanted to survive, to get ahead, he needed to stand up and take what he wanted. At ten, that had meant pulling rank over the babysitter so he could sleep over at a friend's house. Now it meant that he was tired of avoiding Shelby and pretending he didn't want her so bad he hurt.

"So?" he asked her, kissing her neck. "I want to spend time with you. Alone. I'm not going to get it if I don't ask, am I?"

"Except you're not really asking," Shelby said, breathless, back arching and fingers digging into his upper arms.

"You're free to say no at any time." He lifted his head and pinned her with a stare so she'd understand his meaning. "To anything."

"I know."

Her eyes dropped to his lips and Boston's gut twisted. "Are you saying no?"

"No."

The first sharp kick of lust subsided into panic. What if she meant *no*-no? Boston sought clarification. "No, you're not saying no, or no, you don't want to give me a private tour?"

Shelby smiled and swept her thumbs over his shoulders. He took it as a good sign. "No, I'm not saying no. I'm saying yes, I will give you a private tour." Her nails scraped across the buttons of his shirt. "But you might want to change first. It's a walking tour. Dusty."

He was reluctant to let her go, but eager to be with her, so he released her and started to move past to the door.

"Hey, Boston? You're not seeing anyone back in Chicago, are you?"

It was a valid question and he paused, sorry they hadn't cleared that up earlier. Maybe it had contributed to Shelby's reluctance. Cupping her cheek, he said, "No. Absolutely not. I haven't even been on a date in six months."

Shelby nodded, and her eyes showed clearly that she knew just as well as he did where this evening was heading. And was looking forward to it.

Boston turned and jogged into the house to change, already undoing his buttons to save time.

Shelby watched Boston hit the hallway running and sagged back against the porch railing. This acting sexy business was a strain.

But in the two days since her dinner with Danny, she had come to a conclusion. She wanted to have an affair with Boston Macnamara. She wanted to know once and for all whether or not she was capable of feeling passion, or at least of achieving an orgasm without an act of God.

If even the hot feelings she had for Boston resulted in so-so sex, well, then she'd go back to Danny and take him up on his offer.

If the sex with Boston turned out to be more explosive

than the Cuttersville Fourth of July fireworks, well, she would still remarry Danny and settle down once and for all.

Because Boston couldn't give her the cozy country home and children she craved, and he would never even want to try. Whereas Danny cared about her, and they knew each inside and out, and they could have a good solid life together.

Running her tour was fun and she didn't regret leaving Danny and exploring life out on her own for the last three years. She'd needed to prove her independence to herself and to search for that illusive passion. But she couldn't see herself at forty-five, still traipsing people through the White House, single and living with Gran.

She wanted to have a child, to stop ignoring the grief she'd felt when she'd miscarried, and get on with her life.

But first, she wanted Boston.

And he looked perfectly willing to oblige her.

He came back out the door wearing jeans, a T-shirt, and expensive-looking hiking boots. "Aren't you going to be hot in that?" she asked doubtfully. Even though it was six-thirty, it was still hovering in the upper eighties.

"You said to change."

"I meant casual clothes and shoes other than sandals, that's all."

Boston was down in the drive already. "These are my walking shoes. So, where are we going first?"

He seemed incredibly eager to be off. Shelby sat on the steps and pulled her gym shoes over to her side. She'd taken them off because her feet were hot after walking over from Gran's, but the prospect of pulling sweaty socks back on wasn't very appealing.

"Well, this is usually the middle of the tour, so we're going out of order, but first we'll go down to Miller Road, where a jilted lover waits to interrupt amorous couples. He shakes their cars during make-out sessions."

"This town is full of jilted lovers, apparently. First Rachel, now this guy." He stood with his hands on his hips while she dragged on her socks. "And the curiosity is killing me . . . who is the Blond Man? You never told me."

Shelby laughed. "It's not worth losing sleep over. No one knows who he is, but a young man with blond hair and an early twentieth-century suit has been seen in the parlor and the dining room. He's usually just standing there and he's smiling. Sometimes he winks or waves or laughs before shimmering out of sight. They say he looks real enough to touch."

"Maybe he is. Maybe some enterprising local guy is dressing up to freak people out."

Now he was reaching. "That's totally irrational." She finished lacing her shoes and stood up.

"No more irrational than seeing ghosts."

Shelby started down the road past him. "Maybe. So are you sure you don't have a female friend with blond hair, long legs, and designer clothes?" That woman on Main Street had been bugging her, especially since Gran had confessed she'd rented the Gray House on Bell Street to her for two months, and that she was in fact from Chicago. She'd also never hesitated to pay Gran four thousand dollars rent up front, which Gran had been pleased over and Shelby had been appalled by.

Her grandmother was raising her rents left and right to unsuspecting newcomers and not feeling the slightest ounce of remorse for doing so. Gran had actually sported an ear-to-ear grin when she'd told Shelby the news.

"I probably know a lot of women like that, but I don't have a specific female friend that meets that description. Why?"

Boston was keeping a fast pace and Shelby felt a little winded already. "No reason."

He shot her a suspicious look but let it drop. "So, does the town advertise your tour and its Most Haunted status? Cuttersville could cultivate a whole bed-and-breakfast clientele interested in the paranormal."

"You know, I don't really think so. I mean, it's kind of just word of mouth."

"Does the town have a web site? They could promote there, and maybe have a town Halloween party every year. Register the various sites on your tour and document all the alleged sightings to distribute and generate interest. People would enjoy popping down here for a weekend."

Shelby crunched gravel beneath her feet and thought over the whole idea of taking her tour and Cuttersville to the next level. Her first reaction was no way, she did not want a bunch of ghost-seeking strangers invading her quiet town. But then she thought about the locally owned restaurants, gas stations, drugstore, and candy shop. As well as the half-dozen or so folks who had big old Victorian houses that would serve well as B and Bs. It could strengthen the local economy, but she wasn't sure how the locals would feel about it.

It was worth thinking about, she supposed.

"You could call the Cincinnati and Columbus news channels and have them run a story on Haunted Cuttersville, right in time for Halloween this year."

"Cuttersville on the news?" The idea was unfathomable.

"Shelby Tucker's tour on the news." Boston grinned at her and reached for her hand, stroking her thumb beneath his.

Except in six months there probably wouldn't be a Haunted Cuttersville Tour. She would probably be hunkered down on the farm for the winter and counting the days of her cycle to get pregnant.

The thought made heat rush through her body and her heart pound in anxiety.

"Hey, you alright? Your face just lost all its color." Boston stopped walking and bent over her in concern, pressing his lips to her forehead. "You feel clammy."

Clammy. How sexy. "I'm fine, just the heat got to me for a second." The heat and a sudden overwhelming panic that she didn't know what the hell she was doing. What she wanted or where she was going or why five minutes earlier she'd thought it all made sense.

Except she knew she wanted Boston—that was the only thing she seemed to be clear on.

"Do you want to hang out in the shade for a minute?" Boston started to tug her off the road to an overgrown copse of trees.

His concern was sweet, and truthfully, more than she would have expected of him when she'd first met him. But the Boston she'd come to know over the last few weeks was more than that aggressive corporate shark he portrayed to the world. He was kind, and funny, and just a little bit needy, whether he realized it or not. He wanted someone to love him.

Shelby thought it wouldn't be that hard to let herself do just that. And maybe it would be okay to fall a tiny bit for him, while she had a wild summer affair to remember fondly in her old age. To give something back to Boston and to feel daring and alive and sassy once before she settled down and did what was right with her life.

"No, I'm fine. We're here anyways." She pointed to a little pull-off in the road that dead-ended with a sign that read NO DUMPING.

"This is it?" He looked dubious. "Why would a ghost haunt this place?"

"Because this is sort of like Cuttersville's Lovers' Lane. Cars park off the road here and couples make out."

"Here?" Boston looked horrified. "There's nothing but a scrubby bunch of trees and a pitted road. What's romantic about that?"

Nothing if you thought real hard about it. But most people who came there were thinking only about each other, not the scenery.

"No one from the road can see you," Shelby said wryly. "And when you're eighteen and every living soul in town knows you, your car, and your parents, you'll take any hidden spot you can."

Boston turned back to her. "Did *you* ever make out here, Shelby Tucker?"

His tone was teasing, so she tossed him a saucy grin. "Of course. All the time. Still do."

"Oh, really?" Boston started toward her, obviously going to put her words to the test.

But Shelby darted back onto the road, out of his reach, laughing. "So the story goes that William Sherman loved his lady most devotedly."

Boston followed her, stalking her, looking intent on getting his hands on her. "I don't care."

"Of course you do. You want to hear all about Haunted Cuttersville—that's why you wanted a private tour."

"I wanted a private tour so I could be alone with you."

Even though his words sent a sharp pang of desire below her belly, she teased him again. "But with the spirits of the undead around, we're never really alone, are we?"

He gave a grunt as he reached for her, a sound that could have meant agreement, disgust, or a rock was wedged in his boot. Shelby laughed and took off running, his fingers slipping over her elbow but not getting a good enough grip on her to halt her progress.

"But William Sherman's girlfriend fell for another man and stood poor Will up a month before the wedding," she called over her shoulder. "So he killed himself, as distraught brokenhearted lovers are wont to do, and now when couples are out on the road here, getting fresh with one another, William doesn't like it."

The thick sultry air moved around her, the sweet scent of wildflowers clinging to the air, and Shelby breathed deeply as she ran.

Boston was keeping pace by jogging, just behind her. She knew he could catch her easily if he wanted to, but he merely watched her with dark, dark eyes that raked over her body and seared her with lust. "Oh, yeah? What does he do?"

"He chases people, just like this, down the road for a long frightening mile and just when they think he's gone . . ." Shelby stopped running and whirled around. "He jumps on their car and shakes." She gripped Boston's shoulders and rattled them back and forth. "Until the terrified couple speeds on, vowing never to engage in sinful behavior at Lovers' Lane again."

Boston jerked a little under Shelby's powerful grip and felt an arousal he had never experienced in his entire long and lust-filled life. Shelby's eyes were wide, bright with humor and the mischievous tone of her tale, her voice eerie and quiet, rising at the proper places to spook him, and he thought she was the most fucking gorgeous woman he'd ever seen in his life. He wanted to take her right there in the goddamn road, then whisk her away to the White House and let Nanny Baskins lock her up in his bedroom forever.

Being with her, under the Cuttersville sky, on a dusty road in the middle of nothing, listening to her silly story, was the most fun he had ever had in his adult life, and he wanted to show her that, appreciate her fully and completely.

"Did you ever see William Sherman?"

She shrugged with a crooked smile. "Nah. I never saw anything at all until you came along."

Her pale soft lips were calling him, and he was close enough, her hands still on his shoulders, that if he leaned down, he could taste her there, on the side of Miller's Road where the jilted lover haunted.

"If I kissed you right now do you think he'd chase us?"

Shelby pushed back some of that wild horse's mane she called hair and glanced around, breath catching in excitement. "I suppose he might."

Boston bent with the intention of taking her mouth, possessing her fully beneath him, and slaking his burning hunger for her, but she darted backward. "Just where the hell are you going?" he asked.

"To the Bigleys' barn, just down the road. Next stop on the tour."

Her sexy little behind sauntered off, a definite feminine sultry swagger in her walk that he'd never seen before. She was toying with him, turning him on intentionally. He suddenly realized she was *seducing* him, with the tight shorts and the no bra and the teasing comments.

He liked it. It was working. He was just about completely fried into a drooling idiot in desperate need of sexual release.

"Does the Bigleys' barn have another victim of love's cruelties?"

Shelby veered off the road into a field, mindless of weeds tall enough to rival her. "Nope. The Bigleys' barn has a cow."

"You're taking me to see a cow?" He had no interest in livestock. The only way he wanted to encounter a cow was medium-well on his dinner plate. "We could probably skip this one, Shelby. I prefer to meet cows after their death."

She laughed and ducked around a particularly violent-looking weed with spikes. "Well, you're in luck. This cow is dead."

Boston gave the weed doubling as a weapon a wide berth and was grateful he'd worn his jeans. "Dead? You know, let me rephrase that. I don't want to meet any cow, ever, that isn't cooked into some sort of meal. Before it reaches that state, I'm not interested."

Shelby popped out of the weeds into a clearing, and a big red barn rose in front of them. It had an Ohio bicentennial flag painted on the side and looked a lot more solid than he had been expecting. He glanced around half expecting to see a cow corpse littering the ground.

Hands on hips, she shook her head at him. "You're just downright ridiculous, you know that? This cow, Strawberry, is a ghost. She died in nineteen eighty-six, struck by lightning."

"Cows can get struck by lightning?" The things he was learning were just phenomenal. He would be returning to Chicago with intimate knowledge of mosquitoes, bacon grease, and paranormal cows. How many Samson execs could boast that?

"Strawberry went to that big grassy field in the sky sure as shootin', but for whatever reason she's still here in the Bigleys' barn, mooing on many a summer night."

He'd heard enough. "You've got to be kidding me. Why would a cow be haunting a barn? Did the lightning blind her and she couldn't find her way to the light?"

Shelby snorted and slapped him on the arm, giggling. "You know, you really make me laugh sometimes."

Whether that was a compliment or not, he was going to take it as such. "No one's ever really thought I was funny before."

"Really?" Shelby headed toward the barn. "You're kind of witty in a pretentious sort of way."

He should have quit while he was ahead.

Shelby shoved open the big door and disappeared into the barn.

"Aren't we trespassing?" Though they had actually approached the property from the back, he could see a white farmhouse not too far ahead. A dog was barking as he ducked inside after Shelby.

"No, I have a standing invitation to take my tour through here. In exchange, I take the groups by the Bigleys' produce and honey stand. They usually sell about fifty to a hundred dollars a week to the tour-goers so they consider it worth it to have me in their barn. But this week they're in West Virginia visiting relatives for the holiday weekend."

It wasn't a big barn, in Boston's ignorant opinion. It was also empty except for a tractor and a big pile of hay. It didn't even smell.

"I thought barns had animals. This is just a tractor garage."

Shelby turned to face him, hands on her hips. "It is, really. The Bigleys built a bigger barn ten years ago, but they can't tear this one down for historical preservation reasons. This barn is a hundred and fifty years old. So they just store the tractor here."

"What's the hay for?" Boston walked over and stuck his toe into the big pile.

"It's actually straw, not hay. And it's used for the dirt drive when it's muddy so the tractor doesn't get stuck."

Shelby picked up a handful and poked him in the middle with it. "It won't hurt you, you know. It's actually very soft."

The pile rose behind her, and she was smiling, a teasing glint in her eye, and the urge to tumble her back onto that straw was strong and arousing. He could just give her a little push, she'd fall back, legs splaying apart, breasts bouncing in that sexy little top, and he could go down between her thighs with his mouth . . .

"Boston?" Shelby peered closely at him. "What are you thinking about? You look awfully serious all of a sudden."

Good God, he was actually fantasizing about taking a tumble in the hay. How was that for ironic. And actually it would be a tumble in the *straw*.

Ironic, maybe, but also a damn good idea. He was throbbing hard and unwilling to ignore the fact any longer.

"I was thinking how you'd look laid out on the straw, spreading your legs for me."

Shelby's brows shot straight up under her hair. Her mouth slipped open, and a little raspy gasp of surprise flew out. She gave a nervous laugh. "You can't be serious."

"Very serious." Boston took her hand and set it on his shaft jutting against his jeans.

Her hand was hot and her fingers jerked, and he closed his eyes for a split second before letting her go, allowing her to pull back if she wanted.

"This does seem serious," she said, giving his cock a squeeze before moving away slowly, dragging down the length of him in a firm caress. "What should we do about it?"

"I think," Boston said as he stuck his foot behind hers and gave her a push that sent her off balance, "that you should lie down and spread your legs."

Shelby windmilled her arms, grabbed for him with a little squawk, but he sidestepped her and let her stumble backward into the straw, landing on her sexy little ass, shirt riding up to the curve of her breasts.

It was better than his fantasy, because in reality Shelby looked up at him with a raw sexual excitement, her eyes flashing with desire, her tongue dragging over her lip. Her succulent breasts strained beneath the little girl halter top, and her shorts hugged her crotch tightly, outlining the folds of her sex for him.

Then she dug her fingers into the straw and dropped her thighs wide open for him.

Boston let a moan escape, then bent down to experience his first romp in the straw.

Chapter Ten

Shelby couldn't believe she was about to do it in the Bigleys' barn, but even Strawberry the dead cow sitting on her couldn't stop her now.

The way Boston looked at her, like she was the sexiest thing he'd ever seen in his life, made her feel willing to do just about anything. As he knelt between her knees, he just stared at her, eyes roaming from her lips to her breasts, to her crotch and up again, while his breath hitched, his eyes darkened, and that impressive bump in his jeans grew longer still.

And the longer he stared at her, the more she wanted him to touch her. The slicker her inner thighs became, saturating her panties with her want for him. Her shorts had ridden up, nudging into her behind and cupping her in front, and Boston ran his finger over the stitching right under the zipper. Right along the seam that separated her lips and her cheeks, and when he reverently slid his finger up and down, from her pubic bone down around, she gave a tiny whimper.

"Are you comfortable?" he asked, nose nudging into her belly button, lips skimming over her waistband.

"Yes." The straw against her back was fine, but the ache pooling inside her was unbearable.

Still she knew she needed to tell him not to have high expectations for her. It was only fair to warn him so he wasn't disappointed.

"Boston, you should know something," she managed to say, clamping her eyes shut in embarrassment, while he pulled her shoes and socks off.

"What's that?" The button on her shorts went, and his hot breath hit her skin as he took the zipper down.

"I . . ." She what? Shelby lost her thought when Boston sucked her flesh into his mouth, right above her panties, a strange restless longing ripping through her. She loved the action, the feel of him, but it was the wrong place. There he was only teasing, when she really wanted his mouth on hers, or her breasts, or down between her legs . . .

"What, beautiful? Tell me."

Shelby forced her eyes open, watched the top of his head bent over her, felt his teeth graze her, nipping, tugging her panties down an inch. It felt so good, her body sensitive and straining up against him, but she had to tell him.

"I don't have orgasms," she blurted out, then nearly groaned when he went still against her.

His gaze was hooded when he glanced up. "Ever?"

"Well, not very often. I'm not a very passionate person," she said as she lay on a straw pile in a barn with him draped all over her between her thighs. It occurred to her maybe she wasn't being very convincing.

"You could have fooled me," Boston said, sitting back up.

"I just thought you should know, so you don't expect too much." Shelby felt her cheeks burning and, with belated modesty, started to move her knees together.

His hand stopped her. "What do you think you're doing?"

"I was going to stand up. Finish the tour." Crawl into a hole and die.

"Okay," he agreed, tossing her legs back apart and pressing them against the bed of straw. "But first, I'm going to make you come."

"You can't," she protested weakly, knowing she was right but enjoying the sudden look of determination on Boston's face. Clearly he spotted a challenge.

"You don't think I can?" He came in right over her, his erection pressing against her leg, his chest covering hers, his mouth hovering an inch above her lips, his eyes staring right into hers.

Shelby shook her head, a little frantic. Why wouldn't he let her save him from mediocre sex? She couldn't hold out much longer if he kept at it. "It's not you, it's me. Some people just don't enjoy sex the way others do."

Boston kissed her, hard, with lots of tongue and possession. Shelby groaned against him, her nipples strumming, thighs clenching around him.

He jerked back just as quickly and slid down lower and lower until he was hovering over her undone zipper. "You look aroused to me. Your eyes are wide, your breathing is hard. Your nipples are popping out of that little top, and if

I'm not mistaken, your panties are damp." He drew in a deep breath. "You even smell wet."

Shelby shuddered, rolling her head back. He did have a point.

"Are you wet, Shelby?"

She shook her head, a strangled "No" coming out of her mouth.

"I don't believe you." He sat back on his haunches, pulled his T-shirt off, and tossed it in the dirt. Then he reached for her shorts. "Let's find out. If you are wet, I bet I can make you come in less than five minutes. If you're not, give me ten."

It sounded so good, but he just really didn't understand that she wanted to come, she really did, she just couldn't. It was like her body got right to the store and then couldn't walk inside. She could get real close, but could never tumble over the edge.

Her shorts went down, so tight from her attempt to look sexy that they dragged her panties to her knees on their downward path. Boston pulled her shorts over her ankles and sent them over by his T-shirt. He left her panties alone, hugging across her thighs, but baring her mound to him and making her feel very naughty.

The straw poked her backside a little as she slid around restlessly, but it was nothing but another turn-on. She had her pants down in a barn and Boston was determined to make her come. Dang, she wanted to oblige him, just for trying so hard.

Another tug behind her neck and he had her halter top undone and was sliding it past her hips, down over her panties, dragging them with it, until suddenly in the still dusky air, she was completely naked before him.

"Oh, Shelby," he said, sucking in hard. "You are absolutely *hot*."

For a response, her nipples hardened. Boston actually smirked, the sexy bastard. Shelby threw a piece of straw at him. "Stop staring at me." A girl could only take so much without being mortified to death or expiring from want.

The straw landed in his black hair and he ignored it. Instead he propped himself up on his elbows and spread her apart with his thumbs, taking another one of those long and searching looks at her most intimate spot.

Shelby squirmed, equal parts turned on and embarrassed. "Boston." The tips of her toes were probably even blushing.

"You definitely look wet." Boston dipped his index finger between her folds, just dusting across her clitoris and skimming over her swollen and slick flesh, never really sinking in. He spread her moisture back over the curve of her cheeks, then backtracked, and trailed hot wetness over both of her inner thighs. "You're so wet you've got plenty to spare."

And as if to prove his point, he drew his finger into his mouth and sucked.

Shelby was never so shocked in her whole life, and a squeaky "Oh!" flew out before she could stop herself. Because, while she was shocked, she was also titillated, eager to see what Boston would do next.

"Mmmm. You taste good." Then he made a show of checking his watch. "I've got about four minutes left, right?"

Shelby had no idea, the very concept of time suddenly seeming ridiculous, for stodgy people who weren't getting sexually tortured in the most exquisite manner in a barn.

Boston's body was taut, tense with arousal, his chest far from brawny, but powerful, lean, tightly coiled muscles that were hard and bunched beneath his skin. His jaw was locked, but he still managed a cocky grin.

His wet finger fell onto her nipple, brushing over it, dampening her areola, plucking at her until she arched toward him. "Boston!"

Any other desperate plea she was going to make was cut off by his kiss, heavy and open, his tongue swirling over hers while he teased first one nipple, then the other, cupping her breasts and nudging them together.

When he pulled back, he took her up with him, leaning her against his chest. Then while his mouth moved across hers and she struggled for oxygen, without the least little bit of warning, his finger sank into her, going deep as her muscles clenched around him and quivered with pleasure.

Breaking the kiss, he pushed her head against his chest. "Just lie there, Shelby, while I make you come. Do you want to come?"

Could there be a stupider question on this earth? "Yes."

Nudging her thighs apart with his knee, Boston pulled his finger back and dragged it across her clitoris, pausing to make little circles around the swollen button. "Do you want to come hard?"

Eyes half closed as she let his chest hold up her head, Shelby breathed in the sweaty sexy scent of Boston's skin, felt the sheen of moisture on his flesh in the humid barn, and arched her back as he drove into her.

"Yes, I want to come hard." More than anything, she

wanted to break right then over Boston's hand and soak up the satisfaction.

He moved in and out with excruciating slowness, stilling her with a hand on her back whenever she tried to rock him to a faster rhythm. She was pulsing, building, aching toward that all-elusive orgasm, and she shuddered, clawing into his abdominal flesh.

"Yes, yes."

The hand behind her skimmed over her backside and suddenly there was another finger nudging into her, coming from behind to join the one from the front, sliding into her hot cocoon with ease. Shelby gasped as her body stretched to accommodate him and he stroked her over and over.

Squeezing him, arching her back, burying her head in his chest as he drowned her in pleasure, Shelby cried out into his flesh, so close, so close, straining too hard, reaching for it, wanting to find it, but always staying just far enough back to keep her from it. Desperate, she sensed it slipping away, passing her over again, the train on the verge of rolling out without her, leaving her frustrated and unfulfilled yet another time.

Then Boston wiggled his back finger, while the front slid out and pressed her clitoris, and her head snapped back as her body jerked her out of her thoughts. There was an agonizing pause, everything stilled, goose bumps racing over her damp flesh, then suddenly she was there.

She came with great shuddering sobs, intense waves of ecstasy passing over her while his fingers stroked, stroked, milking maximum pleasure from her.

Clinging to him, she rode it out all the way, amazed and shocked and deeply, seriously pleased.

"Oh, my," she said, sagging against him, burying her face in his smooth chest, the rapid beat of his heart filling her ear.

"You feel so good, Shelby." He wiggled his finger still inside her. "I loved feeling you clench down on me, pulse as you came. You're damn sexy."

Shelby gave a little laugh. She couldn't believe it. She'd had an orgasm in the Bigleys' barn, and it had been *good*. Maybe just about the best she'd ever had.

"And I had thirty seconds to spare," Boston said as he pulled back and kissed the top of her head.

There was no mistaking the arrogant satisfaction in his voice. "Give you a gold star."

"Is that sarcasm?" He gave her a mock frown. "You could be a little more appreciative."

Stretching her arms over her head, Shelby rolled her neck and gave a soft sigh of sated approval. "Oh, I am, trust me."

Then he got a little gleam in his eye that worried her. He started nudging her back into the straw. "Let's see how much you appreciate me when I make you come again."

Shelby resisted falling back. "Now you're just being ridiculous, Boston. There is no way I can do that again right now. It'll be at least a week before you should even bother trying again. Give me time to get . . . you know, *worked up*," she whispered.

Flustered and blushing and abandoning hope for reaching her clothes tossed who knew where, Shelby let him pin her back and figured she'd warned him. If he wanted to waste his time it was all the same to her.

She waited. Exasperated and embarrassed and a little bit excited.

"Now is the best time actually." Boston kissed her chin, her neck, the swell of her breast. "See, you're still wet, you're still swollen, your body still wants more."

Shelby seemed to be going shy on him, but Boston wasn't interested in allowing that. Watching her come apart in his arms, rocking against his touch, digging into his skin with short nails, had been triumphant and sexy and primal. He'd never taken that much pleasure just from watching, and even though he was more than ready to sink inside all that giving warmth, he wanted to taste her first, drag her under until she was so hot and so ready for him she begged.

Not a passionate person, his ass.

Boston enjoyed the feel of her soft and pliant beneath him, her limp arms draped across the straw, her slumberous satisfaction giving way to impatience. Shelby thought she was done with playing and probably really wanted to continue on with the tour, but for whatever reason wasn't shoving him away. Either curiosity or politeness kept her there, waiting to see what he would do.

What he was going to do was make her come again. And then maybe again. Not to prove the point to her that he could, but to prove that *she* could.

Boston suckled her nipple, slowly, leisurely, rolling his tongue over the plump nub before pulling back and blowing on it. Shelby shifted beneath him, her sigh a sign of the first stirrings of renewed desire. He moved to her other breast, tasted the underside, nipped along the side, pulled her nipple firmly into his mouth, and sucked hard.

Her breathing changed minutely, the steady rise and fall shifting into a rhythmic pant, and her relaxed shoulders tensed slightly.

He'd felt her before, when his fingers had been buried inside her, felt her struggle, the way she thought and strained and clawed toward an orgasm, and Boston wanted Shelby to forget to think. To forget to worry, to forget about pleasing and performance and to have nothing in her but the rolling need and want of her body. To let her body take her where it wanted to go.

Kissing down her firm abdomen, Boston ducked his tongue into her belly button. She jerked, then settled still again. He'd never considered himself a selfish lover, but loving Shelby showed him he'd never been selfless either. And he wasn't now. He was taking just as much as he was giving, feeling her smooth body beneath him, and he hadn't even removed his jeans—with good reason.

If he took off his pants and shed his boxers, it would be damn near impossible to prevent himself from pressing her back into the itchy straw with a quick thrust of his cock.

Which he couldn't do because he wanted Shelby to have a chance to ache for him, to walk away satisfied yet unfulfilled.

And he didn't have any condoms anyway.

So the pants were staying on as a security measure.

Boston brushed his lips across her dewy curls, darker than her head of golden-brown hair. "What have we here?"

He roamed over her thighs, light teasing strokes that had her wiggling.

"Boston . . ."

The way she said his name, so exasperated, so aroused, so different from the women he'd dated before, made him smile over her mound, giving a little laugh that sent hot breath dancing over her. The country in her voice was more pronounced, drawing out his name to twice its normal length, and while there was much to find annoying about Cuttersville, that wasn't.

Thumbs on her folds, he kissed her clitoris. "Yes, dear? Did you want to say something?"

Shelby gave a snort of derision. "Yes! You're driving me nuts, and you're crazy if you think I'm going to have another orgasm."

He looked up over her stomach, rising ribs and full, plump breasts. "It's not all about the O, you know. There's just as much to be said for the trip there as the final destination."

Drawing his thumbs back, he opened her sex for his viewing. Shelby sucked in her breath when he blew lightly on her. "Shelby, it's not a failure if you don't, as long as you have fun along the way."

Though she was going to pull all the way into the station with a roar if he had anything to say about it. But he wanted them both to enjoy every step of the process.

Just the tip of his tongue connected with her glistening flesh and he closed his eyes. Damn, she tasted good. Like sex and want and sweet, honest woman. He forced himself to pull back and stared at her again, drinking his fill of the sight of her spread out for him, little gleams of moisture sliding down the longer he watched.

His attention was getting a positive reaction.

But she whacked his shoulder. "What are you looking at? Geez Louise, you'd think you'd never seen a naked woman before."

The ruddy flush in her cheeks showed she was embarrassed more than disgusted by his behavior.

"I've never seen you naked before. It's the best damn view in Cuttersville." He kissed her clitoris a second time, pausing to suckle it gently.

Shelby bucked on the straw. "Oh, shit! What is *that*?"

He had a winner. Boston sucked harder, darting his tongue down once to swipe over her.

Shelby panted. She swore. She begged him to stop.

So he did.

As he sat back a couple of inches, rubbing her dampness off his bottom lip, she cried out in anguish.

"You're stopping?" she asked in condemnation, as if he'd suggested stealing candy from kids.

"You told me to," he pointed out, hiding his grin in her thigh.

"I didn't mean it." Shelby flopped back on the straw, long yellow strands of the stuff sticking to her hair, her breasts bouncing. Her legs tried to squeeze together as she moved restlessly, but he was in the way.

She groaned.

He took pity on her. "Oh. I'm sorry. Would you like me to do it again?"

"Yes," she said, and added in a soft voice, "duh-uh."

Boston laughed, amused and enraptured with Shelby. "Watch it, Ghost Girl."

"Quit talking, City Boy." Her voice came out as an anxious growl, fingers digging into his hair and urging him forward.

The aggressive move shocked him, and set his low-burning lust into high heat. Shoving her thighs apart with his forearms, Boston bent over her and tasted her thoroughly, all the way up and all the way down, licking, sucking, eating, biting.

He wanted all of her, to absorb her scent and feel and to drive her mindless. Shelby clung to his hair, thumbs pressed to his temples, thighs quivering as she gave little soft cries of ecstasy. The air was heavy with the earthy scent of straw and dirt, the sweet desire of Shelby's wet sex, and her ragged moans.

Boston felt her muscles tighten in anticipation and he knew the exact moment she careened into an orgasm. He swirled around her clitoris and down to slip inside her as she writhed, yelling his name with enough passion and satisfaction to make him thrill from the sound of it.

His cock rested against her lower leg, wanting in on the action, but he ignored his own needs and held on to Shelby and stroked his tongue over her leisurely, even after she'd settled back and tried to push him away.

Drawing out her orgasm on and on, while she whimpered and strained, had him fighting not to join her.

When he finally sat back and saw the look of wonder on her face, the drowsy shock and satiation, Boston pushed himself up the pile. Sweat curled her hair at her temples and ears, and moisture clung to her upper lip, a plump rosy red. Everywhere her skin glistened, and he kissed a trail between her breasts and up her neck until he was pressing his mouth onto her open lips.

"Okay. I guess I'm big enough to admit I was wrong," she said after breaking the kiss to gasp for air.

"But at least it worked in your favor."

"True." Her arms came around his shoulders and she glanced down hungrily. "If you're still functioning after the eyelet spread incident, I think it's time for you to take your jeans off and put that thing to work."

He would love nothing more than to do just that, especially since her thighs had wrapped around him. The heat from her body soaked through the denim and tortured him.

He could be inside all that warmth. After a deep breath, he spoke as calmly as he could under the circumstances. "I am functioning very well, thank you, and I'd prove it, but I don't have a condom with me."

"No?" Her question was heavy with disappointment.

"Nope. Don't worry, we'll get to it soon enough." If he didn't die from sexual frustration first. But it had been worth the pain of a rip-roaring hard-on to watch Shelby relax and enjoy herself.

"I suppose I could give you head," she said, with the enthusiasm normally reserved for a root canal.

He almost laughed. "While I'm sure I would enjoy that, I can wait."

She tried to hide her sigh of relief, but wasn't quite successful. "We can go to the CVS and get some condoms. I'll just call Gran and tell her I'll be out late." Rubbing the tip of her nose on his shoulder she asked, "You got bricks for doorstops, right?"

It was almost too good to be true that she was willing to spend the night with him. He'd been afraid that she was done for the night and he would have to wait. But while she was willing, he needed to reassure her quickly about the alleged ghosts before she changed her mind about returning to the White House. "Shelby, nothing is going to happen. The house has been quiet as a tomb since last week."

She didn't look convinced. "Maybe it's us together then that causes activity."

Maybe it was nothing more than wind and the power of suggestion.

Boston shoved back up, his thighs straining from the awkward position. He shook out his legs and adjusted his jeans before reaching for Shelby's hand to pull her cute naked butt out of the straw. "I don't think so, Ghost Girl."

And a sudden loud moo had him just about jumping out of his skin.

Chapter Eleven

Shelby heard that big old cow moo-
ing in the empty—yes, empty—barn and almost wet the
pants she wasn't wearing.

Boston turned around, hands out in loose fists. "Jesus
Christ! Did you hear that?"

Shelby did. The sound of a complaining bovine was replaced with her own scream at top lung capacity as she
leaped out of the straw and searched for her clothes. "Oh,
dear God! I'm naked! Help me find my clothes."

Boston gave her the most outrageous look of disbelief
she'd ever seen in her life. "Who gives a shit if you're naked?
An invisible ghost cow doesn't care what you're wearing."

It did sound stupid when he put it like that, but she just
felt vulnerable as hell standing in the buff with hay stuck
all over her ass. Swiping her hands across her skin, she
took a few cautious steps toward her shorts, hoping she

wasn't going to inadvertently walk into Strawberry. "That's easy for you to say, you've got your pants on!"

Boston put his hand on his snap, looking exasperated. "I can take them off if that would make you feel better."

"Yes, as a matter of fact, it would." She hadn't gotten to see a darn thing but his chest, and had gotten to touch even less. It had been *The Shelby Show* for the last half hour, and even though they needed to pick up condoms, at least she should be entitled to a peek.

As Shelby pulled on her panties, giving her rear a little shake to get everything in place as she settled the elastic on her waist, Boston popped his jeans snap open.

Then took a step toward her, with a look she was starting to recognize as his dominating sex look. But then he stopped and said, "Eyaahhh!" and jerked backward.

"Holy shit, something just licked me."

"What?" Shelby looked at the hand he was holding out for her in horror and damned if there wasn't a slobbery streak across his palm. "Oh, my . . ."

"Nasty!" Boston swiped it back and forth on his jeans. "Grab your clothes, babe, let's get the hell out of here."

He didn't have to tell her twice. Pulling on her halter top, she left it untied, scooped up her shoes, and dragged on her shorts as they jogged through the barn door.

Heading back to the road, Shelby fiddled with the top strings behind her neck and burst out laughing. "You forgot your shirt, you know."

"Let the damn cow have it." He stopped and grinned at her. "Here, I'll get that."

Gentle fingers worked the straps into a loop. "Is this too tight?" A soft kiss fell onto her neck.

"No, it's fine." And Shelby shivered, because Boston

was many things that she'd never expected. He was funny and kind, and he was responsible for her feeling that maybe there wasn't all that much wrong with her sexually.

Maybe she'd been too young when she'd married Danny. Maybe she'd worried too much about having an orgasm, thought about it all the time, and once she'd relaxed with Boston, things had happened naturally.

Or maybe she was falling for him in a big, big way.

She couldn't go home with him tonight, she realized as they walked down the dusty road, the orange sun sinking in the western sky. Not when she was raw and excited and all too willing to tumble herself into something she couldn't get out of. She had no barriers from him right now and she knew she needed some.

"Hey, Boston, I just remembered I'm supposed to pick up Gran's car tonight at the garage."

"Okay. I can drive you there, then we can go pick up those condoms." His eyebrows rose up and down and she was sorely tempted.

"Not tonight . . . I wasn't thinking . . . I can't." She didn't want to lie, so she didn't offer any more than that.

He looked like he knew exactly what she was doing, given the serious way he studied her. But he just asked, "What about tomorrow? I'm going to a picnic at a coworker's, can you come with me?"

"I have a family picnic I have to go to, at my mom's and her boyfriend of the month."

There was a long awkward pause during which Shelby brushed at the seat of her shorts self-consciously as they walked.

"How about tomorrow night, then? We can just get a movie, hang out together."

She should say no. But she couldn't. She wanted to be with him and that was the whole darn problem. So she just said, "Sure. Sounds good."

Then because he was silent and the awkwardness was her own fault, she tried to lighten the mood as they turned onto Gran's street and strolled toward the Yellow House. "See, I told you things happen when we're together."

It was meant to be a joke, but Boston took her hand and dragged her to a stop before Gran's front porch. "Oh, I never doubted it for a minute. There's all kinds of things happening between us."

Before she could think to even think, he took her mouth in a soft but passionate kiss that left her lips trembling and her heart quaking. It was over before she could catch her breath, and he was tapping her rump and urging her toward the house.

"Go in the house, Shelby Tucker, and I'll see you tomorrow."

Since she couldn't think of a damned thing to say, her mind a jumbled mass of confusion, she just nodded and did as he suggested.

When the front door closed behind her and she leaned against it, breathing in the lemony pine of Gran's wood cleaner, she closed her eyes and folded her hands across her breasts. "Damn. I think that ant-size attraction I felt for him has grown to about as big as an elephant behind."

"You say something, Shelby?" Gran called from the kitchen.

"Just thinking." That she was totally and completely screwed.

*   *   *

Jessie sat in the kitchen wondering if she was suffering from the onset of Alzheimer's. What the hell had she been thinking to rent one of her houses to a woman who was very likely her granddaughter's stiffest competition?

Boston knew it wasn't Shelby knocking on his door at the crack of dawn. Shelby would never bother to knock. She'd stroll her sexy little self into his house using that key he'd had visions of wresting from her on several occasions.

But when he woke up on the Fourth of July to pounding downstairs, he was thinking how nice it would have been if Shelby had used that key, slipped into his room and into his bed . . . complete with a box of Trojans and some slutty black underwear.

He'd tried to hold on to the fantasy, but the pounding persisted. Stumbling out of bed, Boston pulled on the wrinkled jeans from the night before and headed down the stairs. He didn't bother with a shirt, and thought of how much money he was saving in dry-cleaning bills. Half his time in Cuttersville had been spent without a shirt on, thanks to Shelby and the lack of air-conditioning.

Boston tripped over the fringe on the deep blue rug in the foyer, but recovered before he clipped the wall. The bell pealed again.

"What?" he said in annoyance, yanking open the door, fully expecting to see Brady Stritmeyer blowing smoke in his face.

It wasn't Brady.

It was a tall, lean blonde, wearing a denim skirt that was

about the width of a stick of gum, along with spiky sandals and a pink skintight shirt that said SO JUICY across her breasts. Enormous sunglasses tinted pink were shoved up on her thick blond hair and she smiled brightly.

"Amanda?" Boston said in astonishment. Even a dead cow licking his hand wasn't quite as unbelievable as seeing his boss's daughter standing on his front porch in Cuttersville, Ohio.

"Hi, Boston. Long time no see." Amanda Delmar leaned forward and kissed his cheek with a light airy movement, then slipped her skinny body around him and into his house.

"What a . . . surprise." Boston turned around, his mind not quite wrapping around the concept of Amanda, a spoiled, albeit intelligent, socialite popping into Podunk. "Is Brett with you?" He peeked out to the driveway, almost expecting to see his boss.

Amanda laughed, spinning on her toothpick heels. "Of course not! And my father's just going to freak when he finds out I'm here."

Without waiting for an invitation, Amanda went into the parlor, touching tables and peering at the lace curtains. "This place is sort of cool in a stodgy esoteric kind of way. If you're into the antique-y thing."

Her voice left no doubt that she wasn't one of them. But Boston had no comment, still feeling slightly poleaxed.

"So, are you visiting?" Cuttersville? That was about as likely as someone swinging by a nuclear power plant just for kicks.

"Yes." Amanda smiled again at him, a calculating practiced smile that made him want to edge back out the door. "I came to visit you. If I'd have known you were staying in this big old house by yourself, I would have just stayed here and saved myself some cash."

"Where are you staying?" he asked, heart suddenly pounding. Something was wrong here. Someone was not making sense. There was no logical reason for Amanda, who spent her days shopping and her nights partying, to travel four hundred miles to see him.

They were barely acquaintances, only seeing each other occasionally when she visited her father at the office, or at corporate parties where Amanda was usually draped appealingly over the bar.

"I'm staying in a little gray house that looks like the seven dwarves might pop out at any minute. The ceilings are so low I have to duck to go through the doors." She waved her hand, adjusting her Hermès bag on her shoulder. "I can't imagine why I rented it for two months."

"Two months?" He sounded like a castrated parrot, but damn, he couldn't help himself. Amanda Delmar was like glass—beautiful to look at, but capable of slicing you to ribbons.

She wouldn't be so dangerous if she wasn't smart, but she was. Smart, bored, and rich, a bad combination all around.

And her boredom had brought her here to Cuttersville, for him, apparently.

He was so fired.

All his revenue generating, increased plant efficiency, and years of dedicated loyal round-the-clock service to Samson Plastics would mean nothing if Brett thought he was bouncing his only daughter.

"Yes, two months, isn't that just absurd? But four grand seemed so reasonable for rent and I am *so* bored in Chicago, I've been doing nothing but lying at the pool and counting my mai tai umbrellas. I decided it's time to see America."

"Starting with Cuttersville, Ohio?" he asked wryly, already trying to think of a way to get her back to Chicago. Maybe he could tell Amanda about the vengeful ghosts, get Mrs. Stritmeyer to refund her money, and have her on a plane by dinner.

"Sure." Amanda shrugged. "I was thinking the relaxed setting would give us time to get to know each other, away from Dad and all the pressures of Samson."

"I do work here, you know." He was just going to ignore that comment about getting to know each other. Maybe if he played dumb, she would get bored with him, just like she did with everything.

Brett had told him Amanda ran through men just like she had colleges, a new one every quarter. Her father had made the comment blithely after discovering that Amanda had maxed out her credit card buying gifts for a boyfriend, and she was *destitute,* as she'd put it.

She wasn't looking destitute these days if the five-thousand-dollar bag on her shoulder was any indication. Shelby could probably live for five months off the money invested in that pink bag. Amanda had probably taken an entire three minutes to buy it.

"I know you work here, you dolt. Why do you think you're here? Daddy sent you away to save you from me." She looked incredibly amused by the idea.

Boston wasn't amused at all. He was astonished, followed quickly by red-hot searing anger. He had been sent there, to the land of dead cows, cornfields, and back fat, to *protect* him from Amanda Delmar's expensive clutches? It was infuriating, offensive, unprofessional . . .

"Well, don't look so pissed, Boston. It means Dad likes you. He wants to keep you financially solvent and focused on your job." She ran one glossy fingernail over her pouty lip. "I have a reputation for distracting men from their careers and forcing them into bankruptcy."

Boston knew the only way to play this with Amanda was to be as nonchalant as she was. He could not let her know that he was even a tiny bit concerned. Which he was. Exactly how long did Brett plan to cloister him here like a Victorian virgin?

But he could handle Amanda. Probably. "So is it true?"

She laughed. "It's exaggerated. It's true, I probably do distract men when they're dating me. I tend to dive into new relationships whole hog." Amanda smirked. "Listen to that, I'm picking up the local lingo already."

There was something appealing about Amanda, and it wasn't just her looks. She was so cavalier, so confident, that Boston could see men getting sucked into her vibrant vortex. He wasn't one of them, though. His tastes ran more to natural, no-game-playing tour guides.

"And the bankruptcy charges?" He smiled at Amanda, gesturing for her to sit down on the sofa.

She did, tucking those long thin legs under her, the little skirt covering only the essentials. "Is it my fault if men want to buy me things?"

Boston laughed, seeing straight through Amanda Delmar. Underneath the flirtation and the designer clothes and the self-deprecation, she was lonely. He should know. He'd felt exactly the same way until he'd come to Cuttersville. Until he'd met Shelby.

He decided that whether it jeopardized his career or not, he needed to play it straight with Amanda. Boston dropped into an armchair that he usually avoided because it was rickety and narrow. He shifted and looked at Amanda.

She was waiting expectantly, features carefully amused, but just a touch of wariness in her eyes. Boston thought most people wouldn't notice it, but he did. "I appreciate your stopping by to see me, Amanda. And I'll be happy to show you the charms of Cuttersville, such as they are. But just to be up front with you, I'm dating someone here."

There was no reaction. Amanda was good at covering her emotions. She tilted her head a little, the sunglasses starting a slow slide out of her heavy hair. "Really? I never would have imagined that. Well, enjoy your little down-home dalliance."

She reached up to adjust the sunglasses, her tight top stretching way up on her thin frame, exposing ribs and the concave flesh between. Amanda was a gorgeous woman, and maybe once upon a time he would have seen that bare flesh and been aroused. Now he could only compare her glossy perfection to Shelby's natural beauty, and Amanda fell far short.

"She's special."

Now Amanda did blink. Then she threw back her head and laughed. "That's unbelievable, God, Boston Macnamara falling for a girl in the sticks. But I wish you all the best and all that other pleasant bullshit."

He thought she meant it, as much as Amanda could. Her attraction to him had never been about him, but another way to jab at her father. It was a feeling he understood, had entertained himself, though he'd never acted on it. Of course, he didn't know where his father was.

"Thanks." Boston tapped his thumbs on his knees. It

wasn't any of his business. But he had to ask. "What gives between you and Brett? Why the animosity?"

He expected her to laugh and pretend she didn't know what he meant. Or to tell him to go to hell and take her father with him. But she just shrugged. "He wants me to be you, that's the problem. I was supposed to be a boy. Instead he got a girl, complete with breasts and a brain and a penchant for eye shadow. He never knew what to do with all of that."

She didn't want him to say anything, and he didn't know how to respond anyway. He couldn't fix Amanda's relationship with her father any more than he could fix his with his own. "So are you planning on telling him you're here? Or is this a secret?"

"It wouldn't be any fun if it was a secret. But I guess I won't be here as long as I originally planned since you're busy. I'll leave in a day or two. Right now I couldn't handle that cab ride back to the airport." She rolled her eyes. "God, these people here are crazy, Boston. The cabbie wanted to *talk* to me, can you imagine? For an hour and a half!"

He laughed. "Why don't you stay a week? I'll show you around and by then you'll be bored, but Brett will have had time to get wind of the fact that you're here. And your landlady is a shark, by the way, but since I'm seeing her granddaughter, maybe I can get you a refund on the rent."

"Sounds like a plan," she said breezily. "Only I need a rental car then."

"No problem. We'll hook you up." He stood up. "Now how about we head down the street for the parade, and I'll show you all that picturesque Cuttersville has to offer."

"Oh, goody." Amanda sounded less than enthused. "A parade."

"Do you want to change?" He eyed her shoes dubiously. "It's a casual kind of thing."

Amanda looked at him like he was insane. "I am casual. T-shirt, denim skirt. What do you want? Pajamas?"

He cleared his throat. "It's the shoes, Amanda."

She stuck her foot straight out and inspected her stilettos. "These are Jimmy Choo shoes, appropriate for all occasions."

He just shook his head. "Trust me." If his hair gel warranted discussion, he couldn't imagine what Amanda's five-hundred-dollar shoes would do to the good people of Cuttersville.

"Okay." She dug into her bag and pulled out a pair of pink flip-flops. She exchanged the heels for the rubber sandals and asked, "Better?"

"Better." At five-ten, blond, and dressed like a supermodel, Amanda was still bound to attract attention, but at least in flip-flops he wouldn't have to pull her out when her heel got stuck in the dirt.

"Aren't you going to put a shirt on?" she asked, gesturing to his chest. "Or is that casual for men?"

He'd forgotten he wasn't wearing a shirt. "Hang on, I'll get one."

"Do we have time to grab a latte?" she called after him.

He wished. "Not since grabbing one would be an hour round-trip."

Chapter Twelve

Shelby waved her American flag at the Shriners in their little cars riding down Main Street and tried not to wonder where Boston was.

She should have gone to him this morning and asked him to come to the parade. Heck, she should have gone to him last night. No, she should have never left him in the first place.

Except that going home with him would have meant admitting that she was falling for him, and the night before, she hadn't been ready to admit it.

This morning, after a long frustrating night alone in her twin bed, she was ready to fess up. And if she was all prepared to be honest with herself, she could sleep with Boston and be alright when it was time for him to leave. Because she knew she had feelings for him and it wouldn't be a sucker-punch surprise, so therefore she could deal with it as she went along, sleeping with him while fully understanding she cared about him and he was leaving.

It all made sense. Sort of.

Not really. But she was running out of options.

Danny touched her elbow. "Look, there's your mom."

That wasn't something to improve her mood. Her mother was riding triumphantly in a Chrysler Sebring convertible with her boyfriend, Dave Henchen, mayor of Cuttersville. Giving a queen's wave, her mother beamed beneath her bleached hair, and thrust her always-burgeoning breasts out at the crowd.

"Hi, Shelby, honey!" her mom called out.

Shelby loved her mother. She just wasn't entirely certain she hadn't been adopted. Given the territorial satisfaction on Dave's face, her mother didn't have any trouble having orgasms. Or giving them.

Fighting a shudder, she smiled and waved back. It really wasn't a good idea to think that through when it wasn't even ten in the morning yet and coffee was a distant memory.

"You know, your mom's held up pretty good," Danny said thoughtfully.

Shelby rolled her eyes, but he missed the effect. He was nudging her again. "Look over by the hardware store, in the crowd. Jesus, look at that blonde with Boston. She's . . . tall."

Given the tone of awe in Danny's voice, that wasn't all he was thinking. But Shelby didn't give a care what Danny thought, not when Leggy Blonde was with Boston. Her Boston. Not her Boston, dammit. She had *known* that woman was here for him and she'd rolled in the straw with him anyway.

It didn't make her feel any better when she followed

Danny's gaze and was visually reminded that Boston came from a world of beautiful women, who dieted and worked out and waxed and chemical peeled. Including that beautiful woman, who was standing way too close to him on the sidewalk as they watched the parade.

The crowd had shifted away from them, as if they were afraid to wrinkle the city folk's expensive clothes with their John Deere T-shirts and jeans.

"Aren't you going to say hello?" Danny asked.

"I don't know her," she answered testily. And didn't want to.

"I meant say hello to him."

"Oh." Shelby thought about it. Shelby watched Boston whisper something in Blondie's ear. Shelby looked down at her voluminous American flag T-shirt and dingy white shorts. "No."

"That's rude, Shelby. See, he's looking right at you." Danny nudged her again, until she wanted to nudge him flat on his ass.

What was his obsession with having her chat up Boston? Before the question even finished forming, or the drool stopped puddling in the corner of Danny's mouth, she realized the answer. Duh. He wanted to meet Sex and the City over there.

Which infuriated her. Geez Louise, she couldn't even count on Danny anymore. One minute he was suggesting they remarry, the next he was gawking at a blond wig on a stick.

Men. Annoying creatures.

Danny was right, though. Boston was staring at her. He gave her a smile—a hot, promise-filled smile that about seared her shorts right off even clear across the road. Bastard.

She gave something that could pass for a wave or a flick of her bangs and turned resolutely in the other direction. The parade had come to a stop fifty feet back due to a Cuttersville Marching Cougar Band member dropping his tuba. Three flag bearers were trying to hoist it back over him with little success.

"Let's cut across the street," Danny said.

"No!"

Resistance was futile in the face of Danny's enthusiastic tug of her arm. Manual labor had made him strong as an ox, and he dragged her across the street like a dog with a toy sock.

Boston felt like he and Amanda were getting as much attention as Siegfried and Roy strolling through the supermarket in full sequined costume.

Jaws were dropping in their wake and people were giving them a wide berth. He could only be grateful Amanda had taken off the heels.

"So what do we do?" Amanda asked, leaning a little closer to him as if she realized they were garnering more attention than the parade.

"We stand by the street and watch the stuff go by."

"Oh, okay. I can do that." Amanda stood with her hands digging into her pockets. "Who are those men in those little cars? I've never seen anything like that."

It was odd, to say the least. Men wearing fez hats were driving around in little go-carts, whipping back and forth in circles and honking their horns. Boston just shrugged. "Beats the hell out of me."

"I'm seeing America, Boston, and it's freaking me out."

Amanda pried her sunglasses off to study the scene more closely.

Boston didn't answer. He'd caught sight of Shelby across the street from him, and dammit if she wasn't with Farmer Ted, Danny Tucker, ex-husband extraordinaire. The guy didn't seem to realize that once two people filed divorce papers, they weren't supposed to spend every waking moment together.

Shelby waved to a woman in a convertible heading down the parade route, then she caught his eye. And immediately looked away.

What the hell was that all about? When he'd left her the night before, he'd gotten the distinct impression that something was wrong. That despite the positive outcome, she was regretting having rolled in the straw with him. Her skittering gaze today confirmed it.

"Boston, look at that, some kid dropped his tuba. You know, this is kind of entertaining after all." Amanda tilted her head, then jumped when a young girl in the parade shoved a little American flag into her hand.

Her ponytailed friend tossed one to Boston with a giggle. He caught it and he and Amanda stood there, both uncertain. "Is she giving these to us?"

"I think so." Amanda waved hers back and forth experimentally. "Here, I've got it. You just wave it like everyone else. Now we'll blend."

That didn't seem likely, especially when Amanda tucked the flag in the waistband of her miniskirt.

"My, oh, my, they do grow them big here," Amanda said, eyes peering out from over her sunglasses.

Boston stopped fiddling with his flag, and looked up. It was Danny Tucker, who he could do without, but he was dragging Shelby with him through the break in the parade, and for that Boston was grateful. He wanted to talk to her. "That's Shelby. And she's not big, she's got a fabulous body."

The image of her staring up at him from the straw rose in his mind, her beautiful naked body tense with anticipation. Boston shifted on the sidewalk, wishing he had worn shorts instead of jeans. Things were getting hot.

Amanda laughed. "I meant the guy, you geek. And I'm guessing Shelby is the local attraction, hmm?"

He nodded, preoccupied with trying to get Shelby's attention, but she was staring at the ground.

Something hit him in the head. "What the hell?"

Amanda bent over and retrieved a plastic-wrapped oval from the ground. "It's candy." She jerked when a Tootsie Roll clipped her in the shoulder. "Why are they throwing candy at us?"

Shelby snorted quite distinctly right in front of them. Danny Tucker cleared his throat and looked down at Amanda, giving her his friendly farmer smile. "It's part of the parade. Everyone throws candy."

Amanda stood up and pelted Danny in the chest with the Tootsie Roll. The chocolate hit, bounced, and dropped to the ground.

Boston bit back a grin. Shelby scowled. Danny looked astonished. "What'd you do that for?"

Amanda looked partially confused, partially amused. "You said everyone throws candy. I'm participating. I'm trying to get into the spirit of things."

"Oh, dear God," Shelby said, and shot Boston an accusing glance, as if he were personally responsible for Amanda and everything she wore and said.

Danny laughed. "No, that's not what I meant. The people in the parade throw candy to the crowd, and the crowd just keeps it." He pointed to a little boy on the curb, his T-shirt tail bursting with a cache of candy. "See? It's just tradition, fun for the kids."

"Oh. Well, sorry then." Amanda turned back to the parade, flip-flopped foot tapping in time with the Cuttersville marching band.

Boston took the opportunity to touch Shelby's arm. "Hey. How are you?"

"Fine."

She didn't look fine. She looked pissed off, and there was something that burned in her eyes a lot like jealousy. Jealousy he liked. It meant she felt something for him. But he didn't want her to get the wrong impression. "Shelby, let me introduce you to Amanda Delmar, my boss's daughter."

Her eyes narrowed further. She didn't look appeased. "Uh, Amanda's just here for a little visit from Chicago."

Nothing but mean little slits were staring back at him now.

"How nice for you," she said, jaw locking, arms crossed over her T-shirt.

"Amanda's just an acquaintance," he said, leaning over to whisper in her ear.

Shelby whirled to face him, hitting him in the chest with her shoulder. "Oh, please, like she's going to haul her skinny little butt all the way to Cuttersville to see a man who is just an acquaintance. I may not be book smart, but I can still add two plus two. And in this case they equal you're a big fat liar."

"I'm telling you the truth," he said, locking his jaw and

feeling annoyed. "And this isn't the place to discuss it anyway."

"Where's the proper place to have an argument?" Her words cracked out at him like a whip.

"Shelby, you've just got to trust me. There's nothing between Amanda and me. She's just come here to irritate her father." He kissed the tip of her ear, staying close to her even when she slapped back at him. "Come to the White House tonight and I'll prove to you you're the only woman I'm interested in."

Now. Shelby could almost hear the disclaimer tacked on to the end of his sentence. Boston only wanted her now, because she was a novelty, and eventually he'd tire of her.

And what exactly was the problem with that? That was nothing less than she had expected right from the get-go, and nothing less than what she wanted anyway.

There was no future with Boston, and she didn't want one. She couldn't picture him staying in Cuttersville, and she could never leave. She'd known all of that when she'd dropped her drawers for him in the Bigleys' barn.

So why was she acting like a jealous girlfriend?

Because she was starting to care about him, damn him, and she needed to get her priorities adjusted before she went and made a total fool out of herself. She needed to remember that she'd made a decision to remarry Danny one way or the other at the end of the summer.

She could have her fling with Boston, or not, but either way she was settling back down with Danny to live the rest of her life. The question was whether she could restrain her emotions enough to enjoy Boston Macnamara in the short term.

"I don't know, Boston." But the words sounded weak.

He must have sensed her capitulation. Boston held her at the waist, stroking with his thumbs, and he nuzzled in her hair with his mouth and nose. "Please, Shelby. I want to see you spread out on that big bed, and I want to be inside you."

Apparently she wanted that too, if her restless body was any indication. Her panties were damp and her nipples were standing at attention.

"It's disturbing staying in a haunted house, Shelby. You'll be keeping me from getting scared."

She snorted and looked up at his teasing face. "Oh, right. You look just terrified."

"Terrified you'll say no." His fingers had worked under her shirt and the feel of his warm flesh on hers was tantalizing.

Spared from answering by Amanda turning around, Shelby struggled to dredge up some resistance, but found she didn't have any. Not a single stinking drop.

"Boston, aren't you going to introduce me to your *cher amie*? I want to meet the woman who has you basking in small-town life." Amanda flipped back that long blond hair that Shelby wanted to strangle her with, and laughed. "I mean, look at you. PDA-ing at a parade at ten A.M., who would have ever thought that of *you*?"

While she was sure Amanda was nice in a rich, bitchy kind of way, Shelby couldn't help but hate her on sight. She was the kind of woman Boston should be with—thin, educated, stylish—and the irony of Shelby's finally finding a man who could stir her passionate side, while being all wrong for her, wasn't the least bit amusing. And Amanda was the living, breathing example of reality butting into Shelby's lust-filled thoughts.

If Boston thought anything of Amanda's comments, he

was too city-smooth to say anything. He gave a bland smile, left his hands on Shelby's waist, and spoke. "Amanda Delmar, Shelby Tucker and Danny Tucker."

Shelby murmured a "Nice to meet you," trying not to sound like she was lying, which she was. Women like Amanda Delmar just drove home all her insecurities and that annoyed the spit out of her.

She'd never been one to worry about appearance, and she didn't want to start now just because Blondie was blessed with good DNA and wealth. At the end of the day, Shelby had the sneaking suspicion she was happier anyway. Amanda looked malcontent behind her expensive pink sunglasses.

But she couldn't stop herself from thinking she shouldn't have eaten three doughnuts for breakfast.

"Likewise," Amanda said with a brilliant pearl-white smile. "Are you brother and sister?" she asked Danny.

Danny, who looked his usual impassive and friendly self, seemed to have recovered from his earlier fascination with Amanda's height and breasts, and just shook his head. "Actually, Shelby's my ex-wife."

Danny locked eyes with Shelby, his gaze dropping to Boston's hand resting on her. She read the question in his expression and, embarrassed and not sure why, she took a step forward, forcing Boston's hand to drop.

Before Amanda could voice the question that seemed to be floating from her unnaturally plump lips, Shelby smiled at her. "I run a haunted house tour, Amanda. Maybe you'd like to come one day while you're here and see the local spirit spots. You look like a thrill seeker."

Maybe the Bigleys' cow would moo and scare her back to Chicago.

"Haunted houses? How intriguing. Sure, give me the details and I'll come."

"Boston's house is haunted," Danny offered. "And so is the house you're staying in, Amanda, though it's not on Shelby's tour. Too far out."

"The house I'm staying in is haunted?" Amanda looked thrilled at the prospect.

"My house just has drafts," Boston said, still in denial. Then he shot Shelby an intimate look. "And I still haven't gotten the complete tour, Shelby."

And Shelby knew precisely why. Because he'd made her moan in a barn, and she'd panicked. But she wasn't going to give him any Haunted Cuttersville Tour. He didn't give a crap about the ghosts, and she knew it. It was just an excuse for him to remind her of how he'd made her feel with her clothes off.

"Absolutely, the house is haunted," Danny said. "Both of them."

"Who's haunting it? Short people?" Amanda asked wryly. "The ceilings were not made with twenty-first-century women in mind."

"Who haunts the Gray House, Shel, honey? I can't remember," Danny asked.

"The woman in the mirror."

"Oh, that's right."

"What mirror?" Amanda looked like she thought it was hooey, but was still curious.

"The one in the second bedroom, the room with the glass in the door."

"Why is there glass in the door anyway? It's not exactly private."

"That was a porch at one time, so that door was an exterior door. No one knows where that mirror originally came from, but rumor has it a young virile German man was passing through town, and stopped to rest for the night at the local drinking establishment." Shelby lowered her voice. "He met a girl here in Cuttersville that night, and married her, and built her that cute little gray house, a love bungalow. Only one night he disappeared, the only sign of anything wrong a large black dog waiting outside in the yard. Some say it was the devil set to escort the man to hell. For it turned out he was a murderer back in Germany, and carrying a stash of stolen money."

Danny was grinning.

Boston was rolling his eyes.

Amanda was affecting boredom, but her eyes gleamed with interest.

"So the widow died broke and brokenhearted, ashamed that she had bedded down with the devil's helpmate, and they say if you look in that mirror, her face stares back at you, beseeching you to understand. And she cries sound-less tears, eyes locked on yours . . ."

The Cuttersville fire engine let out a blast of its horn as it rolled by and they all jumped. Amanda gave a screech before clamping her hand over her mouth.

"Jesus! What the hell is that?" Whirling around, she ad-justed her enormous bag on her shoulder. "Oh, shit, it's just a fire truck. What are they making so much noise for?"

Shelby wanted to laugh. Amanda glared toward the fire engine, and just about every fireman perched at various spots around the truck almost fell off as they gaped at the full frontal view of her. Shelby suspected the ladder wasn't the only thing rising as eyes plastered all over Amanda's chest and that offensive T-shirt she was wearing. Walking behind the ladder truck, Howie actually gathered enough nerve to smile and wave at her.

The truck ground to a halt as the parade slowed down, and Howie slammed into the back of the truck, clipping his shoulder. Shelby didn't think he even noticed, though, especially not since Amanda had deigned to wave back, retrieving her little American flag from her skirt and raising it in salute.

"There are a surprisingly large amount of attractive men in this town," Amanda said thoughtfully, still eyeing Howie.

Howie? Shelby thought hair dye must have addled the girl's brains. "Howie's pretty cute," she said to be polite, which earned her an evil glare from both Boston and Danny.

"Hey, look, those sweet little boys are throwing candy to me." Amanda started casually grabbing at the candy the middle-school-aged Boy Scouts were flinging at her by the handful, their eyes as wide as Frisbees.

Amanda bent over and Shelby swore she heard a collective gasp from the boys. It was a day they'd probably remember all through puberty. Amanda stood back up with a dozen pieces of candy and dropped them into her voluminous bag.

Shelby was a little shocked to find out that Amanda actually ate.

"What is *that* thing?" Boston asked with a frown. "It says SAMSON PLASTICS on the side of it."

"It's the Samson float, can't you tell?" Shelby thought this year's was the best yet. "It's made entirely out of two-liter bottles, the primary product manufactured in Cuttersville."

Of course, Boston would know that and Amanda wouldn't give a darn, but somehow she wanted to stress that Cuttersville wasn't just any old run-of-the-mill hick town. They had spooks *and* plastic. Not every town could claim that.

"It's very creative," Boston said wryly. "Oh, and look, there's a mock-up of a soft drink pouring into a giant bottle. Corporate dollars hard at work."

"It's called community involvement," Shelby said. "It shows Samson cares about this town and the people who live here." Unlike Fancy Pants there. She glared at Boston for good measure.

"You're right," he said, shocking her speechless. "I never thought of it that way."

"This whole down-home parade business is kind of fun," Amanda said with a smile and another triumphant wave of her flag, this time at the veterans' group who all appeared to be saluting her.

Shelby figured she could have this much fun sorting her laundry into whites and darks. "The sun is getting to me. I'm heading home."

Danny turned to her solicitously. "Maybe you should get some water. I'll walk you home."

Boston looked ready to wrest Danny's hand from her arm, but he paused, watching Amanda, looking torn.

His first responsibility obviously was staying with his boss's daughter, and the knowledge of that didn't make Shelby feel any better.

Danny would always be there, true and comforting. Boston was a flash of passion, a hot forbidden desire, like a crack of lightning in the summer heat.

Boston watched her edge away from the street, but before she could fully escape, he leaned down and whispered in her ear.

"I'll be there to pick you up tonight, Shelby, eight o'clock." His fingers brushed back her hair, and she shivered as his warm breath danced across her cheek. "Pack your toothbrush and whatever else you'll need to spend the night."

Then he turned back to Amanda and the parade.

Just as casual as you please.

Damn, the man was sexy.

Chapter Thirteen

Boston pulled onto Turkey Trail and found Bob's house right away. As he took in the picnickers in their shorts and T-shirts lounging around in white plastic chairs, he was extremely grateful that Amanda had declined his invitation to join him.

She'd had enough of Cuttersville for one morning and had gone back to the Gray House to take a nap, and probably buff the country air out of her pores. Considering Amanda was about as subtle as a raging bull in designer clothes, he couldn't say he was sorry. He actually wanted to enjoy this picnic.

And he did. A beer and a plastic plate loaded with carbohydrates were shoved into his hand, and he found himself mingling with Samson employees and the Turkey Trail neighbors.

Kids ran around the yard shooting water pistols at each

other, occasionally pausing to stuff potato chips in their mouths, but otherwise left unfettered.

Never once in his entire childhood had Boston run unfettered.

He found now that he was kind of enjoying being part of this casual group, sitting around, talking about nothing. He didn't even mind when someone grabbed a camera and forced all the company employees to stand together for a group photo.

When his Samson acquaintances stood up to refill their plates, a woman took the empty seat next to him.

"I'm so glad to meet you, Boston." She smiled at him with round cheeks flushed from the heat, her brown hair sitting like a cap around her face. "I'm Cheryl, Bob's wife."

"Oh, nice to meet you too." Boston stuck out his hand. "Thank you for inviting me, I'm enjoying myself."

"Well . . ." Cheryl looked around the yard with pride. "Bob and I have done this every year since we got married. It's fun."

She crossed her feet. "So are you here for long? Are you liking Cuttersville? It takes some getting used to when you rely on big-city conveniences."

"A little." A lot. But Boston sat under the hot sun, listening to the roar of the men laughing over the grill, the chatter of the women, the shrieks of the children playing in the crunchy browning grass, and he thought there were some really good things about Cuttersville.

"I like it more than I anticipated."

And it occurred to him, for the first time in startling clarity since Amanda had revealed the reasons behind his banishment, that Brett's purpose in sending him to Cuttersville was not being served. Amanda had followed him, and while she appeared to have no interest in pursuing him, Brett didn't know that. He might just turn around and whisk Boston, and Amanda, right back to Chicago, where he could at least keep an eye on them and protect Boston from her alleged poverty-creating clutches.

Boston didn't know how he felt about that.

Two weeks before, he would have willingly shredded his season tickets to the Cubs for a chance to shake the Cuttersville dust off him and go home. But now he wasn't so sure he'd be in the same frenzy to pack his bags.

Not yet anyway. There were a few things he still wanted to achieve before he left.

Like ensuring the Samson plant was on solid footing.

Not to mention getting Shelby Tucker down on that eyelet spread in his bedroom and following things to their natural conclusion after a quick stop at the drugstore for essentials.

No, he definitely wasn't ready to leave just yet.

"Mom, I don't want another cupcake, thanks." Shelby waved off the proffered treat her mother had shoved under her nose, the blue-sprayed frosting turning her stomach.

She'd already eaten too much.

Displaced physical longing was what it was.

She'd spent all day pondering Boston's toothbrush comment and wondering if the barn had been a fluke occurrence owing to the alignment of the planets or the supernatural powers of a dead cow, or if she'd actually have another orgasm under Boston's tutelage.

Or under his mouth, or his hands, or his tongue . . .

Her mother's hand slapped on her forehead. "Are you coming down with something? You're turning down sweets and you look all hot and sweaty."

"It's almost ninety degrees out. Everyone's sweating." Except her mother, who looked fresh and patriotic, an Uncle Sam top hat perched on her blond head.

Dave, her mother's boyfriend, wandered over and rested his hand on her behind, like it was just magnetically drawn there. "Susan, honey, is there more beer? The boys are going thirsty."

Her mother got flustered. "Of course there is. I bought just absolute tons, so we wouldn't run out. Where on earth did it all go?"

She rushed off, in a hostess panic, Dave following at a more leisurely pace, surrendering his hold on her mother's cherry red backside. The vibrant capri pants were topped with a white tank top sporting a giant blue star in the middle.

Shelby took a swallow of her diet soft drink and wondered if she could muscle her way into the shade, where the seniors were all holding court under three giant elms. There were no lawn chairs left, but she could sit on the ground, none too worried about her shorts. Between Amanda Delmar and her own mother, she felt like a troll anyway.

There were Chihuahuas with better wardrobes than hers.

And there she was, thinking about it again. Dang it, she did not care what she looked like.

Making her way across the lawn, she took in the back of her mother's little white ranch house. She'd grown up in that house, had broken her arm on the hard-packed dirt under the metal swing set, and had struggled through her homework at the scarred oak table in the peach kitchen.

This was home, where her roots were.

She'd made out with Danny Tucker, feeling grown up and daring, behind that dilapidated shed, right where Brady had Joelle pinned right now.

Shelby veered past him, giving him a little shove. "They can see, you idiot, and Mom's wondering where all the beer went."

Joelle jumped back with a guilty flush, but Brady held on to her. He rolled his eyes at Shelby. "I didn't sneak off with any beer. How lame is that to steal my aunt's beer at one in the afternoon?"

"Lame," she agreed.

"Hey, where's Mac? I thought he'd be here."

Shelby couldn't think of Boston by that nickname Cuttersville seemed determined to saddle him with. "He's with the Samson people. And since when are you all chummy with Boston?"

"We hang out sometimes."

"What?" Shelby tried to envision Boston and Brady watching MTV together and couldn't manage it.

"He's hot," Joelle ventured, raising shiny brown eyes toward Shelby, her hair slipping from its thin ponytail.

Now it was Brady's turn to be astonished. "What do you know about him being hot? He's old enough to be your *father.* Man, that's just sick."

"Brad Pitt is hot too, and he's like forty," Joelle said with a giggle. "And Russell Crowe and Sean Connery."

"Sean Connery?" Brady made gagging sounds.

Shelby left them to battle it out, Brady's outraged voice floating behind her.

Brady's older sister, Heather, was standing in a circle of women, absorbing the admiration of all for her newborn baby girl.

"Two weeks old and sleeping through the night," she proclaimed proudly.

All the women oohed and aahed and told Heather how fabulous she looked. Which she did, despite the slight dark circles under her eyes. She had that almost palpable glow of a new mother, and Shelby couldn't help but smile at her.

"Want to hold Rose, Shelby?" Heather held out the infant in offering.

"Sure." It would insult Heather if she said no, and she did have an itch to get her hands on that downy blond hair.

After a tricky pass-off, where multiple hands shifted closer to them if needed for a fast catch, Shelby settled Rose into the cradle of her arms, her compact baby body resting with a firm warm weight. Wearing a little pink short-sleeve onesie, Rose was sleeping blissfully, her long pale eyelashes twitching over her red eyelids. Her mouth mimicked sucking in her sleep, and her little fingers shuddered occasionally.

She was just a baby. Just like any other of a thousand born every day.

But staring at her tiny beauty, smelling her soft formula-and-powder scent, Shelby felt everything inside her shift and rise up in a suffocating cloud of longing.

She wanted one of these. One of her own.

For the first time since that long-ago miscarriage, she could admit to herself that she wanted to be a mother now. Not later, not never. But now, in the next couple of years, and that which had seemed impossible a month before suddenly seemed possible.

Passion was fine and dandy, but at the end of the day, a girl had to have something to come home to.

And just in case part of her was thinking that, it sure couldn't be Boston Macnamara.

Boston rang the doorbell to Shelby's grand- mother's house and shuffled his feet a little on the porch, not sure if Shelby would actually come out with him or not. She was clearly having reservations about continuing anything between them, but Boston wasn't going to take no for an answer.

If Brett Delmar was about to yank him right back out of Cuttersville, Boston didn't have a lot of time. And he didn't think he could leave this town until he'd held Shelby in his arms, skin on skin, her warm legs tossed around him, his body deep inside hers.

When Jessie Stritmeyer answered the door a split sec- ond later, he had a boner.

And the old lady knew.

As if guided there by familial protectiveness, she glanced right down at the front of his jeans and raised a whisker-thin eyebrow. Without even giving a greeting, she said, "You been to the drugstore?"

He didn't even pretend to misunderstand. "Yes." Three condoms he'd pulled out of a new box accounted for the other bulge in his pants.

"Alright then." She held the door open. "Come on in while I round Shelby up. I think she's shaving her legs."

Boston didn't need to know these things. The complex- ities of female hygiene had always mortified him, having grown up in such a formal household with no sisters. But for some reason, the image of Shelby damp from the shower, bent over, leg high on the bathroom counter, with her towel slipping, slipping, left him as hot as that imagined shower.

Stepping into the tiny front hallway, Boston prepared to wait uncomfortably with his landlord, but when he looked up the twisting spindled staircase, he saw that Shelby wasn't shaving her legs. She was standing there watching him, hair piled on her head in its usual disarray, rich brown eyes wide.

There was something about Shelby that was timeless, that with just a quick change of her clothes, she could have been a farmer's daughter in the Depression, or a young immigrant bride in the nineteenth century. She had a strength about her, and she was utterly no-nonsense.

Which was what he wanted between them.

No games, no flirtations, no selfish maneuvering, just a humid country night and desire etched plainly across her face.

"Hey there, Boston."

"Hi, Shelby. Want to come and watch the fireworks with me?" And make some of their own?

The picnic had been abuzz with the pending Cuttersville fireworks extravaganza set for 10 P.M., and Boston was hoping he and Shelby could find a quiet corner on Main Street to watch them together. As luck would have it, he'd been freed from the pleasure of Amanda's cynical presence by the arrival of Howie the fireman, who with more earnestness than charm had wooed her away.

Boston had considered slipping the guy a twenty to keep her occupied all week, knowing full well Howie was open to bribes, but he had resisted the urge.

"Sure," she said in a breathless little voice that wrapped around his groin and squeezed.

If it wasn't for her grandmother standing there looking amused, he might have bounded up those steps and pressed her against the nearest wall for a deep kiss.

Struggling to divert himself, he turned to Mrs. Stritmeyer. "So who haunts this house?"

Jessie gave him an incredulous look. "No one. You think I'd share a house with a bunch of dead people? No thanks."

Shelby came down the stairs and waved to her grandmother. "Good night, Gran. Don't wait up."

"I wasn't planning on it." Jessie headed toward the kitchen. "Not that I'll get much sleep tonight with all those fools shooting off fireworks in their backyards."

Shelby laughed, and leaned in to whisper to Boston. "She's one of those very people, you know. She's got a box of Roman candles and bottle rockets set out in the garage just ready to go."

"I don't know what you're talking about." Jessie was all old-lady innocence.

"Uh-huh. Just don't let Fran set the roof on fire this year." Shelby leaned over and gave her a kiss.

She turned to Boston. "Bingo ladies. They're wild, I'm telling you."

He could only imagine. "Good night, Mrs. Stritmeyer."

"Night, Boston."

They walked outside, the porch steps creaking under their weight, and Shelby took a deep breath. "I love that smell. Summer."

He loved her smell. Fresh and sweet, like soap and honey, which no perfume or shower gel could ever replicate.

Boston put his hand on the small of her back as they headed toward his car, just to touch her. Just to feel her warm firm skin under her T-shirt, and to tease himself with how close his fingers were to the top of her panties.

"I know a place where we can watch the fireworks," Shelby said. "Alone."

Nothing in his entire thirty-two years had ever sounded better.

"Lead the way."

Shelby had to get a handle on her heart racing, or it was likely to leap out of her chest and run on down the road. Which would earn her notoriety she didn't crave.

"We should probably drive there."

Boston stopped in front of his fancy deep blue car, and the corner of his thin mouth lifted. "Are you taking me to Lovers' Lane, Shelby?"

"Of course not." She grinned, nervousness evaporating. "I would never do anything so tacky. I'm taking you to a cornfield."

He opened the door for her and leaned over, his lips brushing across her jaw. Shelby shivered.

"At least I know you can't take advantage of me in a cornfield."

She snorted.

Boston wasn't touching her anywhere, except for that little dusting with his lips across her chin and around the corners of her mouth. It felt as intimate as sex, that soft coaxing kiss.

"And there won't be any voyeuristic ghosts to interrupt whatever might happen."

"That's true." Shelby shifted away from him and slid into the car. "Let's go."

Before she started making out with him in her gran's driveway.

Boston came around and got into the car. She pointed him in the right direction to drive and he did, but as he turned left, he glanced at her. "So why did you and Danny really get divorced?"

Shelby was startled out of her impure thoughts. "I told you, we just decided we were better off as friends."

"He still cares about you." It wasn't a question.

"Yes." Shelby studied Boston's profile, the firm jaw, the long aristocratic nose, the smooth stubble-free complexion that seemed so unusual for a man with black hair.

It occurred to her that maybe a tiny piece of Boston was just a wee bit jealous of her relationship with Danny. The thought thrilled her more than it should if she were a decent sort.

"Then there had to be something," he insisted. "Did he leave his dirty underwear lying around? Hang out drinking with his buddies too often?"

"No." Shelby ran her fingers over the fringe of her denim cutoff shorts. She'd put these on hoping they'd get dirty. "Love between eighteen-years-olds isn't always enough five years later. That's all. Nothing mysterious or complicated or worth writing home about."

She wanted to be swept away, not tussled back into her past.

Boston didn't say anything, just took a left turn when she pointed in that direction, but she could just about feel him thinking. He wanted a *real* reason, like infidelity or screaming arguments, or irresponsible spending habits.

Sometimes it was both simpler than that and much more complicated.

She hit the button to send her window purring down, the thick night air rushing in. "So did you and Amanda ever date?" The question had been on her lips all day and she couldn't contain it any longer.

But his genuine laugh reassured her. "No. I don't even really know her. She's been at corporate functions and flits into the office looking for an advance on her allowance occasionally, but that's the extent of our relationship. I have no idea why she showed up here." He shrugged. "Just bored, I guess."

"Turn here and park, and we'll walk in." Shelby rolled the window back up. "You know, there does have to be something boring about getting everything you want just handed to you. But I hope Amanda doesn't mess around with Howie's head. He's just a simple kind of guy, you know, nicer than anything, and eager to please. I'd hate to see her take advantage of him."

Boston opened his door. "She won't be here long enough to mess around with anyone. I can almost guarantee she'll be gone in a matter of days."

She waited for him to come around and open her door, knowing that's what he would do. When he opened it, she stared at the buttons on his black shirt and asked, "But Amanda is the type of woman you date, right? Has there been anyone serious?"

Strong hands tugged her out of the car and snug up against Boston's sculpted chest. "I'm a workaholic. Didn't I mention that?"

"That was sort of the impression I got myself," she told his chest.

"I always dated casually. Not enough hours in the day to spend on both a serious relationship and my career."

"Don't you want to settle down someday, Boston?"

She felt a casual shrug, nothing more, then he moved away from her.

"Let me get something out of the car."

Running her hands over the goose bumps that were on her arms for no apparent reason given the temperature, Shelby watched him emerge with a bottle of wine and two glasses. They were flutes from the china cabinet in the White House. He also had a big blanket that looked suspiciously like the bedspread from the yellow bedroom.

But she couldn't find it in her to protest, not when the very thought of snuggling up on that with him was sending a nice warm sensation slithering throughout her body. "We'll be able to see the fireworks just perfect from here," she told him, heading to the edge of the cornfield.

Her uncle owned this farm, so she wasn't worried about trespassing, and there was a little rise between two fields that afforded a perfect view of the night sky over Cuttersville. Dusk was rapidly falling, and the knee-high corn plants swayed in the soft sticky breeze.

"How's this?" She gestured to the grassy slope, and Boston gave her such a hot look she glanced down to make sure her breasts hadn't popped out of her T-shirt when she wasn't looking.

"This is beautiful." Though he wasn't looking at the field, or the sky, but at her. Just her.

Shelby took the blanket that was draped over his arm and spread it down on the ground, then flopped on her stomach with a sigh. Boston dropped down beside her, the glasses in his hand clinking a little.

"Wine?"

"Sure." She wasn't much of a drinker, but it seemed to match the mood. Rich, robust, reckless.

Out of curiosity, she looked at the bottle in his hand, then got annoyed when the letters shifted and jumbled in her head, the French phrasing throwing her off. She concentrated a little harder, but still wasn't quite sure what she was looking at.

"It's just a Zinfandel," he told her, and something about the tone of his voice had her looking up at him.

"I'm dyslexic," she told him. "Did you know that?" She could tell he did—it was written all over his face—but she wanted to see if he would tell her the truth.

There was only a slight hesitation before he nodded. "Yes, Brady told me."

Little pain-in-the-butt teenager. She felt the urge to snip Brady's sapphire spikes off next time he was sleeping. "Nice to know my cousin goes around running at the mouth."

"Does it matter that I know? That you are dyslexic?" he asked her earnestly.

"No, I guess not." Except she'd never quite been able to shake her shame off, even though intellectually she knew it wasn't a big deal, and it said nothing about her smarts. Part of her just couldn't help thinking that she wasn't quick enough, high-powered enough.

Boston popped the cork on the wine. "Sometimes, Shelby Tucker, I think you and I have more in common than we ever could have imagined."

Lust maybe, but that's as far as she saw the resemblance.

Still on her stomach, Shelby picked a milkweed and ran the tip back and forth over her fingers.

He poured the wine, not looking at her. "I never thought I would ever settle down as you called it. I didn't exactly have good role models for raising a family." His fingertips brushed hers as he handed her a glass. "Put me in a board-room and I have unlimited confidence. The thought of any-one depending on me totally strips me of that."

"That's why I didn't go to college. I didn't want to fail." She took a sip of the wine, rolled the sweetness around her tongue. "But you know, sometimes I wonder if failing isn't better than always wondering."

"But failing out of college isn't as detrimental as failing as a husband or father. In that case, you're screwing up an-other person's life as opposed to just your own."

Shelby set the glass in the weeds and rolled onto her back, peering up into the limitless sky. "Maybe we are more alike than I thought."

"Shelby . . . I'm leaving, you know." He settled down closer to her, his thigh pressing against her arm.

It wasn't unexpected, and she had thought all along she was okay with it, but when he said it out loud, she didn't want to hear it. "Soon?"

"No. I don't know. It could be. There's some politics in-volved in this transfer and I don't know when I'll be sent back to Chicago, but it will probably be sooner than later, and when it happens, I'll be leaving and not coming back."

Shelby folded her hands across her tummy and kept her eyes trained on the sky, dropping into inky black darkness. "I know that, Boston. I've always known that."

"I just wanted to be honest. Because whatever happens between us, this is all there is. Right here, right now."

"Then we'd better make the most of it."

Chapter Fourteen

Boston was leaning toward Shelby to claim that promise in her eyes, when a rocket launched into the sky and exploded over their heads in a purple cascade.

"Ooh!" Shelby said and jerked back away from him, propping her head up with her arms and smiling in delight at the fireworks.

Personally, he could care less about what was happening in the sky, focused as he was on what was occurring right there on the blanket between them. When Shelby spoke, when that wistful expression broke over her face, he wanted her, totally and completely and in all the ways that mattered.

He wanted her to be his, and that just couldn't ever happen under any circumstances for whatever reason. It was insane even to contemplate.

But he'd told her the truth, that he was leaving, and his conscience could be clear that he'd never misled her. So when he made love to her, she would be there with him, and they'd enjoy each other for the short time they had.

"Look at that one!" she said, pointing up. "It looks like Christmas lights. And that one is crackling, like grease in a hot pan."

And he still couldn't drag his gaze off her long enough to appreciate a greasy firework. Draining his wine, he watched her watch them, the wonder and enthusiasm in her voice and on her face creeping into the jaded corners of his heart and warming it.

He had the sneaking suspicion that he was starting to fall in love with her.

Contrary to what he'd always assumed, he didn't feel weak and frustrated, jealous and distracted. He just felt, well, good. Like he'd finally stopped running that race for just a minute and was standing on the sidelines admiring the view.

God, he needed something stiffer than wine. He was starting to feel freaking poetic.

So he ditched the glass in the weeds and lay on his side next to Shelby, dropping his hand onto the dip of her stomach. Corn plants were lazily swaying behind her and he almost laughed. He could honestly say he'd never made it with a woman in a field of corn.

Instead, he kissed the spot on her shoulder where it rounded the corner to her upper arm, startling a squeak out of her.

"What're you doing?" She continued to watch the sky, but her breath had already picked up speed, her mouth parting in silent invitation.

"Kissing you." Boston tasted down to her elbow, flickering out his tongue to slip into the crease there.

Shelby wiggled. "That tickles."

With a quick shift, his mouth was on her waist, and he shoved her shirt out of the way, licking across the length of her and dipping into her belly button.

"Oh, stop that." Her tone of voice wasn't very convincing, even when she added, "I'm trying to watch the fireworks."

"So watch them," he murmured, nibbling across her abdomen, his fingers popping the snap on her ancient denim shorts.

He shifted his leg across her calf for better leverage, and let his thumb drift beneath her shorts, trailing over the front of her panties. They were crisp white cotton, glowing in the dark field, and he pictured her golden brown curls beneath the fabric. The fireworks sent a labyrinth of color over her body, and he brought her T-shirt up to her shoulders to better view her.

There was no bra to slow him down, just ripe round breasts and taut nipples. When he slowly drew one into his mouth, Shelby shuddered, eyes resolutely trained on the display in the sky. He sucked harder. She whimpered.

He pressed his thumb against her, deeper and deeper until he felt the moisture releasing from her, seeping through her panties. His erection was nudging painfully into her thigh, reminding him that it wanted part of the action too, but he ignored his own ache, enjoying the pleasure he could give Shelby.

Enjoying the pinch of her fingers into the blanket, the glassy desire of her wide-open eyes, the rich little moans that were coming faster and faster now as he slipped under her panties to cup her. Working her breast harder, he just let his hand rest on her, feeling the heat and dampness of her curls, until she thrust her hips off the ground in a blatant invitation for him to move.

"Do you want this?" he asked, sliding his finger along her clitoris and down into the hot wetness below.

"Yes."

Out of vanity, out of jealousy, out of deeper emotions than he cared to admit, he asked, "I make you feel good, don't I, Shelby?"

And he sank inside her.

"Yes," she moaned, breasts arching up toward him, nipple brushing against his lips.

It was an offer he wasn't going to refuse. He bit her.

Lightly, but with enough force that she jerked beneath him and said, "Oh, Lord, Boston!"

Her hips had fallen wide open and he stroked inside her with one finger, then two, feeling her stretch to accommodate him, growing slicker and slicker, while he teased the tip of her nipple, rolling his lips back and forth.

Glancing up, he saw her head tilt back, her mouth forming a moan, before she said breathlessly, "Take my shorts off."

If he did, he'd be in her faster than she could say foreplay. "No. I want you to see that I can make you come with your clothes off, and with your clothes on, and with me inside you . . ."

And before he could even finish the thought, she was gone, letting out a cry as her body broke, her hips thrusting to meet his fingers, nails raking across the blanket. He kept his head between her breasts, breathing in the salty scent of her warm flesh beneath his lips, while he kept his fingers still and let her ride out her pleasure.

But the minute she relaxed back, her eyes drifting shut,

he pulled back, ripped his shirt over his head, and undid his jeans. The noise alerted her, and when she saw what he was doing, she wiggled her shorts and panties down to her knees.

Boston paused to remove them the rest of the way, caressing down her knees and calves, feeling the smooth firm muscle. "Nice clean shave."

A strangled laugh left her mouth. "Thanks."

"Take that rubber band out of your hair." He wanted to see all that hair loose.

While he sat back and shoved off his jeans, Shelby went up on her elbows and reached into that pile of hair, jerked once, and snapped the band right out of her hair. It fell to her shoulders and below, big bouncy waves, thick and lustrous.

The sight about ripped the air right out of his lungs.

She was so feminine, so beautiful, that he could only shake his head. "Damn, you are incredible."

A smile flashed at him, while the slow and leisurely one or two rockets at a time Cuttersville Fourth of July celebration continued. He had his boxers off in record time and didn't bother to wait. He slapped a condom on with more force than finesse and looked up as Shelby tossed her shirt to the side.

She lay back on the blanket, hair spread around her, chest rising and falling with quick staccato breaths. Then she slowly and carefully dropped her legs wide, exposing her to him, and her arms opened, a come-hither look on her sexy face.

She didn't need to ask him twice.

Boston moved between her thighs, and used one hand to open her swollen sex to him. He nudged at the entrance, teasing himself with her soft wetness while Shelby gripped his forearms and begged.

"Please, please . . ."

He couldn't wait another second. With his own groan, he drove into her, thrusting her back against the blanket. Too late, he remembered it had been three years since she'd had sex, and the wince she fought to cover up reminded him. As did the tightness of her body, caressing him, wringing an agonized curse from his mouth.

"I'm sorry." Boston bent to her and kissed her mouth softly, holding still inside her as he watched her face.

"I'm fine." She pulled his head back to hers and kissed him this time, her tongue licking at his lips, demanding entrance.

He opened his mouth for her, and the kiss went hotter, her hands in his hair, and Boston gripped the smooth skin of her back and rolled them both over, still embedded in her.

Shelby lay across his chest, her breasts pressing over him, her hair tickling his chest. Without moving inside her, he kissed her again, over and over, stroking her dewy flesh, cupping her backside until she started to thrust and grind against him.

"Oh, yeah, that's it. Take what you want, Shelby."

Her eyes locked with his, Shelby pushed herself back until she was sitting up, hair tumbling over her rosy nipples. She adjusted her hips a little, fussed with her wrists, brushed her thumbs over his chest. Then she lifted and sank back down, her eyes drifting shut, her cheeks flushing, little pants of pleasure slipping out.

Never in his whole life had he seen anything as sexy as Shelby finding her rhythm on him, riding him faster and faster. He ground his teeth together, dug his heels into the blanket, and forced himself to not do a damn thing.

It was worth every tense muscle when she ground that swollen button against him and yelled out loud enough to wake the dead, who probably weren't asleep anyway. Shelby shuddered and pressed through her climax, eyes half closed, inner muscles trembling over him, and Boston fought his own release.

"No way," she said with a shaky laugh, squeezing his shoulders. "I can't believe that just happened."

He was so goddamn glad it had. Reaching out with a growl, he buried his hands in the lush caramel strands of her hair and twisted them around his knuckles. He tugged her forward. "Come here."

Shelby had barely recovered from her orgasm, in fact was still shaky and trembling, when Boston used her hair like a leash and jerked her down onto his chest. "What?" she managed, trying to prop herself up a little so she wasn't squashing him.

"I'm going to roll you over," he said tightly, jaw clenched and breathing hard.

"Okay." She didn't think he was actually asking permission, but she was feeling like she'd agree to do just about anything after he'd delivered twice in one night again.

Then he flipped her smoothly, returning her to her back on the hill. The slight incline had her sliding down a little until he pressed his chest against hers and held her in place. Hands still tangled in her hair, bodies still intimately connected, he sucked her bottom lip. And then moved.

With a raw determination, a hard territorial thrust, fingers fanning her hair out and inadvertently pulling. But she didn't care, not when he was moving, not when he was sliding into her with reckless, out-of-control drives.

And Lord have mercy, when she wrapped her legs around his hard thighs, she saw the Cuttersville fireworks grand finale bursting over her head behind his shoulder, the loud booms drowning out all sound but the rush of his groans past her ear.

His forehead pressed to hers, his eyes closed, hot breath fanning across her nose, and she felt him come inside her with a last pulsing thrust that had her moaning with him. Boston made her feel like the sexiest woman he'd ever gotten naked, and as she lay back on the ground like an overcooked noodle, she realized that this was much more than she'd ever bargained for.

"Oh, boy," she said on a swallow, seeking reassurance in his eyes that this was ordinary sex to him, standard procedure that didn't mean anything at all about the state of her heart.

But he just nuzzled against her with his mouth, nodding. His black eyes locked with hers. "Oh, boy," he agreed.

"Nice fireworks," she ventured, sure she was wrong, and that no doubt he'd had cornfields full of sex better than what they'd just shared.

"Best I've ever seen," he said, confirming for her that they could never do this again.

Chapter Fifteen

Boston showed up for the Saturday six o'clock Haunted Cuttersville Tour on July fifth, right on time but full of trepidation.

For one thing, there was a large crowd of twenty gathered on his front porch, waiting for him.

For another, after the incredible blanket bonanza under the stars the night before with Shelby, he felt a little bit like Red-Eyed Rachel had conked him on the head with a candlestick.

Shocked. Stunned. Dazed.

It wasn't every day he realized he'd just about fallen in love with a woman. In fact, this was the first. And given the vague, glassy expression on Shelby's face when he'd dropped her off the night before, and the single-syllable replies she'd given him, she had also been experiencing something other than unadulterated bliss.

Neither one of them had thought to suggest Shelby grab her toothbrush and stay over. Boston thought maybe they'd both known they'd had all they could handle for one night.

Having Amanda accompanying him this evening wasn't helping either. She wasn't doing anything that could be classified as annoying, although her lip gloss was a little blinding, but having her around was a reminder of Chicago, where he belonged, his real life.

And when he was in Cuttersville, and holding Shelby in his arms under a pollution-free sky, he didn't want to be reminded of reality. He wanted to play small-town house for a while.

Only his house was full of T-shirt-wearing gawkers and Shelby looking like she'd eaten week-old fish. Even from the driveway, her skin looked an alarming shade of green, somewhat like mint chocolate chip ice cream, without the chips.

"Shelby looks upset," Amanda said, her voice lazy and knowing.

She did. Boston wanted to shove everyone aside, walk up those stairs, take Shelby in his arms, and claim her as his with a kiss in front of all those people.

He wasn't so totally far gone as to actually do that, though.

Instead, he just nodded to the people standing around and offered a forced smile. Shelby was sidling behind a middle-aged man who looked to be hiding a beach ball under his shirt. While Boston wasn't sure what to say to her, he didn't want her avoiding him.

So he called to her. "Shelby, can I speak to you, please?"

Her green cheeks pinkened, so she looked a bit like peppermint. She'd worn an incredibly oversized orange T-shirt that said DICK'S HARDWARE, which struck Boston as redundant, but that she'd probably worn solely for the coverage. Nothing above the elbows was showing, and he couldn't even get a good shot of her cute little backside with that thing hanging down over her dingy gray shorts. Dirty gym shoes were on her feet, no socks, and Boston read her meaning loud and clear.

She didn't want any attention from him.

Well, she could be wearing head-to-toe multilayered fleece and he'd still be turned on.

Especially since he'd seen her hair down over her naked shoulders and breasts.

"Yes?" she asked, her little chin jutting out toward him, her eyes wary but determined.

"What do you want me to do? Just go into the house and stand there? Sing maybe, or play the piano?" He tried to tease a smile out of her.

No smile, but she loosened up, shoulders relaxing, hands letting go of the hem of her shirt. "You can just do whatever you normally do. Work or read or eat, whatever. Thank you for doing this, I know it's uncomfortable for you."

"No problem." He couldn't resist squeezing her hand a little, but she pulled it right back. "Listen, Shelby, we need to talk."

Her eyes snapped shut for a split second, and she shook her head just slightly before blowing a big breath of air out, scattering the loose hair over her forehead. "I know we do."

"Can you come back after the tour?"

"Sure." She nodded resolutely. "We need to clear the air about some things."

It had an ominous sound that he didn't understand or like. Confusion mixed with fear, which warred with the euphoria that he had found a woman he could really fall in love with, until he thought programming his cell phone made more sense than the thoughts running around his head.

Boston opened the door, walked in, and just managed to duck in time when a plate came flying at his head.

Shelby only saw a flash of white go past Boston's shoulder before it collided with the door, in an explosion of shattering shards. Jumping back with a shriek, she bumped into the soft stomach of the woman standing behind her.

"Show's on," Boston said wryly, moving into the foyer with total confidence, like he wasn't the least bit scared.

Which she had to admit was appealing. If he had knocked the tour-goers down in an attempt to escape the house, she didn't think she'd be in love with him.

Which she was. In love with him, darn it.

Miserable and irrationally annoyed that exciting things seemed to happen only when *he* was around, Shelby took a tentative step in behind him.

Boston's hand shoved her head down right as another plate came spinning past. Shelby caught a glimpse of Scarlett's drapery dress go flying by from her bent-over position.

"Hey, those are Gran's limited-edition *Gone With the Wind* plates! She's not going to be real happy."

But Boston laughed. "Frankly, Shelby, I don't think they give a damn."

"Who's they?" She was afraid to stand up, and grabbed on to the belt loops of Boston's black pants for leverage.

A quick glance back showed half a dozen people crammed into the doorway watching, more in the windows of the parlor.

"I'm guessing it's Rachel."

All the lights came blasting on, pouring from the chandelier, scattered lamps, and from the fixture at the top of the stairs.

Shelby inched closer to Boston's butt.

Bless his heart, he took pity on her, and put an arm around her, his suit jacket obscuring some of her view. Which could be a bad thing if Rachel winged a plate at her, but a good thing if an entity decided to show itself. She could do without seeing any dead people until she was good and dead herself.

"Nice to see you again, Rachel." Boston spoke like he was at a corporate lunch. "You remember Shelby? She's stopped by to visit."

Shelby smacked Boston's leg. She didn't want to be dragged into this. She'd never had a problem with Rachel until he'd shown up.

"Stand up, love," he said, urging her with his hand.

Shocked from the endearment, which tripped off his lips so casually and sweetly, Shelby stood up and gaped at him. He just smiled and touched the tip of her nose.

"I want to kiss that expression right off your face," he said.

This time, when Rhett Embraces Scarlett came down off the plate rack above the curio cabinet, Shelby saw it. Sticking her hand up, she shielded the side of Boston's face and let out a yelp when the china crashed into her.

Her hand stung, and tears popped into her eyes. Boston's eyes went wide, then furious. He grabbed her hand, and cursed at the blood that flowed from a two-inch-long gash.

"Alright, Rachel, that's not funny!" He glared around the foyer. "If you have something to say, get your dead self out here and say it, but you cannot hurt Shelby ever again, understand me?"

Shelby didn't think it was such a hot idea to be issuing commands to psychotic ghosts, and she started inching toward the front door, clutching her bleeding hand in her T-shirt. Boston stilled her, pulling her against his hard side, his muscles bunched as if bracing for a fight.

Don't let Rachel appear, just don't . . .

Squeezing her eyes shut, Shelby tried to pretend she didn't hear the footsteps in the kitchen, coming toward them, loud and ominous. Click, click, click, they grew closer and closer, and Shelby's heart beat so fast she couldn't catch her breath. With more courage than she'd known she possessed, she forced her eyes open.

And saw Amanda standing in the kitchen doorway, wearing high heels and a tangerine orange strapless sundress.

"Amanda, what are you doing?" Boston asked, his fist relaxing.

"I couldn't see a damn thing." She shot a glare at the women stuffed into the front door frame. "So I came around the back."

While Shelby remembered to breathe again, Amanda assessed the situation. "I don't see anything going on."

The God As My Witness plate hurled at Amanda. She shifted and watched it crash into the rose-colored wall. "Well, someone's not getting any," she remarked.

"How many plates are there?" Boston asked, glancing to the rack. "Jesus, there's a ton of them."

"It was a long movie." Shelby strove for some of Amanda and Boston's nonchalance, but found she didn't have a whole lot. "And I'm not waiting around for the whole thing."

Boston tried to pull her T-shirt off her injured hand, but Shelby held it tight. She wasn't crazy about the sight of blood, even a little.

"I'll drive you to the ER for stitches, Shelby."

The very thought made her woozy. "I don't need stitches. We need to save the plates."

One-handed, she started to drag a dining room chair over to the plate rack.

"Don't be ridiculous. Amanda, you get the plates while I take Shelby to the hospital."

"Do what?" Obviously the thought of any task other than primping herself baffled Amanda. She was staring at the chair blankly.

Shelby just rolled her eyes and climbed onto the chair, keeping her head tucked behind her uninjured arm. In a minute she had all the plates down, stacked in Boston's hands. The practical action made her feel less hysterical.

"Put them in the cabinet." Shelby pointed to the mahogany hutch in the dining room.

While Boston secured the plates, Shelby peeled her T-shirt back, hoping to convince herself it was just a scratch and she didn't need to go to the ER. The sight of red blood smeared all over her hand greeted her, and she became aware of how wet and sticky it was.

The room tilted, her mouth went hot, her breathing desperate. "Oh, God."

Boston caught her just in time before she hit the floor. She didn't faint, but came awful close, her vision blurring, everything going black for a split second. Things were just starting to clear when Boston lifted her off the ground into his arms, which made her dizzy all over again.

But there was something comforting in being carried, even as she sucked in gobs of air to try and still her nauseous stomach. Shelby wasn't a woman people cosseted, not even as a kid. To have Boston holding her tenderly like she was Amanda-skinny, whispering soft little words of encouragement and distress, was a good feeling.

She settled against the crisp white dress shirt covering his chest and was pleasantly distracted by his arm under her backside. Shelby sighed and let her eyes roll closed.

Boston barked for the gawkers to get out of the way, and then he was settling her in his car.

"I'm fine," she protested, trying not to slide down off the leather passenger seat. "I just don't like blood."

"You need stitches," he said in a voice that brooked no arguments, his jaw locked.

"But the tour . . . those people . . ."

"Can all go to hell."

Easy for him to say. He didn't need those people to eat.

As he backed out the driveway, he softened his tone. "Those people will probably still be there when we get back. They got exactly what they wanted—a ghost—and it will be all over town in half an hour."

He was right, and she should be thrilled. But all she wanted to do was lean her head against the window and try not to gag.

*　　*　　*

Boston sat in the chair in the ER cubicle and watched Shelby resting on the bed, eyes closed, cheeks pale. The doctor had given her six stitches, assuring them it was a minor cut, but that the fleshy part of the hand bleeds a lot.

Boston had yet to find a part of the body that didn't bleed a lot when sliced, but Shelby had seemed reassured. They were waiting for the discharge papers from the nurse, and Boston was content just to watch Shelby lying there. He'd ditched his suit jacket and tie in the car before coming in, and he'd rolled his sleeves up, but he still felt over-dressed next to Shelby and her grubby dig-in-the-dirt outfit.

Yet he thought she was beautiful. And he was in love with her.

It was all there, clearly before him. Nothing else could explain the feeling in his chest when he'd seen Shelby clawing to stay conscious, blood running down her wrist in red rivulets. He'd experienced blind panic. The primitive urge to protect. He would have taken on a whole houseful of spirits, if need be.

This wasn't supposed to happen. The last thing in the world he'd expected when he'd been forced figuratively kicking and screaming to Cuttersville was to fall in love. But there it was, and he had indigestion.

Having never expected to ever even fall in love, he was unprepared to deal with the fact that he not only had fallen in love, but had done it with the wrong woman. Or more accurately, he was the wrong man for her. He had nothing to offer Shelby Tucker that she valued.

Her eyes fluttered open, and she gave him a weak smile. "I'm a total wimp, aren't I?"

"Nah. And you saved the *Gone With the Wind* limited-edition plates. Not many people can say that."

Shelby laughed, propped on her side. "It's only eight o'clock and I feel like going to bed."

"So do I." He didn't even try and hide the innuendo in his voice. He just let his lust hang out there for her to see and do whatever she wanted with it.

She sighed. "We can't."

"I'll be gentle," he promised, teasing a little, his heart growing heavy. She was only saying what he already knew. That they needed to stop before it got worse, before one of them got seriously hurt. Before he did something stupid like try and drag Shelby off to Chicago or promise that he'd stay in Cuttersville.

Neither one of them could make that sacrifice, and it was better to cut things off now.

Except the thought of that made him unaccountably sad.

"You know what I mean." Shelby sat up and he moved to help her. She let him touch her, hold her hand, her body soft and pliant, his. She leaned toward him, allowed him ownership. But her words said the opposite. "Last night was it, Boston. I can't have a casual affair. I thought I could, and I certainly don't regret last night, but I can't do it again. We can't . . . I'm really sorry."

So was he. But she was being honest, like he'd been honest the night before about going back to Chicago. He should have had the sense to know Shelby wouldn't be comfortable with that kind of temporary arrangement.

He should have had the sense to stay the hell away from her in the first place.

He should have quit Samson before agreeing to come to this little dot of nothing.

Because now when he left, he was going to leave a golf-ball-size piece of his heart in Cuttersville.

He stroked her hand. "I'm sorry too." More than she could ever understand.

Her gaze locked with his for a brief second, then skittered away.

No one was at the White House except Amanda and Brady when he returned from dropping Shelby off at her grandmother's.

"Where's the tour?" he asked as he walked up onto the porch.

Amanda was sitting sideways on the swing, sundress tucked around her legs stretched out in front of her. A whole hell of a lot of thigh was showing, and her efforts at modesty had only accentuated her hips and waist, the soft orange fabric clinging to her body. It didn't take a genius to figure out exactly why Brady was hanging around.

Brady was sprawled across the floor, and his grin indicated to Boston the view from below was even better.

Amanda blew out a stream of smoke from an almost-gone cigarette. "They left, Thank God. Those people are nuts. They went through every inch of your house, and some even had tape recorders."

"Don't worry. They'll be back tomorrow." Brady ground out his own cigarette on the bottom of his shoe. "Is Shel okay?"

Boston figured the hell with his suit and dropped to the porch floor next to Brady, resting his arms on his knees. "Yeah, she's okay. They stitched her up."

He couldn't prevent a hearty sigh from escaping. He

wanted to be with Shelby, taking care of her, teasing her to laugh. Instead he got blue hair Brady and orange ass Amanda to share his evening with.

"Well, I guess I'll shove off," Brady said. "I just didn't want to leave Amanda here alone."

"Thanks, man." Boston let Brady knock their fisted knuckles together before he stood up.

"Sure, Mac. Catch you later, Amanda." Brady waved and vaulted down off the porch.

Amanda exerted herself to wave, then stared at Brady's back as he headed down the street into the dusky night. "You know, it's weird to me that a fifteen-year-old would even think to give a shit about a woman he doesn't know being left by herself. Howie is like that too, and Danny Tucker. It's like a freaky sort of code of honor with the men here."

"Is that a good thing or a bad thing?" And Boston was wondering if he even came close to having it. He liked to think he did, but he'd been raised by selfish people and taught to fend for himself.

Maybe at the root of Shelby's dumping him was that she didn't think he had enough integrity for her.

That was a depressing thought.

"It's a good thing," Amanda said thoughtfully. "Though I'm not really sure why."

She started to flick her cigarette over the porch railing, then caught herself. Giving him a shrug, she dropped it into her empty Diet Coke can on the porch floor.

They sat there in silence, something he never would have expected of Amanda. But she just kicked her foot out so the swing rocked back and forth, and stared over into the copse of trees on the right of the house.

Boston drummed his thumbs on his knees, listening to the crickets and wishing something, anything was different. He'd experienced disappointment and frustrations in his life, but he had never been quite this restless, anxious, unwilling to give up. It seemed like if he thought long and hard enough, he should be able to present a solution to their problems that would address all of Shelby's concerns.

He snorted out loud. That sounded like he was going to sit down and give her a PowerPoint presentation about why she should continue to sleep with him.

"You know, Boston, I'm sorry you got sent here because of my father's hysteria."

"It's okay." If he hadn't come, he'd have never met Shelby. He'd have never appreciated that there were people who didn't give a damn about what he did for a living, or where he lived, or his net worth. He'd have never seen that there was something to be said for living in vinyl happiness on Turkey Trail.

"We'd have never been able to date each other anyway," Amanda added.

Boston looked over at her, amused. He could think of a half-dozen or so reasons why he couldn't have dated her, but he wanted to hear hers. "Why not?"

"Because the truth is, we're both too needy."

"What?" No, that was most definitely not on his list. "I'm not needy."

She gave him a patronizing smile, but it wasn't unkind. "Are too. You and me, we both grew up with workaholic parents, right?"

He couldn't deny that. He nodded.

"And while we've taken different approaches to our own lives, deep down we both just really want someone to love us. To give us that total all-consuming unconditional love."

Isn't that what everyone wanted? Of course he wanted someone to love him.

"The problem is, we want it on our terms. You want Shelby to come back to Chicago with you, don't you?"

"Yes. What's wrong with that?" Boston forced his hands to relax. He had fisted them listening to Amanda.

Amanda stretched her left leg to the floor, and her dress hiked up to the danger zone. She didn't bother to adjust it, just turned to him with a lazy sympathetic look. "But you wouldn't do the same for her."

Move to Cuttersville permanently? The very thought made a chill run up his spine. "It would be career suicide."

"I'm not asking you why, I'm just saying you wouldn't."

"So you think I'm selfish?" He whacked a mosquito that was getting too friendly with his forearm. He put more force into it than was necessary, annoyed at Amanda's probings of his psyche.

"I don't think you're selfish, I think you're needy. We put up these walls, defense mechanisms, and have standards that no one could ever possibly meet."

"What are you, my conscience?" he asked, determined to ignore that Amanda might actually be on to something.

"Your guardian angel, I think." She gave him a dimpled smile.

"More like the devil," he grumbled, rubbing his chest with his fist. He really did have a pain there, like he'd eaten overly spicy Mexican.

"No! The devil wears Prada." Amanda laughed. "This is Juicy Couture."

He rolled his eyes, amused in spite of himself. "Amanda Delmar, I do believe that your father is doing you a disservice. You have the logic of an attorney and the legs of a supermodel. You're Brett's untapped asset."

"And will remain that way," she said, all traces of amusement gone. "He sees what he wants to see."

Boston fell back onto the porch and stared up at the wooden boards of the ceiling. "I thought that by the time I reached thirty-two, I would have figured it all out. I think I was more confident at twenty than I am now."

"God, don't tell me that! I'm only twenty-five and I don't think I can get any more aimless than I already am."

He turned his head on his side and grinned. "That *would* be difficult."

Amanda stuck her tongue out at him and laughed.

Chapter Sixteen

Saturday the TV crews showed up.

Gran warned her, having fielded the phone call from the television station as the owner of the White House. They were on their way to conduct interviews and shoot footage.

Shelby ran, her gym shoes pounding the gravel harder than they had since high school track, but when she turned the corner, sweaty and out of breath, she saw she was too late. A van was in the drive, and Boston was on the porch waving his hands at the crew, looking ticked off.

Retreating would be cowardly. She only considered it for a split second. Especially since he glanced up and saw her. She offered a tentative smile and a shrug.

Lord only knew who had called the news. It certainly hadn't been her. But given the way gossip about the *Gone With the Wind* plates attacking her and Boston had ripped through town, it could have been just about anyone.

Surreptitiously wiping the perspiration off her forehead, Shelby glanced down at her outfit. It revealed to her exactly what she had expected. She looked like a slob in denim shorts and a T-shirt she'd gotten for participating in the March of Dimes. In 1997.

You wouldn't think it would be hard to take herself to the mall and just pick out a few casual, comfortable, yet moderately stylish outfits. It seemed that it was, however, because she hadn't, and here she was again, looking like a neglected stepchild.

Boston wasn't announcing her presence. In fact, he seemed to be gesturing for her to take off running, if she wanted. His head kept tilting to the side as he met her eyes. Coward though she was, she couldn't do that to him. She'd brought him more aggravation than one man should have to endure over the last three weeks, including being so monumentally stupid as to sleep with him and then suggest it was a bad idea.

Yet he still protected her.

She cleared her throat and walked right up to the porch, weaving her way through the two cameramen and stopping behind a woman wearing a floral skirt and peach sleeveless shirt. "Excuse me. I'm Shelby Tucker, the tour guide for the Haunted Cuttersville Tour, and my grandmother owns this house. Can I help you?"

The woman turned so fast Shelby feared her head might spin off. "I'm Adrienne Ashley, Channel Five Action News."

She put her hand out and Shelby took it.

Adrienne Ashley gave her hand one good pump, then abandoned it. "We would like to conduct a series of interviews with the people who witnessed the ghost sighting, run some footage of the house, that sort of thing, but Mr. Macnamara doesn't seem interested in cooperating."

Red lips pursed and her dark blond helmet hair deigned to shudder in disapproval.

Boston rubbed his jaw. "I wasn't going to do anything without Shelby's permission. It's up to her."

Shelby paused to wonder how he'd spent his day off. With Amanda? Working? She didn't even know what he liked to do in his free time, and that made her feel her decision to stop seeing him was the right one. They didn't really know each other at all.

But they could have. And they did, in the ways that mattered.

Shelby shut up her inner dialogue and tried to focus on Adrienne Ashley's long self-important nose. "Well, Ms. Ashley, I don't know."

Now that sounded intelligent. But for the life of her, she couldn't decide if it would be a good thing or a bad thing to have the White House immortalized on the eleven o'clock news. Likely, it would just embarrass them all.

Or it could bring business—big business. When Boston moved out, Gran could convert the house into a bed-and-breakfast.

Her answer didn't please the reporter, especially not when Boston nudged around her and picked up Shelby's injured hand. "How are you feeling today? Did you take a pain pill?"

He inspected her like he was waiting for her to puddle on the ground again.

"I'm fine, thanks. It doesn't even hurt." And she regretted that she'd been such a weenie about the whole thing the night before. It had made it all that much harder to stick to her guns and tell Boston they couldn't see each other. When he'd stared at her in that hospital ER, his eyes the most delicious rich blue, and looked at her like he wanted to sweep her off to a deserted island and worship at her feet, well, she'd been sorely tempted.

"If you want to do the story, I don't mind," he said in a low voice. "I want whatever you want."

She wanted him, darn it all to hell and back again.

But that wouldn't pay the bills or pop a bun in her oven, and she was first and foremost a practical person. "It makes sense to do the story. More business."

He nodded. "That's what I would do."

She was probably going to regret this, but then what was life for but regrets? Shelby made no effort to remove her hand from Boston's as she called for the reporter, who was impatiently pacing the porch. Her professional smile had warped into a gritted lip pull.

"What exactly did you have in mind?" Shelby asked.

"I want to interview everyone who was here yesterday who's willing to talk on camera. I want to tape myself walking through the home, and I'd really like to have a ghost expert come into the house and make an assessment."

"A ghost expert?" Shelby didn't like the sound of that. It seemed like a surefire way to tick Red-Eyed Rachel off, and Shelby imagined Gran wanted to keep intact whatever valuables remained in the house. "I don't think so."

Adrienne was persistent. "Well, then, how about we set the cameras up to run day and night and see what we can record? We can run this story in a special segment in a week."

"Like reality TV?" she blurted out before she could stop herself.

The reporter nodded. "In a way. But we would edit out any time when nothing's happening. We're only looking for activity. People will flock here if we get something on tape."

Oh, swell. Shelby tried to work up enthusiasm. "But then Boston would have cameras invading his privacy."

"It's only for a couple of days," Adrienne scoffed, like she wouldn't mind having a camera catching her without makeup or hair products.

Boston squeezed her hand. "I don't mind," he said, though he looked like a cow had sat on him. In pain.

"You don't have to do that!"

"My source tells me that the ghosts seem to respond with the most force when the two of you are in the house together," the reporter remarked, giving their entwined hands an interested stare.

"Who is your source?" So Shelby could hunt them down and kill them.

"Normally I don't reveal names, but since we need your cooperation in order to do this, I'll tell you. It was Brady Stritmeyer and Amanda Delmar."

"What?" Shelby squeaked. Her own flesh and blood . . .

"I guess it wasn't wise to leave them together at the house," Boston said, looking more amused than annoyed.

"What are you smiling at? You're the one who's going to get stuck with a camera watching you sleep for two days."

"Well, actually," Adrienne interjected. "I was hoping you'd stay in the house as well to ensure that we get things, uh, riled up."

She was getting all riled up, alright.

Because Boston was now grinning.

*   *   *

He should tell Adrienne Ashley, reporter, to leave Shelby out of it. He should remember his own resolve to respect her wishes and stay away from her, for both her sake and for the safety of his heart.

But it was too good of an opportunity to pass up. Shelby sharing the White House with him day and night, torturing him with her sweet natural scent and her no-nonsense attitude. It would be difficult not to want to make love to her, but with the cameras playing Peeping Tom, he figured he could control himself.

And it was a way to steal more time with Shelby before he had to leave Cuttersville behind.

It might not have been the wisest thing he'd ever done, but he nodded enthusiastically. "I think that's an excellent idea, Ms. Ashley. You can set the cameras and sound equipment up and let them run for the remainder of the weekend. Monday I have to go to work, so I need them to be removed by then."

Before Shelby could interject, he swept his arm open. "Come on in and get started."

"Excellent." Adrienne gestured to her cameraman and they went in the front door.

Ignoring the expression on Shelby's face, he said, "I'll call Brady and have him come over and keep an eye on the house while they're setting up, and I'll take you home to pick up your overnight bag."

He pictured Shelby in a filmy white nightgown, the ultrafeminine kind that stopped above the knee, with a high waist and a little ribbon running through it under her breasts.

His mouth went dry.

"I'm not spending the weekend here." Shelby didn't look as if she had filmy nightgowns on her mind as she glared at him.

"I'm doing this all for you," he said with a manipulative wheedling that should have made him feel ashamed of himself. But it didn't. "Nothing ever happens unless you're here with me, and think of the business a story like this could bring. I bet the Columbus channels pick up on it too, and you'll have more tour-goers than you know what to do with."

Shelby crossed her arms over her chest and looked torn. "You won't . . . try anything will you?"

"Why? Afraid you can't resist me?" he teased, running his thumb over her wrist that wasn't injured.

"You know I can't!" she snapped.

While he'd been fairly certain that was the case, he'd expected her to lie about it. That she didn't thrilled him. "I can't resist you either. So why are we?" He remembered there had been reasons, but they just didn't seem relevant anymore. He wanted to tuck Shelby Tucker up into his bed and romp the weekend away.

"Because."

"Because why?"

She shot him a look of exasperation and tried to tug her hand away. "Because . . . because!"

"Because because why?"

He wanted to laugh at the outrage distorting her pretty features. He should have been concerned about her unenthusiastic response, but he wasn't. In fact, he was feeling pretty damn good. Shelby was his for the weekend whether she liked it or not.

Shelby was his, period. He loved her. She made him

feel younger and happier and freer than he'd ever felt, and he didn't want to give that up. It was just going to take a little coaxing, that's all.

"Because you're a bossy brat, that's why." She wrenched her hand from his.

Okay, so a lot of coaxing. But hell, they had all weekend to work on it.

Boston leaned forward and nuzzled her neck. "Yeah, but you love me anyway."

Shelby didn't say anything, but when he looked up, the truth was there, for him to see plain as the charges on Amanda's credit card. Shelby loved him. He had been teasing, but she did.

Nothing had made him feel so triumphant, so joyous. The other stuff didn't matter. She loved him, and they would work out all the minor details later.

He cupped her cheeks, tilted her head, closed his eyes . . . and met empty air.

Shelby had ducked out of his touch and turned her back on him.

Minor details. He had all weekend to work them out.

Jessie Stritmeyer watched her grandson hang up the phone in her kitchen and grin.

"Boston wants me to come and watch the house while the TV crew is setting up."

"So he agreed?" Jessie was a little surprised, truth be told. Boston Macnamara wasn't a man who liked his hand forced.

"Yep." Brady had the nerve to pull out a cigarette and stick it in his mouth.

Jessie gave him a withering look. He tucked it back in his pocket. Blue hair or not, Jessie loved Brady as dearly as she loved Shelby. Unlike Shelby, who was wont to hang back and let life pass her by, Brady's flaw was trying to stir it up if it was too boring for his taste, which was a good deal of the time.

It was a definite that Brady would leave Cuttersville and test the waters somewhere more exciting, and Jessie was resigned to that. The trick was to see that he didn't screw his life up before he graduated high school.

Brady pushed her copper flour canister over and vaulted onto her countertop. She didn't even want to think about where the butt of his jeans had been before he'd sat them on her counter. Where she planned to fix dinner in a few hours.

"So you think Boston will really want to stay in Cuttersville?" Brady acted like no one sane would consider that.

"Men will do strange things for love," Jessie told him, hoping she was right on this one. As sure as she was that Boston was the right man for her granddaughter, she didn't want to be wrong and have Shelby hurt. "Besides, this is where his job is."

"For a while anyways. Unless Amanda has her dad assign him here permanently. Then he'd have to quit his job if he wanted to go back to Chicago."

"Except that would be manipulative." Jessie headed for the refrigerator. If Brady was going to hang around all afternoon, she might as well feed him. The kid was a goat—he'd eat anything, and all of it in large quantities.

"Isn't calling the TV channel manipulating?" Brady fiddled with a blue tip of hair.

It was possible. "If we didn't call, someone else would have."

Brady laughed and hopped off the counter. Next thing Jessie knew, he had her up in the air in a big bear hug. That was the injustice of being five foot two and having a grandson almost six feet tall and not even fully grown yet.

"Gran, remind me never to go against you." He kissed the top of her head, messing up her combed-out bob haircut.

"You remember that," she told him, unable to resist smiling and patting his cheek. "Now set me down, damn it."

Chapter Seventeen

Boston had the nerve to follow her into her bedroom. Shelby was determined not to talk to him, but when he came up the stairs in the Yellow House and down the hall and right on into her room like he had a right, she whirled on him.

"Do you mind?" Lord almighty, the man was so annoying.

His eyebrow rose. "What? I'm just trying to help you." Reaching out, he plucked a lacy pillow off her easy chair, which had been reupholstered in a pink floral chintz the summer she was sixteen.

She'd loved that chair and had requested this room in Gran's house after her divorce solely for the pink chintz. Now Boston was fondling the pillow and she knew she'd never be able to sit there again without thinking of him. Remembering their night together.

The man was disturbing her peace.

The last thing in the world she wanted was to have him invading her own private personal space and cluttering it up with memories of him. When he left, which he would, and soon, she wanted to forget him. To shove him in a little box in her heart marked PASSION, USE SPARINGLY, and keep it locked for eternity.

"I don't need your help." Shelby bent and grabbed a duffel bag from under her bed, wondering if keeping the tour going was worth the dangers of spending the weekend with him.

Truthfully, though, she wasn't doing it for the tour, which could fold and not really hurt her in the end. She had Danny to go back to, after all, or her gran would help her get back on her feet. The real reason she was agreeing to have cameras record her every move was because she was into masochism and wanted to spend this one last weekend with Boston.

Not having sex. Just being together.

Boston made a low growling sound in the back of his throat.

Whirling, she caught him staring at her behind, a feral gleam in his eye.

Shelby stuck the overnight bag behind her back, so her butt was covered with olive canvas.

"That just makes your breasts stick out," he told her.

Before she could finish a gasp, he moved to her dresser and started inspecting the objects scattered over it. Her fingers twitched with the urge just to grab everything he picked up right back out of his hand.

It was absolutely unbelievable to her that Gran had not said a single word in protest when Boston had followed her upstairs. Her grandmother had always been a stickler for Shelby not having boys in her bedroom. But then again, she was a grown woman and Gran had offered birth control advice.

"You're very neat." He said it like he was surprised.

Shelby went to her closet and pulled a couple of T-shirts off metal hangers and stuffed them in her duffel bag. "Why does that shock you?"

"You don't exactly treat your clothes with reverence." He nodded at the duffel bag.

The unmistakable feeling of a blush stole over her cheeks. "Some of us wear clothes to keep from getting sunburned and to show a measure of modesty, not to make a fashion statement."

His lip twitched. "There's functional and then there's just ugly."

Shelby wanted to get her bras and panties from the dresser, but there was no way she was doing that with him standing right there. She nudged him out of the way, opened her shorts drawer, and pulled out a pair.

"Of course, I'd be happiest to see you *out* of your clothes."

Though his words sent heat rippling through her, she glared up at him. "Are you trying to talk me out of this?"

"Of course not." He caressed the ceramic angel on her dresser. "I like seeing this side of you."

"The one that's griping at you? You see that all the time."

"No, this softer side. Angels, antique perfume bottles, floral chairs, and a lacy bedspread." Without warning, he opened the top drawer with one sharp yank. "I bet you have whimsical panties, don't you?"

Somehow instinctively he'd picked the one drawer Shelby didn't want him in, and she refused to let him see the satin push-up bras and barely there panties shoved to the back. Moving slowly so as not to alert him, she scoffed. "You've seen my panties. They're cotton and I've never thought of cotton as whimsical."

She started to pick out her biggest, softest, most faded pair when Boston's big hand slid past hers. Those hands with the sprinkling of dark hair on the backs of them shifting through all her underwear disturbed her. That seemed nearly as intimate as sex.

The bastard somehow emerged with a satin set. "Well, look what we've got here." He dangled the emerald green intimate wear up in the air. "Take this pair." With his own lack of reverence, he crammed them into the duffel bag alongside her oversized T-shirts.

"Boston . . ." Shelby warned him. One glance at the front of his jeans showed her he was picturing her wearing those ridiculous underwear.

She'd worn them only once, near the end of her marriage when she'd been desperate to crack the code on orgasms. It had been futile.

That wouldn't be the case with Boston, and her nipples knew it. They were winging out at him like tree roots to water.

Boston smiled and kissed the tip of her nose. "Let's go."

Shelby had spent the afternoon avoiding him.

Boston was frustrated and horny, not necessarily in that order.

Not to mention that if Shelby refused to be in the room

with him, there was not going to be any ghost-like activity. At least he didn't think there would. And after all, this was all for Shelby and her financial security. His nefarious plan to convince her to make love to him, marry him, and move to Chicago was just a side bonus since they were alone together.

Except she wouldn't come near him.

When they'd discovered the cameras were in place and the crew and Adrienne Ashley were out interviewing witnesses, Boston had sent Brady home and prepared to coax Shelby out of her clothes. She was faster than he was, though, and had disappeared in the yellow bedroom with her bag, shutting the door in his face.

Three hours ago.

He'd thought about knocking on the door but had been afraid she was actually taking a nap and hadn't wanted to wake her. But he was bored and restless. He'd worked in the parlor for a while, clearing out his e-mail and leaving a few messages for Monday morning.

But then he had found himself standing outside Shelby's door again listening with his ear pressed to the wood to see if she was awake and moving around. Nothing. She was either asleep or she'd crawled out the window and shimmied down a tree. He wouldn't put it past her.

Edgy, he went down to the kitchen to distract himself with food. Mary was coming in the back door.

"Hello, Boston." She gave him a wide smile in her soft round face.

Boston had a real fondness for Mary. She popped in right when he really needed her, and she baked some mean sugar cookies with little candies pressed into them. She was no stranger to a Pledge can either, and kept him out from under a layer of dust.

"Hi there, Mary. How are you today?" Boston leaned against the counter and tried not to salivate. Surely Mary would cook something for him.

The TV channel's camera was on the refrigerator, he noticed, and the red light blinked steadily, showing him it was recording.

"I'm fine, as usual." Mary set down a package wrapped in brown paper and string. "I baked you some raisin bread."

"Thank you." He wondered if it would be rude to dive for it.

Mary didn't keep him waiting. She reached for a knife, cut the string, and unwrapped the bread. "I hear Shelby's staying here."

"Yes, for the weekend. In the yellow bedroom." He didn't want to lose his housekeeper by offending her.

"She loves you, you know." Mary sliced the bread, not looking at him.

Boston was a little startled. "I hope she does," he said honestly. "Do you know Shelby?"

"Since she was a little girl." Mary pointed the knife at him. "And she's worth the sacrifice, Boston Macnamara."

"What sacrifice?" He felt a little uneasy for some reason. The conversation seemed odd.

"Here you are," Mary said briskly, the loaf fully sliced. "I'll be back to do the house on Monday."

And she left, as quickly as she'd arrived.

Boston bit into the bread and wondered.

He'd almost finished the loaf when Shelby walked in. Her presence was announced by her stomach growling in the quiet room.

"Where did you get that?" she asked.

"From Mary." He took the last remaining slice and walked over to her. He held it in front of her lips.

She didn't take it. "Who's Mary?" Something like jealousy laced her voice.

Which was satisfying, but amusing. Mary was fifty if he was inclined to be generous. "My housekeeper."

"You have a housekeeper?"

"Yeah. She came with the house." He tapped her lip with the bread.

"What's her last name? I never heard of a Mary who cleans this house."

"I don't know. She's older, wears a bun and an apron. Makes great bread."

Shelby opened and took a bite. "Mmmm. It's good. But you know, I think your housekeeper is dead."

"Why? What she'd do? The bread is awesome."

Her head shook back and forth. "No, I mean, she's dead. Like she died fifty years ago."

"Whatever." He leaned forward and kissed the crumb off the corner of her mouth.

"You don't care?"

"I don't believe you." Nor did he care, for that matter. Boston wrapped an arm around her waist.

"Rewind the tape, Boston! We might have caught a spirit on tape!"

If he hadn't been so interested in kissing that shiny spot in the corner of her mouth, he might have stopped and thought about what she was saying. But after a frustrating afternoon he finally had her in his arms.

She shoved him.

Or not.

"Stop it! The camera is right on us."

"And if it wasn't?"

"I still wouldn't want you to."

"Why?" he asked in annoyance, knowing it wasn't smart to push Shelby but unable to stop himself.

"You know why," she said with one of those cryptic female statements that means nothing to a man except that he won't be getting any. She gestured to the camera.

Boston raked his hand through his hair.

Shelby smiled a little. Her finger reached up and touched his head, brushing her arm against his and giving him a taunting view of her lips hovering near his.

"Bread crumb." She dropped it in the sink. "Now don't you want to take out the tape and see if Mary was recorded? That would really be something to show that reporter."

Yeah, his housekeeper slicing bread. Exciting stuff. He'd seen Mary, talked to her many times, and there was no way she was a spirit. No dead person in their right mind would hang around washing a man's dirty clothes and scrubbing the toilet.

"Want to watch a movie first?" he asked, trying not to sound desperate. If she retreated to her bedroom again, he was going to either howl in frustration or just beat down the door and drag her out à la King Kong. He didn't think she'd appreciate either gesture.

"What movie?" Her voice dripped with suspicion.

Did she suspect him of wanting to entice her with porn? "Whatever you want. Amanda rented twelve videos yesterday because she couldn't decide what she wanted to see. Then she realized she couldn't watch twelve videos in three days so she brought me eight of them."

The TV in the parlor was small and the VCR ancient, but they worked.

Shelby rolled her eyes, but laughed. "We don't need the Haunted Cuttersville news story; we have Amanda as a one-woman boon to the local economy."

"Too bad she won't be here very long."

The smile fell off her face. "Yeah, too bad."

And it hung in the air between them, the fact that he was leaving not long after Amanda.

"Shelby, we need to talk . . ." He reached for her.

She turned away from him. "I don't want to talk about this on camera," she whispered urgently. Popping another bit of bread in her mouth, she tried to smile. "Now let's go watch a movie."

Chapter Eighteen

If he touched her one more time, she was going to pull a Red-Eyed Rachel and clobber him.

Oh, he wasn't being obvious about it. He wasn't actually trying anything. But at regular intervals he was managing to stick his sexy man hands somewhere on her body, and it had her so wound up and sexually stimulated that one more arm brush was liable to make her groan out loud.

Picking a horror movie had seemed like a good move, since there wouldn't be any sexual innuendos at all. But Boston had just used it as an excuse to turn the lights out to view the film with full effect. And in spite of herself, she couldn't help jumping from time to time or shuddering in fear, and there he was, all over her with comforting hugs and massaging fingers on the back of her neck.

By the time the darn credits rolled, she was just about in his lap.

His arm was wrapped around her, and in spite of herself, she managed to let her head rest on his shoulder. And it was such a nice shoulder. Strong, but not brawny. It didn't slump or slouch, but stayed upright, solid, aggressive. A man who liked to win.

Like he was going to tonight. He wanted her, had been very honest about it. And he was just going to be there, ready, when she gave in.

Shelby was already giving in. He smelled so good, a musky soapy scent that tickled her nose and reminded her of what it had felt like to be under him out in the cornfield. From time to time his bare feet brushed over hers, and his soft jeans were thin and worn and she could feel the heat from his thighs under hers.

The red blinking light of the Channel Five camera kept her sane.

When his finger brushed over her breast, she shoved away from him. "The camera," she said under her breath, curling her legs under her on the opposite side of the couch.

Boston didn't say anything, and she thought she'd finally made him angry. But when she looked, he was standing and eating up the parlor with long determined strides. He yanked the camera from the curio cabinet and turned it off. "There, it's off."

Uh-oh. He set it down none too gently and turned to her. It was too dark to see his expression but she could feel his frustration, his desire, rolling off him in pulsing waves and just about knocking her over flat.

"It's not just about the camera," she said, crossing her arms so he wouldn't think she was actually interested in responding to him.

"What is it about?" He took several steps toward her, the moonlight from the lace-covered windows spilling over him in a spidery pattern. "I know you said you don't want to have a casual affair, but I don't see how it can be called casual when I'm in love with you."

Shelby froze. "Come again?" He could not have said that, she must have misunderstood, because it was just plain ridiculous for Boston Macnamara, city slicker extraordinaire, to have fallen in love with her, Shelby Tucker.

He leaned over, putting his arms on either side of her, boxing her in between his chest and the floral sofa. "I'm in love with you. Never in thirty-two years have I told a woman those words, so I hope you appreciate the enormity of what I'm saying to you."

Shelby's feet fell to the floor as her heart swelled. Oh, Lord, he loved her. That was so wonderful and incredible and tragically horrible. She sucked in a shuddering breath and lightly touched the front of his chest.

"Oh, Boston. I love you too, I really do."

His jaw twitched, and a sigh of relief fell from his lips. She stroked his chin, felt the stubbly beard growing there, brought his face down to hers. The kiss he took and she gave was passionate, open, vulnerable, tongues meeting with a kind of aching appreciation.

The video had rewound and ejected and the TV was a bright blue screen, sending an eerie cobalt glow across Boston's skin as he stood up and ripped his shirt off in one forward motion.

"Can I make love to you, Shelby? I want to show you what you mean to me." His hands were on his leather belt with the silver buckle, and she could see how important this was to him.

It was to her as well. When he left, which he would, she couldn't go with him. She wanted to be with him one last time, knowing they both loved each other.

"Let me make love to you first," she said and scooted forward on the sofa.

Her fingers brushed his aside and she undid his belt. He swore and pushed her away.

"You don't have to do that."

"I want to." She wanted to see him, to feel him. Popping his snap, she kissed his stomach, enjoyed the jerk he gave when her lips touched him.

There was a soft cluster of dark hair there that she nibbled at. She let her hands roll over his stomach, his sides, his tightly muscled back, wanting to taste him and explore, learn every inch of him.

He was standing still, but he wasn't passive. His muscles were tense, his breathing labored and hard, his hands gripping her shoulders.

She took down his zipper, ran her fingers over the bulge in his boxer shorts, peeled back his jeans on either side. Then she nibbled at that bump, feeling the heat kiss her nose and lips as she tugged on the material and rubbed across him.

"Shelby . . ."

"Am I doing this wrong?" She hesitated, concerned that her pleasure wasn't pleasing him.

"Absolutely not. You're just making me insane with want, that's all."

A glance up showed his eyes were closed. He looked tortured and vulnerable. It made her swallow a small moan and clench her thighs together. "Have other women done this to you?" she asked, knowing the answer, not even sure why she was asking. She didn't want to imagine cool blond businesswomen down on their knees in front of Boston.

She reached into his boxers and pressed her hand against his hot skin, finding him on the first try this time, even in the dark.

"Yes. But not one of them ever made me feel like this."

"Like what?" She took a tentative lick across the head of his penis.

Boston shuddered. "Out of control. Immersed. Totally and completely in love."

She covered him with her mouth and took the length of him into her as he swore again, cruder this time. Shadows covered them both, making Shelby feel bolder, more curious, more willing to go with her desires and throw caution aside. Hands on his hard thighs, she pulled him in and out, over and over, shocked at how with each stroke her own need grew and built and ached for release.

Slippery and eager, her lips fell off him and they both groaned in agony.

"Oh, Boston, you taste so good." Pausing only to lick the bead of fluid squeezing out, Shelby closed her mouth over him again, flushed with passion, excitement, love.

The room was hot, the air still and humid, the only sounds the hum of the TV, the steady whirl of the ceiling fan, and their rapid breathing. Boston's hips rocked to meet her, a fast hard rhythm, and then suddenly he was gone.

She blinked up at him, wiping her lips, struggling to see him. "What's the matter?" she whispered, already reaching forward again.

He'd moved back, then he spoke, voice hoarse. "No. I'm going to come if you don't stop."

"What's wrong with that?"

Boston dropped to his haunches and held her face between hands that trembled. "I want to be inside you. I want to feel your body wrapped around mine, and I want my eyes locked with yours when we both come together."

He kissed her with such tenderness, such awe, that Shelby thought she might actually cry, something she hadn't done since she'd lost out on head cheerleader to Mitzy Garvey in the tenth grade.

"You know that you're beautiful." Boston pulled back and took her T-shirt off over her head, wishing it weren't so dark so he could see her luscious body. The light from the TV and the filtered moonlight drizzled over her, but it didn't give him the golden glow of her skin, or the pink of her nipples as he dragged her bra down in the front.

"But you hate my clothes, don't you?" she said with a laugh, brown eyes round and shining with moisture.

"Yes," he said enthusiastically, stroking his tongue along the swell of her breast. He didn't want to see Shelby in something that wasn't her personality, like a suit or a designer cocktail dress, but he really didn't think sack-like cotton shirts and shorts reflected her uniqueness either. "Except for those tight shorts and that sexy little halter top you wore when you took me on the tour. That was a hot outfit."

"I think it was off me more than it was on me."

Boston sucked her nipple lightly. "Exactly. It turned me on, so I took it off."

"I like that you wear jeans, yet somehow it never looks casual. It turns me on, so take them off," she said, digging her nails into his head.

He tasted her whole breast, from one end to the other and back again. "And you had the nerve to tell me *I'm* bossy."

"Do it," she said, taking her breasts out of his reach by

sitting back on the couch. In a second, the bra was tumbling to the floor and she was wiggling out of her shorts effortlessly since they were so loose on her.

Boston didn't want to be left behind, so he shoved his jeans down and kicked them aside. His boxers dropped beside them, and he positioned himself over Shelby on the couch. "Lie down, and spread your legs for me."

He almost expected her to tell him to go to hell. But he underestimated Shelby and her ability to drive him mindless with lust.

She fell back, ponytail pushing her hair out on either side of her face, her small lips open, her tongue trailing across the bottom with instinctive sensuality. Her arms went up on either side of her head, her white bandage still covering her stitches. Her breasts pushed out toward him, round and smooth and glowing in the moonlight. Her stomach rose and fell with her breathing, and as he focused on her nest of curls, she dropped her knees and spread her legs for him.

"Perfect," he said with a fascinated nod.

He was holding himself over her and wanted to just push inside her, but he had forgotten a condom. He fell down onto her lightly, and rushing his lips over her belly, he felt around on the floor for his jeans. He'd been carrying condoms in his pants pockets hoping optimistically for a repeat performance, and whether in a barn or a field or the living room, he had wanted to be prepared.

Thank God.

Shelby didn't complain about his weight pressing on her, just wiggled restlessly under him, stroking his back and nudging her hot little mound into his thigh. He could feel her heat, her moisture, and it made him blind with impatience. She kissed his chin, his neck, while he hooked a finger through the pocket of his pants and hauled them toward him.

A second later, he had the condom on and was stroking between her thighs, making sure she was ready for him. She was more than ready, and she whimpered as his fingers slid over her.

"I want you to know," Boston said as he nudged gently with the tip of his cock, "that I really . . ."

He sank just inside her.

"Do . . ."

Straining for control, he went a little deeper.

"Love . . ."

He thrust fully inside her, taking all of her, her muscles clamping on to him, her chin tipped up, her eyes warm with answering emotion.

"You." Boston paused, throbbing, unbelievably close to exploding, wanting to savor the moment, to memorize her face the way it looked right then.

Her legs locked around his back, pulling him deeper into her. Shelby panted, little sounds of passion, her hands gripping the arm of the couch. He needed her to say she loved him—he wasn't going to move until she did, no matter what it cost him. He had to hear it, had to know that he mattered, that she was his to take and keep and live with for the rest of forever.

"Do you love me too, Shelby?"

Shelby was overwhelmed by the riotous feelings ripping through her as Boston caressed the corner of her mouth with his lips and pulsed inside her with an intimacy she'd never experienced. Every inch of her was alive with pleasure, streaming with passion, aching with want.

She felt his vulnerability, was humbled herself by it, was amazed that this man could feel what he did for her. "Yes, Boston, I absolutely do love you too."

"Good." He took her mouth with his and moved inside her, with a wild edgy abandoned thrust that had them both skating into violent release a minute later.

It swept over her, hard and fast and unexpected, and she clung to him, calling out his name, drowning in sensation and ecstasy. Boston dropped onto her, a crushing weight that felt so real and solid she didn't even object.

Turning her head and sucking in air, Shelby didn't see his face when he spoke. He was kissing her forehead when he murmured, "Come back to Chicago with me."

Shelby lost all ability to breathe, and it wasn't because he was lying on her. "What? Why would you want that?"

He laughed softly. "Were you sleeping when I told you I'm in love with you? That's why. Come to Chicago. Marry me. Make my apartment a home."

That was so not fair of him to dangle something like that in front of her. She shoved at his chest to get him to back up a little, give her a measure of space. "Boston, I can't do that. I can't leave Cuttersville, you know that."

He eased out of her reluctantly and gave her such a look of puzzlement, Shelby understood that he truly didn't get it. Boston didn't have the kind of family that mattered and so he didn't understand.

"I can't leave Gran, and my mom, my cousins. And I'd never fit in in Chicago. I'd get lost on the subway thingy, thieves would peg me as an easy hit, and all those women prancing around with fancy jobs and even fancier black wardrobes would leave me feeling like a country cow."

The very thought of living in the city made her feel

claustrophobic. Shelby sat up and fished her panties back out of her shorts with a sigh. She hadn't wanted it to end like this, so soon. She had been hoping that once, just once, she could spend the whole night in Boston's arms. "Why don't you stay here in Cuttersville?"

Boston raked his hands through his short hair. "I can't. When my boss says I have to leave, I have to. And how do you know you wouldn't love Chicago? It's a great town. You could go to college if you wanted to, and get a real job. I'd pay for it."

Shelby froze in the act of skimming into her underwear. "I have a real job. And I don't need you to pay for me to better myself. I happen to like the way I am right now just fine."

"That's not what I meant." Boston was back in his own boxers and dragging on his jeans. "I just meant if money was holding you back, I have that."

Tears were in her eyes, and Shelby had no patience for them. She blinked hard and reached for her T-shirt. "You don't get it, Boston. I don't need money to make me happy. Never have, never will. And while you can give me money, you can't give me what I really want."

Even in the dark she could see his stony gray eyes. "What is it that you want?"

The last thing she'd wanted was to hurt him, but she had to be honest, here and now before they both starting spinning fantasies about working things out. "I want to live here in Cuttersville close to my family. I want a creaky old house just like this with antiques older than Gran. I want a husband who loves me and doesn't care when I wear grubby shirts. I want children, a family of my own that I can raise right here in the same way Gran and my mom raised me."

There was a long pained silence. "You're deluding yourself if you think any man alive would prefer you in dirty baggy shirts over a tight tank top."

He'd either missed the whole damn point or he was being deliberately dumb. "Tell me, honestly, can you give me any of those things? Can you be content to live here without access to hair products? Can you say that it wouldn't bother you if I stayed at home and raised . . . children?" She'd almost said *our* children then had caught herself because it was too painful to say that out loud. "I know you. You don't understand that lack of ambition."

"I don't understand your willingness to just throw in the towel on us without even trying or talking about options." He stood up, brushed her bare leg with his jeans. "Clearly you've made up your mind already."

Shelby didn't know what she'd done except make a huge elephant-ass-size mistake. She never should have slept with Boston, she never should have told him about her feelings, she never should have even spoken to him the first day she'd met him. "Boston, I'm trying to fix this before we hurt each other worse."

Suddenly he bent over, so fast that she jumped. He pressed her shirt and shorts against her bare breasts with a scowl. "Do me a favor. Put some clothes on before we continue this discussion."

Embarrassed, she got dressed. "What else is there to say?"

"Just tell me that you'd rather take a chance on staying here and never getting married or having the kids you want than come to Chicago with me. Just tell me that."

Shelby had never been the type who knew how to soothe and comfort, or say the right thing to defuse a situation. She was honest and direct, and before Boston, she hadn't had a relationship with another man besides Danny since she was fifteen. She didn't know how to do this. "Danny asked me to marry him again."

That was the wrong thing to say.

She could feel Boston's hurt and anger, even before he spoke, his voice tight, hard, cool. "When?"

"A couple of weeks ago." Shelby stood up, unable to sit still anymore, hating what she was doing to him, knowing that she had to if she wanted to retain her own bit of sanity and not agree to do whatever he wanted. To not stupidly agree to go with him and then hate every minute of it, hurting them both worse in the long run.

A professional mask had slid over Boston's face. He watched her, assessing, but calm and in control. "And you're going to say yes?" he asked conversationally, like they'd run into each other at the grocery. His hands were clenched into fists, though, revealing more than he probably wanted to.

Shelby could picture him at work, intimidating and always, always coming out on top.

"I was thinking about it."

Very slowly, he leaned back against the end table next to the sofa. "I see. So all this time, while you were making love to me, you were thinking about marrying Danny Tucker."

When put that way, it sounded so gosh darn awful. She'd just sent things from bad to hell in a handbasket. "Boston . . ."

"Shelby," he said with barely contained control, though it felt like someone had hacked out his insides with a machete, "I'm asking you to get your things and leave. I really prefer you didn't spend the night."

She stood there in front of him, rumpled and sexy, her lips still swollen from his kisses, and knew she had just taken the piece of him he'd given her and thrown it back in his face. "Boston, let's talk about this. Marrying Danny would be the practical thing to do."

"Fuck practical." His determination to be rational, calm, unemotional shattered. "I told you that I love you. And you stand there and say you want to go back to a man who can't even give you an orgasm?"

"That's not fair. I was young . . ." She stuck her fingers on her temples and squeezed. "I can't believe I'm having this discussion with you, God. This isn't fair to Danny. I shouldn't have told you."

Her concern was for *Danny*?

Boston couldn't take any more. He wanted to be alone with his hurt, to tamp it down in private. It was a trick he was good at. When he'd been a child and his parents had fought or rejected his attempts to gain their attention, he'd gotten very good at hiding it, nursing his wounds off by himself.

"Shelby, I'll go upstairs and get your bag. You can continue the tour in the mornings, but I'm going to have to ask you not to do the five o'clock tour anymore. I don't want to have to be here for that."

Her mouth worked, but she didn't say anything.

"I hope that you'll be very happy as the farmer's wife, but I'd prefer not to receive an invitation to the wedding." He gave what he hoped was a passable smile.

The thought of her marrying Danny Tucker, warming his bed, taking him into her mouth, had him heading for the door with Olympic sprint speed.

"Oh, Boston," she said, touching his arm as he moved past her.

That sound of pity was like acid on an open wound.

He was saved from having to reply by the TV turning off and the lights turning on, plunging them both into artificial brightness and temporarily blinding him.

"What the hell?" He blinked against the glaring lamplight and looked around the room. All three lamps plus the hall light were on, and the red light of the camera he knew he'd turned off glowed.

"Uh . . ." Shelby was suddenly at his side, standing so close he wanted to throttle her.

Didn't she know he could smell her? Feel her arm brushing his? Didn't she know he was suffering the agonizing painful death of hope while they stood there?

He didn't give a shit if the ghosts in this nuthouse stood up and did the macarena. He wanted to be alone almost as much as he wanted Shelby. As his wife.

The spirits didn't do any line dances, but every cushion on the sofa and the numerous chairs throughout the room were slung to the floor by unseen hands like a toddler throwing a tantrum. The drawers on the occasional tables jerked out with harsh squeaking sounds, and the distinct stomping of angry footsteps did a circle around the coffee table.

For once, Boston felt in total sympathy with Red-Eyed Rachel. If Shelby wasn't standing next to him, he just might throw a tantrum along with her.

"Someone's having a mighty big hissy fit," Shelby said in awe, grabbing on to his arm. "Shouldn't we leave?"

"And miss the fun?" But he did move Shelby behind him, closer to the hallway if it should become necessary to run or dodge flying objects.

"I don't think anybody's having fun in here."

Twin candelabras left the fireplace mantel and bounced on the hardwood floor with an ear-splitting rattle.

Boston wanted to stay, amazed and almost awed by what he was seeing in front of his very skeptical eyes. And it matched his own mood so profoundly, he was almost amused. But he gave Shelby a little nudge. "Just back out of the room, Shel, and go out onto the porch."

Her anxious breathing was loud in the suddenly still room, the silence ominous, the air shifting, waiting. He heard Shelby take two steps backward. And scream.

Whirling around, he saw her standing in front of the pocket door, arms up, statue still. Over her head he saw a man leaning against the door, with thick blond hair and prominent sideburns. He wore a black double-breasted suit and had his head cocked slightly to the left, like he wasn't sure what he was seeing. A puzzled frown was on his face, then he wavered, dissipated, was gone.

Shelby turned back to him. "The Blond Man, Boston, that's who that was!" She covered her mouth. "But he wasn't smiling. He's supposed to always be smiling."

A little stunned by what he could swear he'd seen, yet what seemed so unbelievable, Boston shook his head. "Maybe he doesn't like Rachel's antics."

Or theirs. Maybe the guy was smarter than both he and Shelby and saw they were making a mistake.

It certainly felt like one.

Chapter Nineteen

Shelby had been putting it off long enough.

So she had called Danny and asked him to come meet with her at the Yellow House. He was due any minute, and she paced the length of the porch wondering how she would tell him that she couldn't marry him.

In the week since she'd made love to Boston in the parlor, Shelby had had a lot of time to think. Too much time, despite the numerous TV interviews and influx of ghost gawkers. Because every time she spoke, she thought of Boston. And every time she thought of him, she had a whole series of doubts that ran through her head.

Doubts that maybe she'd made a mistake. Doubts that maybe love was worth giving up everything she knew. Doubts that she could ever find happiness or passion with another man.

Certainly not with Danny. It wasn't fair to him, and it wasn't fair to her. She would be half a wife to him, and that was fifty percent less than he deserved.

Knowing that didn't make it any easier to say, though. By the time Danny bounded up the steps with confidence and a pleasant smile, Shelby was sweating like a cold Coke can.

"Hey, Shel, what's up?" He kissed her on the forehead. "Is anything wrong?"

"Yes. We have a problem." Shelby stuck her hands in her pockets, walked a few paces, took a rigid pass by the porch swing, then circled back around. She stopped in front of him, took a deep breath, met his eyes.

"Danny, I've thought about this a lot. It's been a really difficult decision for me, because I truly do love you as a person, but . . . I can't marry you. It wouldn't be fair to you."

While she held her breath, he just blinked, then gave a big sigh, crushing her with the simple sadness behind it. "That's okay, Shel. I kind of thought you'd say no."

"Why?" she asked, curious.

"Because your heart is on your sleeve, honey. You've fallen for Boston, big-time."

Fresh pain shot through her, and she fought the tears that instantly threatened. She wasn't dealing well with the idea that she'd fallen in love with the wrong man. It just seemed to confirm her idiocy, and that wasn't a pleasant thing. "Boston and I aren't seeing each other anymore."

He studied her. "I'm sorry to hear that. Maybe you'll work it out. You're both nuts about each other."

"Some things you can't fix, and this is one of them. But my feelings for him don't have anything to do with my saying no to you." Shelby took his hand, stroked it. "You're my first love, Danny Tucker, and that's a special thing. I don't regret one minute we spent together. But we can't get married for the wrong reasons . . . because we both want kids and we're comfortable together."

"I think a lot of marriages have started on less."

"That's true. And we could have a good marriage. But I think we both deserve great. I think we should take a chance, risk it, that there's someone out there for us both that we can fall madly in love with." Of course, she already had, but that was beside the point. Maybe there was another man . . . who was she kidding? It was over for her. Time to start her cat collection and slowly grow into eccentric Miss Shelby. But this way, if she didn't marry Danny, there was still hope that he could find true love and live happily ever after.

"Madly in love? I don't picture me falling madly into anything. I'm not exactly a dramatic guy, Shel." Danny gave a grin. "But no, I really do understand what you're saying. And a month ago, I wouldn't have agreed with you. But I don't know, I've been thinking maybe it's time for me to date around a bit, enjoy myself. I've got plenty of years to have kids and I want to get married for keeps this time around."

"It will be a lucky woman who gets you." Shelby meant it. Danny was a good man, and she almost wished she could have loved him. Almost, because if she had, she'd have never fallen in love with Boston, and despite the pain in her chest and the ache in her abdomen, she couldn't regret meeting him.

Danny gave her one of those bear hugs that lifted her off her feet and compromised her breathing. "Let's hope she thinks so," he said, bouncing her a little for good measure.

Shelby fell to the porch and checked her ribs for fractures. Gasping, she said, "Let's hope she's too big for you to pick up."

He laughed. "So you going to keep on with the Haunted Cuttersville Tour then?"

"Actually, all the news exposure of the little incident last week already doubled my business this past weekend. What I really want to do is talk Gran into letting me use the White House as a bed-and-breakfast. I'd really enjoy running that, and I could have Brady do the actual legwork for the tours."

"But Boston's living in the White House still. I saw him just yesterday, having a beer with some of the Samson guys at Walt's."

While it didn't exactly thrill her to hear that Boston was out socializing at the local bar and grill, she wasn't surprised. Boston wasn't a brooder. He was an action-oriented person.

But that didn't mean she thought for one minute he liked the local scene enough to stick around longer than was absolutely necessary. He'd made that clear as crystal.

"Trust me, Danny, Boston Macnamara is leaving, sooner than later. I wouldn't be surprised if he leaves next week."

Boston supposed he ought to be startled, but he couldn't work up the energy. When he opened his front door and saw Brett Delmar watching him with raised eyebrows, he merely nodded.

"Brett. How good to see you. What brings you to Cuttersville?"

As if he couldn't guess. He held open the door and gestured for Brett to step inside, which he did, his hand resting casually in his pants pocket, his blue button-up shirt neatly ironed.

"I wanted to check on the Cuttersville plant for myself," Brett said with enough credible nonchalance to make Boston appreciate how he'd catapulted himself to the top of the plastics industry.

"I also wanted to see how you're doing here. What with you living in a haunted house and all."

Boston winced. Here it came.

"And I wanted to see my daughter."

He'd been waiting for that. Boston went into the parlor and offered Brett a seat. He sank himself onto the sofa and surreptitiously rubbed his eyes. He was getting a headache. "I'm sure she'll be pleased to see you."

"Charming interview she gave on television about her experiences with the undead."

"Uhh . . . you saw that?" That was one thought that had never entered his head when he'd been trying to secure Shelby's business by agreeing to tape in the house and allow interviews.

"It's been a slow news week apparently. The entire Midwest has picked up the specialty piece on two Chicagoans in rural Ohio subjected to the harassment of restless ghosts."

"Amanda never even saw any ghosts. What did she say in her interview?"

"Oh, she was appropriately skeptical, yet played it so that in the end you believed in everything from levitation to reincarnation. My daughter is quite convincing when she wants to be."

Brett didn't look amused by that, or proud.

Boston said, "I haven't seen the show. I understand it was made to look a little sensational." Including the reporter focusing in on the segment where Boston had walked into the room, the tape went blank while three and a half minutes elapsed according to the footage, then he was shown eating his sliced bread that had appeared out of nowhere. Boston hadn't seen Mary since that night, and wasn't sure he wanted to. It seemed a little risky to eat chicken cooked by a dead housekeeper, even a friendly one.

Brett snorted. "*Sensational* would be an accurate assessment."

"Did they name the company?" Boston was starting to sweat under his T-shirt, realizing the implications of what he'd done. Brett could be here to fire him for bringing bad publicity to Samson.

"Yes." Brett said nothing more, but stood up. "Is Amanda upstairs? I would like to speak to her."

"Amanda? She doesn't live here. I guess she's at her own house, but I'm not really sure. I haven't talked to her since Tuesday." Boston drummed his fingers on his knees. "You can call her cell phone."

It hadn't seemed like anything could get worse than losing Shelby. Yet losing his job might just add to the fun summer he was having, given the thunderous look on Brett's face.

"You mean Amanda isn't living with you?"

"No, and we're not seeing each other either." He would have thought that would make Brett happy, but it didn't appear to be having that effect. His boss was a trim, healthy, in-shape guy in his mid-fifties. He wasn't losing hair, didn't have a gut, and never seemed out of breath. Right now he looked like he could have a coronary on the plum-colored throw rug.

"She told me she was going to New York to visit friends. But she came here for you, I know she did. That's why I sent you here in the first place, to get you out of her reach. But if she's not with you, what is she doing here?"

Exploring America didn't seem like the answer to give Brett. And truthfully, he didn't really know what Amanda was still doing in Cuttersville. He would have expected her to be long gone by now. Like he wanted to be.

Despite the fact that he'd reconciled himself to Cuttersville, and that he enjoyed living in his big old house, which hadn't had a hint of haunting since he'd last seen Shelby, he wanted to leave. Because every time he stepped into the Busy Bee or drove past Hair by Harriet, or saw Brady, he thought of Shelby.

And wanted her all over again.

He was losing sleep, struggling to concentrate, feeling beyond miserable, and he wanted to slide back into his old life and forget he'd ever spent the summer hot and dusty and with the woman he wanted to marry.

"I don't know what Amanda's doing here, Brett, to be perfectly honest with you. I would have thought she'd have left two weeks ago."

"She does it to annoy me," Brett said flatly.

Boston stood up, not sure how far he could go, but he spoke anyway. "She just wants some attention from you."

Brett looked unimpressed. "She's not a child. If she wants to talk to me, she can call me, not play these damn annoying games that have me worried half to death she'll get herself raped and murdered in some godforsaken place."

Boston didn't know a thing about fatherhood, but he could see the concern on Brett's face and he felt for him. But he also felt like he should talk to his daughter. "Let me give you directions to where she's staying. Then I'm requesting that you transfer me back to Chicago. The plant here is well run, and I'm superfluous."

His boss paused and looked him over before nodding. "I'd be happy to grant your request."

But it wasn't relief that surged through Boston, it was sickening regret.

The problem was, when you had a good plan, there were other people who just went and messed it up. Take Boston and Shelby for instance, Jessie Stritmeyer thought as she weeded out her petunias, cursing the prickers. Damn things had the flowers in a chokehold.

What was Boston about, leaving Cuttersville? She had walked that horse to water, knew for a fact that he'd even taken a drink, and yet he'd just strolled right out of the pasture.

She didn't like being wrong. She didn't like being right and having no one listen to her.

Jessie yanked with fervor, tossing a spiny plant into her lawn refuse bag.

It was time to have a talk with her granddaughter.

Chapter Twenty

There was miserable, then there was scum-sucking, life-draining, pit-of-despair agony. Shelby was experiencing the latter.

As she dragged herself through to the end of another day, she wondered why doing the right thing was so god-damn awful. Stepping into the Yellow House, she pulled at her sticky hot T-shirt and reminded herself that she had done what she had thought was best in breaking things off with Boston.

There hadn't been any better options, and when she walked herself back through her thought process, she could see that she'd made the only logical decision. If the last two weeks had been something akin to hell on earth, well, she'd get better eventually.

"Shelby Louise, come in the kitchen. I need to talk to you."

Gran sounded crotchety, which was a little out of char-
acter. Shelby sighed and forced her feet to take her in that
direction. She was bone tired, not sleeping well at night,
and taking tours through the now-empty White House was
like a fresh slap every day.

She loved Boston Macnamara. And she had sent him
away.

No. He had left, and she'd do well to remember that.

"Hey, Gran, how are you?" Shelby kissed Gran's cheek
as she came into the kitchen.

Her grandmother was standing by the sink, making iced
tea and looking severe. She had on aqua blue capri pants
and a white shirt with a little nautical anchor front and cen-
ter, making Shelby feel a little better. She may not have
Boston, but she had a family who loved her.

"Shelby Louise, I'm kicking you out."

Or not. "What! What do you mean?"

"I mean you have until the end of the month to find another place to live." Gran stirred the pitcher of tea vigorously before setting it on the windowsill above the sink.

To say that she was shocked was an understatement.
She was flabbergasted, and hurt. "Why? Do you want me
to pay rent? I can do that, Gran?" Shelby just didn't think
she could deal with finding another place to live right then.
She wanted comfort, the familiar.

"The rent is six hundred."

"I can't afford that!"

"Guess you'll have to move out, then. Now you can do
a couple of things. You can move in with your mother."

And listen to her mother and Dave cooing over each
other night and day. Shelby shuddered.

"You can find an apartment. Or you can haul your butt

up to Chicago and throw yourself at Boston. I'm hoping that's the one you'll pick."

So that was what this was all about. Gran wanted her to get back together with Boston. Yeah, well, Shelby wanted that too, but this was the real world.

"Gran . . . I can't do that. I can't live in Chicago, away from all of you. What kind of job would I get? It's not practical. I'd hate it there."

"How the hell do you know?" Gran asked with a vehemence that had Shelby opening her eyes wide. "You've barely ever even left Cuttersville. You might love it there."

Which was what Boston had said and what someone always says when they're trying to convince you to do something you don't want to do. "I don't want to leave my family."

Gran's face softened. She put her wrinkled hand on Shelby's cheek. "Shelby, honey, I don't want you to go either. I've loved having you here in the house with me for the last three years. But the good thing about family is you can take us for granted. We'll always be here, we'll always love you, and there will always be room for you."

"For six hundred dollars," Shelby retorted, though secretly pleased to hear Gran liked having her around.

"Wiseass." Gran patted her face, then dropped her hand. Her eyes, the same cocoa brown as Shelby's own, studied her. "But you've got to have your own family now, honey. You deserve to have a husband who loves you and children of your own to raise. Home is where your heart is, Shelby Louise, and your heart is with Boston."

Shelby felt all the weight of logic pressing down on her, all the pain of the last two weeks, and knew that her grandmother was absolutely right.

It didn't matter where. She truly wanted to be with Boston for the rest of her life.

Boston was coping. Or so he told himself as his mind wandered off his work for the nine-millionth time. He spun his chair around and faced the wall of windows in his office, gazing out at the Chicago skyline and to the snatches of Lake Michigan in the backdrop.

The day was beautiful. Bright, sunny, a balmy eighty degrees, with thick puffy white clouds in the sky, as July slid into August. He should be ecstatic to be back home. He should be gorging himself at exotic restaurants every night, hitting the theater and cheering on the Cubs.

Instead he was working long days, but not getting a whole lot accomplished, then returning to his apartment and staring into space while claiming to be watching television. Funny how he'd never noticed until now that his apartment was lacking in warmth, full of cool grays and blues, and that he'd never bothered to take the time to meet his neighbors.

Boston tossed down his pen and focused on his computer screen. Moping around like a bad poet was not helping. He needed to distract himself from how much he was missing Shelby, and work was the most productive way to do that.

It helped for an hour. He was so deep into problem solving on a new account out of Indianapolis that he didn't hear his office door open.

"Boston."

His head snapped up and he took in Amanda, heading right for his desk, waving something in her hand, sending her yellow tank top dangerously high on her midriff.

"Hello, Amanda. How are you?" His day had only lacked this. "When did you get back to Chicago?"

"Three days ago." Her yellow plaid bag slid forward on her arm, and a white cotton ball popped up.

"What is that?"

"Huh?" Amanda looked at her bag. "Oh, this is Baby, my new dog. Isn't she sweet?"

Baby's head was about the size of a quarter. All Boston could see was floppy white fur and a black nose. He eyed it skeptically, wondering if the breeder had given her a hamster and tried to pass it off as a dog.

Amanda petted the head and dropped the papers in her hand on his desk. "Anyway, pack yourself a bag. We're going back to Cuttersville."

"Excuse me?" Boston picked up two airline tickets to Columbus, Ohio. "I'm not going back to Cuttersville. And didn't you just leave there?"

"I came back to Chicago for a wardrobe exchange. I don't want to waste the rent on the house in Cuttersville, so I'm going to hang there for the rest of the summer. And you're going with me."

He'd rather be sent through a paper shredder. "I don't think so. Sorry you wasted money on a second ticket, but it's not going to happen."

"My dad paid for the tickets." Amanda grinned. "And I think it's going to be absolutely hysterical when my dad finds out I went back to Cuttersville. He totally won't understand it, and that will drive him insane."

"I'm sure it will. Have a nice flight." Boston looked down at his computer.

Amanda snapped the lid closed, almost taking off his fingers. "Okay, here's the thing. You're coming with me whether you like it or not. Shelby's moping around back there, and you're doing the same thing here, and I won't put up with it."

Like she had any say in it. Contrary to what Amanda thought, the world wasn't hers to order around. He had learned that himself very painfully. Yet instead of giving her a scathing set-down, he asked, "Shelby's moping around?"

"She's turned it into an art form. I'm actually jealous. I don't think I could elevate heartbroken to that level of sincerity. People are *baking* for her, Boston, that's how pitiful she looks."

He was sorry to hear she was so upset. Yet at the same time, he thought, *Hah.* Now she knew what it felt like.

"You need to go down there, marry her, settle in, and have a couple of starched-up kids."

"Excuse me? I can't live in Cuttersville, Amanda. My life is here." And some life that had turned out to be. Work, a lonely apartment, and acquaintances rather than true friends.

She rolled her eyes and set her bag down on the desk. "Wake up, Macnamara. If you want the prize, sometimes you have to sacrifice for it. You certainly wanted Shelby to sacrifice for you. You asked her to give up everything—her home, family, career, such as it is—and move to a strange place that you know she probably won't like. And what were you willing to give up in that little scenario? Nothing, buddy, exactly nothing."

His mouth opened to protest hotly, but he clamped it shut as Amanda pulled her minidog out of the bag. He couldn't refute what she was saying, because she was right. A conversation with Mary, his supposedly dead housekeeper, popped into his head. She had told him Shelby was worth the sacrifice, and damn it, she was right.

Shelby was worth it. He wanted her, at any cost. Even if that meant putting his career on hold, settling for VP of operations in Cuttersville. His eyes fell on the picture of him and the other Samson guys at the Fourth of July picnic. He'd framed it and stuck it on his otherwise sterile desk, in a move that had startled his secretary almost as much as he'd startled himself. But those were real people in that snapshot with him, who cared about their neighbors and their community. They had welcomed him, accepted him.

He could be part of that. He could give Shelby the home and the family and the love she wanted. And he could have it for himself. He could be a husband and a father, and he could be good at it. That was much more important and satisfying than climbing to the top rung on the corporate ladder.

He would mourn the loss of good coffee and Thai food, but the city wasn't that far off, and Shelby was worth the sacrifice. She really was.

Boston stood up and grabbed the ticket, earning a yip from the fluff resting in the palm of Amanda's hand. He leaned over the desk and kissed her on the cheek with a loud smack that had her eyes widening.

"Amanda Delmar, you are brilliant. Let's go to Cuttersville."

Shelby was putting the last of her possessions in a brown box and taping it shut when Gran walked into her bedroom. "You look like you're all set."

"Almost." Shelby took a deep breath, her stomach bungee jumping up into her throat. "Are you sure I should just show up at Boston's? Shouldn't I call first?"

Gran had Boston's Chicago address from his lease agreement and that morning it had seemed like a great idea to surprise him, but now she was thinking all manner of awful things. Like maybe Boston would have a woman with him, or he'd be annoyed at reopening a discussion he'd assumed was closed. Both seemed ridiculous, but she wasn't feeling rational at the moment.

"And have a heart-to-heart over the phone? I don't think so." Gran was firm, a stack of self-stick mailing labels in her hand. She started slapping them on each taped box.

Shelby's anxiety increased when she saw they had her name on them, but Boston's Chicago address. "Gran! Isn't that a bit presumptuous?"

"What? You go up there, tell him you're willing to give Chicago a chance, he scoops you into his arms, you call me the next morning after makeup sex, I mail the boxes with your stuff. I've got it all covered, honey, you just trust your gran."

"Are you sure you're not biased about this? You've had your eye on Boston for me since he got to Cuttersville back in June."

Gran paused over the fourth box stacked lopsided on the bed. "I know this. That man loves you."

Shelby's heart did a cartwheel. She reached out and hugged her grandmother. "Oh, Gran, I want this to work out. And I love you."

"I love you too, hon, and it will all work out, don't worry."

The doorbell rang downstairs.

"Who could that be?" Shelby pulled back and started for the door.

"It's probably just Brady, though I didn't think I locked the door."

They had agreed to have Brady accompany Shelby to Chicago for a few days, so she didn't panic in the airport or in the cab. Not that Brady was worldly, but he had the cocky arrogance of youth to see them through, and he was tall for his age. Shelby had also figured if Boston turned her out, she didn't want to be alone in a strange place. A fifteen-year-old boy wasn't her first choice of a shoulder to cry on, but she'd take what she could get.

"Brady, why didn't you come around the back?" Shelby asked as she opened the front door.

Brady grinned at her. "Hey, Shel, look who I found pulling in the drive."

Her mouth dropped. The room went hot. She had the sudden and embarrassing feeling that she was going to faint right there, with Brady, Amanda Delmar, and Boston staring at her on the front porch.

He'd come back.

And it seemed like whenever she planned something, thought it through to every angle, the actual occurrence was entirely different.

Boston reached out a hand out, alarmed at the way the color drained from Shelby's tan face.

She took a step back away from him, and his confidence wavered. Not that he'd had much to begin with. On the flight down from Chicago he'd been a mass of spineless nerves, sure Shelby was going to reject him all over again. He hoped to God he was wrong.

Her voice quivered. "Boston . . . what're you doing here?"

Something shifted in him as he felt and saw and recognized the love she had for him shining in her eyes. Stepping into the hall, he turned back to Brady and Amanda. "Stay outside," he told them, and shut the door in their faces.

Shelby's lips fell apart.

Boston allowed himself a second to sweep his gaze over her. Shelby looked different, and he realized what it was immediately. He touched the strands of her hair brushing over her shoulders. Her hair wasn't as long as it had been, or as thick, the rich waves having been tamed into straight stylish strands.

"You cut your hair."

"I let Harriet at it finally. She was so happy she gave me the cut half price."

Boston remembered all that glorious hair pouring over her bare breasts in the moonlight. "I liked it the way it was."

Her nose wrinkled up. "Did I ask you?"

He realized he'd sounded rude. "It looks pretty now, I just liked it down over here"—he brushed the tips of her nipples—"when I was making love to you."

Her breath caught as she grabbed his wrists and held him still. She licked her lips, studied the wall behind him. "Why are you here?"

The feel of her tight nipples, the scent of her warm skin, nearly made him forget his own name. He focused on her again. Then he did what he had never in a million years expected to do with any woman.

He dropped to his knee in front of her.

"Shelby Louise, I'm here to ask you to marry me." He took her hand, which was shaking a little, and added, "I'm that man who loves you. I want to give you that home here in Cuttersville. I want to raise children with you in our white Victorian house in Ohio's most haunted town."

"Oh, Lord," she said.

A plea to a deity wasn't the answer he'd been hoping for. Boston's palms were clammy and his heart sick with love and worry that she'd tell him to take his proposal and stick it, but he still managed to rummage around in his pocket and pull out the velvet box that had brought him equal anxiety.

Amanda had helped him pick the princess-cut ring out, assuring him Shelby would like it, and that the size would definitely fit on Shelby's finger. He would hang Amanda by her handbag if she was wrong on either count.

He took the diamond ring out and stuck it on Shelby's finger before she could say no. "I love you," he said, and waited like a man sentenced to lethal injection.

"Yes, I will marry you," she said, a smile starting to split across her face.

Relief had him hanging his head before he kissed her hand.

"Now stand up, you look foolish down there."

That was the woman he loved.

Shelby watched Boston stand up and thought that she was the luckiest woman alive to have a man willing to sacrifice so much for her. But while she could and would marry him, she could also make it easier on him.

He was trying to kiss her, but she tugged his hand and started for the stairs. "Let me show you something."

"Your bedroom?" he asked with a grin, grabbing her about the waist and managing to sneak in a kiss.

Shelby savored the taste of him for a split second before

reason ruled. "It's in my bedroom, but it's not what you're thinking. My grandmother is around the house somewhere, you know."

"So?"

She laughed, running up the stairs while he followed. Shelby stood in the doorway of her bedroom and gestured for him to go on in. He stopped in the middle of the room, turning around. "You moving?"

"Yep. Check the label on the boxes."

He shot her a look of amusement, before leaning over. He stiffened and the smile fell off his face. "Shel, this is my address in Chicago."

"I know that, you goof. I have a plane ticket downstairs in the kitchen, all ready for me to fly to Chicago this afternoon." Shelby came up behind him and slid her arms around his waist, resting her cheek on his solid back. She breathed in his clean T-shirt smell and sighed. "I was planning on begging you for another chance and telling you that I'd live in Chicago. That home is where my heart is, and my heart is with you."

Boston turned around so fast, her nose got bumped. He cupped her cheeks. "Shel, you don't have to do that. I love you for it, but I realized that there's a lot to be said for living in Cuttersville. And it wasn't fair of me to ask you to give everything up, when I don't have any real attachments to Chicago. I don't really have a family or a home and I never have. I can have that here with you."

Shelby almost choked on the lump in her throat. "Yes, you most certainly can." She reached up and kissed him. "You really want to stay here? And you don't mind if I run a kooky ghost tour?"

"How could I mind? That's what brought us together."

He kissed each of her eyelids in a gesture so tender, Shelby felt like someone had pumped helium into her insides.

"As long as we can work your tour around having a baby or two eventually. I'm getting kind of attached to the idea of raising a little Shelby."

The idea of having his child, a little black-haired baby, thrilled her. "We should get in plenty of practice before we try and get pregnant, though," she told him.

His eyebrow went up. "Practice sex? That's a brilliant idea."

She had meant babysitting, but now that he mentioned it . . .

"How about now? I've still got a key to the White House."

Dang, the man was full of good ideas today. "Alright, but first you've got to say what you think of my outfit. I put this stupid dress on for you, so I would blend in with the city, and you haven't even noticed."

"You're wearing a dress?" He held her back at arm's length and Shelby squirmed.

She never should have borrowed the damn thing from her cousin Heather. She felt like Strawberry the cow in it, spotted and wide. It was a black sleeveless dress that Heather had said would show off her tan, but if he hadn't liked her haircut, chances were good he wouldn't like the dress either.

"You look hotter than hell, and I can't wait to drag this dress off you," he said, his hands starting to migrate south.

"Well, enjoy it, because you probably won't see me in another dress until our wedding."

But the weight of that gorgeous diamond rested on her finger pleasantly and she figured she was open to negotiations.

*   *   *

Boston resettled Shelby in his arms and pulled the white eyelet spread up over their naked bodies. "Thank you for wearing the emerald green bra and panties. That was a nice bonus."

"You're welcome," she murmured into his chest, nuzzling his nipple. Her thigh started to press closer against him, rocking back and forth ever so slightly.

His own body stirred in response, but he didn't think he'd actually be able to carry the effort through to completion at this point. He and Shelby had made love twice already, and he didn't plan on getting dressed for another twenty-four hours or so. Plenty of time for another round in a little while.

"That was nice of your grandmother to offer us this house as a wedding present. I've gotten somewhat attached to it."

"You know, it's been quiet since you left." Shelby ran her brand-new engagement ring across his chest, tickling him. "I wonder if things will get noisy again. And if we're going to live here, I'll have to find another house to take in weekenders for the tour. I'm going to cash in on all this publicity we got."

"That's good. And you know, I have a theory about Rachel. I think she's misunderstood, and that's why she haunts this house." Boston closed his eyes and stroked Shelby's back, pleasantly sleepy and satisfied. "I think it wasn't really Rachel at all who killed her fiancé. I think it was the maid, who was caught stealing the silver, or who was spurned by the fiancé. And Rachel was blamed, so she haunts the house looking for her lover, and for justice."

Shelby's weight shifted a little on him, and her chin rested on his chest. "I think you could very well be right. And I think when I'm on maternity leave someday, you can run the tour for me and tell that theory. You deliver a story as good as any ghost tour guide professional."

He laughed and decided that he must have been temporarily insane to walk away from this woman. "Maybe. But I might be too busy sucking up to Brett to ask for a re-transfer to Cuttersville."

"I love you, Boston." Shelby kissed his neck, tasting the slight salty sweat there. She reached a hand down under the spread. "And I think it's time for me to finally finish that private tour we keep trying to do."

Boston groaned when her hand closed over him, changing his mind about what he might be capable of in the near future. "I love you too, Shelby Tucker, soon to be Shelby Macnamara."

Shelby ducked her head down lower, amazed and so very grateful that she'd found her passion and her heart with Boston.

His hands wound into her hair as she moved. "I thoroughly applaud your tour guide skills."

Shelby glanced up at him over his chest and grinned. "I've added a few features since your last tour. Care to have me show you?"

"Oh, yeah."

And the bedroom door slammed shut and locked.

Turn the page for a preview of
the new book by

Erin McCarthy,

My Immortal

Coming in September 2007 from Jove.

Prologue

RIVER ROAD, LOUISIANA, 1790

Rosa Francis was a demon.

She was a spirit, a chaotic blending of French restlessness, Spanish mores, and the pride of the *gens de couleur*. She was the fortitude of a mixed people heedlessly building a city in a tropical swamp at the mouth of the Mississippi, as well as the foolishness.

The father had told her she was the spirit of greed, the result of a ludicrous lifestyle reminiscent of the French Court that had no business among the cypress and the mosquito. It lived inside her, this desire for more, for extravagance, for rich and delicious foods.

For the lusty, erotic company of human men.

Some believed in her, feared her, particularly the slaves who lived in their squat wood houses on the plantations that were cropping up along River Road with increasing regularity. They understood the need to placate her, to keep her ravenous appetite satisfied, and catered to her desires by leaving out their best food for her to steal and offering her bold men as a sacrifice to her complacency.

The Creole plantation owners believed in her as well, though with no fear. Their wealth, their breeding, the arrogance in their own worth, led them to view her as entertainment. Some had seen her when she'd felt the urge to show herself, had widened their eyes in amazement, then run off laughing to tell their friends. She had on occasion flooded a field, or burned a crop to let them know that, while she was amusing, she could still be dangerous.

Their joie de vivre aside, they understood, and faithfully followed the slaves' example of leaving out food and clothing, though they reserved this generosity for only one day per year. On the summer solstice, they created a feast for her and let her roam through their yards, taking all she wished.

Tonight was that night, so long awaited that she shivered in anticipation, her sister Marguerite padding softly along beside her. Rosa preferred to glide, hovering slightly above the wet swamp as they passed through the Bayou St. John. The swamp was never silent, particularly at night. It was alive with the voices of thousands of living creatures humming in harmony—insects, snakes, and gators, weaving in and out of the reeds and living under the protection of the mighty cypress that watched paternally from the shore.

"Slow down," Marguerite complained. "I can't keep up with you."

"Then fly." Rosa was too excited to let Marguerite sour

her mood. She knew her sister resented Rosa's slim body and long limbs, having been given a round and stout figure. Father had said Marguerite was the spirit of gluttony, the embodiment of the Creole love of money and objects, food and wine. Marguerite said her body was nothing more than the love of cake.

"I won't." Her sister's feet slowed even more.

Rosa laughed. "Fine. I'll go without you. *Au revoir.*"

She couldn't slow down for Marguerite, or for anyone. She could practically smell the salmon, the roasted duck, the wild peas and rice, the café au lait penetrating through the moist, hot air, enveloping her and urging her on. The hunger burned inside her and had to be satisfied.

She was stopping first at Rosa de Montana, a thriving plantation that belonged to the equally thriving Du Bourg family, for the simple reason that she felt it brought her good luck to begin her feast in a place of the same name as herself.

Phillipe du Bourg had been a generous man, with his money, his food, and his favors, and as such had been wildly popular in the exclusive circle of planters in New Orleans. He threw lavish parties, had guests living with him for years at a time, and was known to have fathered a good dozen or so children on his slave women. He laughed, he danced, he gambled, he drank, and he lived a full and privileged life that had suddenly ended when he'd ridden off on his horse wildly drunk and hit his head on the low-hanging branch of a magnolia.

His son, Damien, was not nearly so admired. He had returned from France upon his father's death, a vicious, pampered man of twenty-four, with a pasty-faced smidge of a wife who stood four feet ten and weighed eighty-five pounds in her skirts. Damien had been quite the favorite of the princes at court and as such had been given Marie, with the blessing of her titled family, who thought nothing of her health in the disease-infested wilderness compared to the one million livre fortune the Du Bourg's possessed.

Rumor had it that Damien had been making enemies left and right, was penurious with his money, and thought no boudoir beyond his reach, including that of the mayor's wife.

Rosa left Marguerite completely behind, sailing furiously, the wind rushing through her black hair, her wispy red sheath neither gown nor shift, but more an extension of her long, narrow body. She could see the gas lamps illuminating the house, the doors of its upper galleries open to allow the breeze entrance. Its white pillars stood in the shadows, cast-iron balustrades on either side, an impressive structure in defiance of the soft ground on which it was built.

There was nothing in the yard. Fury ripped through her exuberant mood with the force of a cyclone. There were no lamps lit in the yard, no food, no clothes, no giggling partygoers watching from the front porch. There was nothing.

Hitting the ground with more force than was required, she sank three feet into the soft soil and stepped out in a haze of anger. The rumors were true. Damien du Bourg was not the man his father had been.

He was also standing in front of her.

Leaning on a pillar, he watched her as he smoked a cigar, pulling on it tightly before blowing out a wreath of pungent smoke. He was attractive in a way few men could claim. Rosa studied the strength of his jaw, the long cheekbones, and the haughty tilt of his head. His sandy blond hair was pulled back in a short ponytail, and his loose white shirt was open at the chest, revealing a breadth of shoulders that caused her to shiver in feminine excitement. He wore no jacket, but had black tight-fitting pants that showed his thighs were as muscular as his arms, and his black leather boots were expensive, though well worn.

He held a flask in his other hand, which he put to his lips and drank from deeply. His expression was arrogant, his rich green eyes drinking her in as his lips did the liquor.

"Do you know who I am?" Her anger returned tenfold at his bold sweeping assessment of her.

"Since you have just stepped out of a three-foot hole, I imagine I do."

His nonchalance was creating a maelstrom inside her that was pushing and bubbling and popping. "Where is my food then?"

"I don't have any for you."

Her anger boiled over and before she could stop herself her fingers had spasmed, causing a crack of lightning to flash above their heads and a torrential rain to pour down, flattening her hair to her head and soaking her dress.

"That wasn't very smart." He stood dry under his porch roof, the corner of his mouth twitching upward. "All you did was make yourself wet."

Rosa blinked to clear the water from her eyes and frowned at him. "I want some venison or duck before I'll leave."

His foot propped up the column and he took another swig. "You come here and eat my food, and what do I get in return?"

He was missing the point entirely. He'd been in France too long, where the mysteries of the bayou held no sway.

She quickly sailed through the ten feet between them and stopped inches from his face. "I don't ruin your crops, your plantation, your life."

As she brought the rain to a slowing, misting stop, he didn't blink, nor try to move away from her. She could see there was no fear in his eyes. His gaze dropped to her lips. "No one told me you were so beautiful."

Her other vice, her womanly desires, surfaced with the rapidity of the storm she'd created. It was a painful throb deep inside her, this need to feel a man's body wrapped around her own, an all-encompassing and voracious appetite that she indulged in less than she did her need for food. The roasted duck was forgotten, as were his arrogance and overbearing manners. She decided that while Damien had set out no food, he was offering to feed her other ache.

Confident of her charms, she smiled slowly, floating above the porch step, while mosquitoes buzzed around the lamplight. The starkness of his statement caused a sheen of feminine pride to set her skin aglow. She was beautiful, with the exotic look of a Spaniard, and she could have whatever she wanted. She wanted him now.

Rosa laughed deep in her throat, a sensual promise. "Yes, I am."

His answer was to close the inch remaining between them and press his hard lips to hers, the taste of the whiskey droplets on his mouth sending her into a spiral of pleasure. The wetness of his tongue, pushing urgently into her mouth, filled her with the masculine tastes of cigar smoke and whiskey, hot passion and urgent need.

Her hands gripped his head as she tasted thoroughly, enjoying his hard grip on her arms, the quick mating of his tongue with hers, his lustful willingness to succumb to sexual attraction. Beyond them she sensed movement on the porch. A small, pale woman was clutching her hands to her chest in horror, her brown hair unbound, her white nightgown prim and demure.

She belonged to the delicate French-designed house, with its long louvered windows and sweeping galleries, its wide front steps leading from the swampy jungle to the civilization of the drawing room. But her delicateness, her fragile bloom, did not belong with this virile man, whose appetites were as urgent and questing as Rosa's own.

"Your wife is watching," Rosa whispered in his ear now, sucking gently on the lobe.

"Is she?" He turned, still clutching her, and smiled. "Good evening, Marie. Care to join us?"

When she turned with a gasp and ran into the house, he laughed an emotionless laugh. "Poor Marie, she doesn't know how to have fun."

"And you do?"

"I do." He turned back with a ferocity that stole Rosa's breath, pulling her into him and molding her body to the length of his, her wet dress clinging to her small, rounded breasts.

His kisses trailed down her neck to her shoulder, worshipful hot presses that caused her to moan, her body aching with want. As his thumb brushed across her breast, teasing her nipple, she urged him on. "Yes. More."

"More," he agreed, lifting her dress past her waist with demanding hands, stroking her thighs possessively. With sure and greedy movements he went to the bodice of her sheath dress, pushing it off her shoulders to expose her breasts. With a groan of his own, he took her into his mouth, sucking and pulling gently with his teeth, cupping her bare, eager flesh with his soft hands.

Working open his pants, she pulled the hot length of him into her hands as her desire swirled and churned inside her, pushing out everything but the need to be possessed by a strong, reckless, mortal man. The storm brewed inside her, hot and tight, her infrequently indulged desires sparking like kindling, and she felt rather than saw that her thoughts had actually ignited the shrubbery on either side of the front steps.

He barely glanced over, murmuring, "The bushes are on fire."

"Shh, I know." She turned the rain back on with a tilt of her head, keeping her greedy hands on him, laboring over the smooth feel of his hard shaft until his panting breath hitched and he forcibly pushed her away.

"No more."

His ragged groan was her triumph, her glory in bringing a man to the edge of his control.

The gentle drops of water spattered across her arms, rolling down to her fingertips, and a fine swirling mist rose around them as she delicately poised herself over him. His back was flush against the solid column for support and he urged her body downward with his hands, spreading her thighs and easing her toward him until she hovered in breathtaking anticipation.

"I would ask you for something." His muscular arms held her hips tightly, keeping her still, his hardness teasing her softness as he denied her.

"What's that?" She let her eyes flutter shut, not caring in the least what he wanted. There was only her need, her rolling, throbbing desires seeking to burst forth out of her in a cascade of gloriously delicious sin.

It wouldn't be difficult to take control, drop herself down onto him and force the hot joining they both wanted, but he was whispering in her ear, distracting her, asking . . .

Her eyes flew open in surprise. She'd had humans make requests of her, beg for mercy, for more, for release. But this human, this Damien du Bourg, was asking boldly what no one had requested of her before. He looked serious, his eyes filled with lust, yes, but also a cold, calculated determination. She shivered under the onslaught of raindrops. "How do you know I can give you what you ask for?"

"I know who you are. You can do this." His face shined from the rivulets running down his cheeks, the lamplight reflecting off of his empty, joyless face.

She tossed her sodden hair back over her shoulder, pressing her bare breasts against the softness of his damp linen shirt. It was a foolish request, one he would live to regret, but Rosa thought Damien was deserving of regret. He had a black heart, cold and arrogant.

This wasn't the normal way of things, but she was young and impulsive. She thought it would be satisfying to see this proud man forced to serve her and the father, as he would have to if she granted him the escape from death he requested.

She hesitated long enough to warn, "If I do this, I can't undo it. Do you understand?"

Though his eyes darkened, he nodded. "Yes, I understand. Do it for me."

With a shrug, she told him, "It's done."

And with a soft groan, he moved, slamming her onto him, pumping up and down, exploding her mind and body with a thousand little gunshots of pleasure as she threw back her head in utter abandonment.

"Thank you," he murmured into her mouth as he kissed her hotly, the porch steps creaking beneath his boots as they rocked. "You won't regret it."

Though regret was the farthest thing from her mind at the moment, she knew with the clarity of one who can sense without seeing, that there was going to be hell to pay for this one.